"The future shows much success for this series! Fun, vibrant characters (as well as a sexy smolder or two for good measure) give the novel just the right tone."

— *RT Book Reviews*

"I loved the protagonist, Cass. She and her friends were very well developed and felt like a group of people I'd like to get to know."

— *The Book's the Thing*

"The book starts off on a fast pace, and is a quick page-turner. Readers will love the charm, wit, and feelings that these characters show."

— *Bibliophile Reviews*

"It has so many great characters and just enough intrigue to keep me on the edge of my seat. The setting was quaint and the author made me want to live there. The mystery is well written and keeps readers guessing till the end."

— *Texas Book-aholic*

"I love a good cozy book right before bed, and this charming story about psychic shop owner Cass Donovan did not disappoint. I stayed up far too late into the evening because I couldn't put it down. A well-crafted mystery with a quirky cast of characters, and plenty of twists and turns to keep you guessing to the end."

— *The Mysterious Ink Spot*

"This engaging series just keeps getting better!"

— *Cozy Up With Kathy*

Books by Lena Gregory

Bay Island Psychic Mysteries

Death at First Sight
Occult and Battery
Clairvoyant and Present Danger
Spirited Away
Grave Consequences

All-Day Breakfast Café Mysteries

Scone Cold Killer
Murder Made to Order
A Cold Brew Killing
A Waffle Lot of Murder (coming soon!)

GRAVE

CONSEQUENCES

A BAY ISLAND PSYCHIC MYSTERY

LENA GREGORY

BEYOND THE PAGE
PUBLISHING

Grave Consequences
Lena Gregory
Copyright © 2020 by Denise Pysarchuk.
Cover design by Dar Albert, Wicked Smart Designs

Beyond the Page Books
are published by
Beyond the Page Publishing
www.beyondthepagepub.com

ISBN: 978-1-950461-51-6

GRAVE

CONSEQUENCES

Chapter One

Mist swirled around Cass Donovan, enveloping her in a shroud of chaos. Darkness disoriented her, but still, she squeezed her eyes closed tighter, searching for answers, reaching—

Voices assailed her from every direction, all vying for her attention, each begging louder than the next: *"If you ask me . . . no one told me . . . you have to reach out . . . doctor . . . school . . . never come to you . . . the beach . . . lighthouse . . . go . . . loser . . . killed me . . . hidden . . . secret . . . lost . . . love of my . . . help . . . tell them . . ."*

"Enough already!" Cass slammed her palms against the large round table where she conducted her psychic readings and lurched to her feet, toppling the oversized velvet-covered chair behind her.

Bee Maxwell, one of her two best friends, caught the chair on his way past, righted it in one smooth motion, and continued trudging toward the coffeepot on the back counter of Mystical Musings, Cass's psychic shop on Bay Island's boardwalk. "Honey, I did not get up at the crack of dawn to come down here and watch you have a temper tantrum."

"For the record, Bee, ten a.m. is hardly the crack of dawn." Though, in all fairness, it was to him, since he spent most of his nights working on new designs in the back room of Dreamweaver Designs, his designer gown shop down the boardwalk from Mystical Musings.

He grunted in response and filled his big mug to the brim.

"And I am not having a tantrum." Well . . . maybe a small one, but it wasn't for her own sake, it was for Stephanie's, so that didn't count.

Cass groaned and flopped back onto the chair. She closed her eyes, lowered her head into her hands, and willed the voices to stay quiet long enough for her to make sense of what any of them were saying. Even just one coherent sentence.

The barrage continued. *"Not time yet . . . can't find . . . lighthouse . . . climb . . . not fair . . . have to find it . . . get that lying . . ."*

Yet, each time she tried to grasp hold of one, hold on long enough to discern what it wanted, it eluded her, slipping away like a wisp of smoke on a summer breeze. "I'm sorry, Stephanie."

Stephanie Lawrence, the other of Cass's two best friends, a

woman she'd do anything in the world for with no hesitation, stood from her chair across the table from Cass, slung her bag over her shoulder, and shrugged. Though she forced a smile, there was no mistaking the disappointment clouding her eyes. "Don't worry about it. It's not your fault."

"Maybe we can try another color reading later." While color readings usually relaxed Cass, allowing whatever energy she needed to flow freely, her last attempt to do one for Stephanie had left her weak, her hands trembling too badly to hold the colored pencil, her head pounding.

"Sure thing. Thanks for trying again." Stephanie started toward the door. "I've got to get going. I'm meeting with a new client in fifteen minutes."

Cass stood and laid a hand on her arm to stop her. "Please, Stephanie. Just let me try again later, okay? I'm just learning to cope with all the voices who've figured out I can actually communicate with them, and I need a little time to work it out."

Stephanie patted Cass's hand. "It's fine, Cass, honestly. We can try again whenever you have time."

Pain squeezed her heart. It wasn't fine. Stephanie needed her, and she'd failed. No sense apologizing again; she'd just have to try harder.

"Or, here's a novel idea . . ." Bee leaned against the counter and crossed one leg over the other. He blew steam from his coffee mug, took a sip, then glanced up. "Why don't you just wait and see what happens? Maybe there are some things we're not meant to know ahead of time."

Cass shot daggers at him, willing him to be quiet. Why had she asked him to come down to the shop, anyway? Oh, right. Moral support. And so he could take care of any customers that came in while she devoted her full attention to Stephanie.

Stephanie scowled, then huffed out a breath and shrugged. "Maybe you're right, Bee."

"I usually am." Ignoring Cass's *Shut up* look, he patted Beast's head, then took the seat Stephanie had just vacated and set his coffee on the table. "By the way, Cass, I seem to remember today's invitation coming with breakfast."

Beast, Cass's Leonberger, who'd finally grown into his too-big paws, plopped his head onto Bee's lap and gazed up at Cass, longing filling his huge brown eyes.

Bee laid a hand on his head. "I know, Beast. Seems we're both waiting a long time for breakfast this morning, huh?"

Beast barked once.

Traitor.

Cass ignored them and hugged Stephanie. "We'll figure it out, Steph. Try not to worry so much. I know there's a baby for you out there somewhere."

She stepped back, her eyes filled with hope. "Is that something you see? Or are you just being supportive?"

She honestly didn't know. Even if there was a message from beyond to be had, she couldn't hear it past the constant chatter in her head, the constant pleas for her to seek out loved ones and pass on a million messages—some important, like the man who'd been murdered by his own beneficiary and wanted justice, or the woman who begged forgiveness for a sin Cass couldn't pick out amid the chatter, and others less so, like the woman who constantly badgered Cass to tell her ex-husband what a bum he was. While Cass could certainly understand the sentiment, she had no intention of wasting time seeking the man out and fulfilling the woman's request. "Honestly, Steph, I can't tell. Let's just call it a strong gut feeling and leave it at that for now, okay?"

Stephanie chewed on her bottom lip for a moment, then tucked her frizzy brown hair behind her ear and nodded. "You know what? You're right. When the time is right, it'll happen."

"Yes, it will," Bee called to her. "Maybe the reason Cass can't see when you'll get a baby is because it hasn't been decided yet. Maybe the perfect child for you just isn't available at the moment. Seems it's worth being patient until he or she needs you the most, even if that means waiting a while."

Tears shimmered in Stephanie's eyes as she crossed the shop, laid a hand on Bee's shoulder, and stood on tiptoes to kiss his cheek. "You're right, Bee. Again, as much as I hate to admit it. Thank you."

"Of course, dear." He patted her hand. "And since you've admitted twice in as many minutes that I'm right, I'm going to treat you to something special. Can both of you take off for a few hours later, go do something fun before the schools let out next week and tourist season reaches its peak and everything gets too crowded to enjoy?"

Knowing Bee was trying to distract Stephanie from obsessing over adopting a child, all Cass's earlier annoyance with him fled. This was why she'd asked him to come in this morning, because Bee just had a way with people, with friends. "Sure, I can close up for a few hours around lunchtime."

"Okay, it's a date." Stephanie hiked her bag higher onto her shoulder. "Where are we going?"

"You just meet us here when you finish up. I'll take care of the plans," Bee said.

"Sure thing, thanks, Bee." She opened the door, jingling the chimes Cass had hung to alert her whenever a customer entered.

"Anytime." Bee waved.

Cass watched Stephanie cross the small lot and climb into her car, then turned to Bee. "Thank you."

He got up, went to the back counter, and filled a second mug with coffee. "She's obsessing, Cass, to the point of not having an interest in anything else. You have to stop feeding into that."

His judgment put her back up. Who was he to tell her what to do? "What are you talking about, Bee?"

He set the mug on the table in front of Cass's seat and gestured for her to sit, then abandoned his seat across the table in favor of the one next to hers.

She forgave him a little—just a little—as she dropped onto the chair and wrapped her hands around the warm mug.

"Ever since the woman Tank was talking to about adopting the baby decided to go with another couple, you two have been killing yourselves trying to see when another baby would come available. Maybe, if she just accepts that you can't see it, she'll be able to focus on something else until one does."

The fact that he was right only annoyed her more.

He pushed the milk toward her. "It's not like there was a problem with them adopting, just that one birth mother's personal preference."

Cass couldn't blame the woman, and Stephanie had certainly understood.

The woman had explained that after her own father had traded

4

her mother in for a newer model and taken off without so much as a backward glance, she had been raised by a single mother who'd been too broken to be more than a shell for her children. The woman hadn't wanted to place her own child with a detective, was too worried something would happen to him. If she'd wanted her daughter to be raised by a single mother, she wouldn't be giving her up for adoption. She'd ended up placing her with two teachers instead.

So, not only had Stephanie been left with the heartbreak of not getting the infant, she'd been forced to look long and hard at the danger her husband faced every day. Though Bay Island didn't boast a particularly high crime rate, you never knew what each day would bring, despite Cass's attempts to the contrary.

Thoughts of Detective Luke Morgan's deep blue eyes and killer smile slid in. He'd taken a job on Bay Island as the partner of Stephanie's husband, Tank, to be closer to Cass when their long-distance relationship seemed to be failing. She hadn't seen that coming either. The vise on her heart eased a little.

"I know you only want to make things better . . ." Bee gripped her hand, his large hand surrounding hers bringing immediate comfort. "And that's one of the things I love most about you. But sometimes you have to accept that there are some aches you just can't ease."

Bee would understand that. He hadn't grown up easy and had suffered his own share of heartache in the past.

So had Cass. And he was right . . . again . . . Ugh . . .

Sometimes nothing could take away the hurt, but having a good friend to lean on helped. She squeezed Bee's hand.

"Come on . . . say it . . ." He waggled his thick dark eyebrows, like two fat caterpillars dancing beneath his bleached blond bangs.

"Not happening." No way was she saying the words after Stephanie had already admitted he was right twice in a row. Couldn't have it going to his head.

He shot her a grin. "That's okay. You don't actually have to say it; it's enough that we both know I'm right. Again."

She laughed, feeling better than she had in days.

Bee slid his coffee mug over and took a big gulp. "So, where do you want to go this afternoon?"

"Hmm . . . I don't know. We could go to the beach, I guess, but I don't think sitting around doing nothing is going to help Stephanie's mood any."

"No, you're probably right, though I'd love a chance to work on my tan. And shopping's out, because she's trying to save all of her money for the adoption."

Distracted, Cass stared out the back window of Mystical Musings, scanning the beach that would soon be jam-packed with tourists. One word kept repeating itself over and over in her mind. Her own thought, or someone trying to send her a message? Before she could think too much about it, she blurted out the word. "Lighthouse?"

"Yeah?" Bee studied her and narrowed his eyes. "Why do I get the feeling there's more to your request to go to the lighthouse than just keeping Stephanie occupied?"

Cass shrugged. He knew her too well for her to hide the truth. "I'll make you a deal: you stay up and spend a few hours being a good friend and playing tourist, and I'll refrain from telling you there are voices in my head battling for attention, the loudest of which is screaming something about the lighthouse."

Bee huffed, fluttering his bangs off his forehead. "Fine. But I want that breakfast you promised me. And you'd better make sure there's bacon. Beast and I are both running out of patience."

Cass held her hand out. "So, it's a deal?"

He rolled his eyes and shook her proffered hand. "Sure, why not? We could wander through the museum and gift shop then climb to the top and look out over the bay."

"Okay, then, but unfortunately, you'll have to go pick up breakfast since I'm already open." She smiled sweetly. "Make mine a bacon, egg, and cheese on a roll with home fries."

The chimes above the front door sounded as her first customer of the day entered the shop.

Bee muttered something as he grabbed Cass's car keys and called Beast to take a ride with him.

Cass took a deep breath and tried to rid herself of the stress Stephanie's reading had left hanging over her. She had no readings scheduled for this morning, and she hoped it stayed that way. Lately, any time she opened herself up to do a reading, the voices from beyond bombarded her. Now, if she could just get the mess under control before her next group reading this weekend . . . Maybe taking the afternoon with friends would help. At the lighthouse.

Lighthouse, lighthouse, lighthouse . . . The thought taunted her, over and over, seared into her mind along with an image of the Bay Island Lighthouse standing sentinel atop the bluff at the tip of the island. She glanced out the back window at the lighthouse just as a dark cloud slipped across the sun, casting a shadow along the beach and over the bluff, but only for a moment, before resuming its trek east across the bay toward the south fork of Long Island.

Chapter Two

Cass took her time driving up the long, winding road that led to the Bay Island Lighthouse. A thick stand of woods bordered the road, the dense foliage blocking any view of the bay that might be visible during the winter months.

Stephanie sat beside her in the passenger seat, not brooding, exactly, but quiet just the same.

Bee kept up a nonstop monologue, detailing all of the new gossip he'd gathered while picking up breakfast that morning. Though the shop had been too busy for Cass to sit and chat with him before she'd closed up to head out to the lighthouse, she hadn't been asked for a single reading. A fact she was especially grateful for, since it meant the voices had taken the morning off.

"Oh, and I'll give you three guesses who's back in town, but rumor has it he's going to be playing tour guide instead of lifeguard this summer." Bee paused, then gave Cass a nudge from the backseat when she didn't answer quickly enough.

"I don't know, who?" Even if she did know, she wouldn't spoil his fun. The last thing she needed was Bee in full-on sulk mode because he hadn't been the first to pass on good dirt.

"Quincy Yates." The dramatic pause clued Cass in she should remember the name from somewhere, though it didn't sound at all familiar.

"Who's Quincy Yates?" A quick glimpse in the rearview mirror caught him rolling his eyes.

"Oh, come on, Cass. You remember Quince . . . tall, well-built, blond highlights streaking his shoulder-length brown hair, framing those bright blue eyes, and all set off by his ridiculously dark golden tan. Looked like he sashayed straight off the cover of a romance novel."

"Seriously, Bee? You just described half the lifeguards lining the beach."

He laughed out loud, a long, deep belly laugh that had her grinning. "Well, I can't argue that, but Quince is the one who goes with a new gal every summer, left that snotty tour guide—what was her name?—screaming and cursing up a storm at him from the dock when he left her behind and boarded the ferry to go back home the weekend after Labor Day last year."

Stephanie turned toward him. "You mean Piper Bonavich?"

"Yeah, her." Bee screwed up his face as if he'd stepped in something Beast hacked up on the beach. "I never understood what he saw in her in the first place."

"Really?" Cass lifted a brow at him in the rearview mirror. "Could it have been the long blonde hair, deep dark tan, brilliant blue eyes, and legs that went practically up to her neck?"

"She was beautiful," Stephanie added. "And easy enough for a summer fling."

Bee huffed. "Yeah, well, she may have been beautiful on the outside, but she was a monster on the inside."

True enough. The young woman had been downright nasty to almost everyone on Bay Island, locals and tourists alike. She'd even let Bee have it when he'd been kind enough to hold a door open for her at the deli, eyeing him up and down, then passing with a sneer and a rude comment.

Bee was a better person than Cass, because she'd have dropped the door on her as she passed. As it was, she'd had to refrain from sticking her foot out and tripping her when she'd insulted Bee. "You know how it is, Bee."

During the summer months, tourists from Long Island and New York City flocked to Bay Island in droves. Because of that, the less fortunate, those who'd love to spend their summers on the island but couldn't afford the hefty price tags, often took jobs for the summer and spent their time off playing tourist.

"It's a win-win, really." Stephanie relaxed back in her seat, her gaze focused on the view as they rounded the last curve and the woods opened up to reveal an incredible expanse of dark, choppy water, blue skies, and puffy white clouds. A gorgeous day for sightseeing. "We get the extra waiters and waitresses, tour guides, lifeguards, house cleaners, and retail help we need, and they get to hang out on an island for the summer before heading back to reality come the beginning of September."

Bee shrugged. "I don't mind the influx of summer workers, only Piper. Hopefully, she had her fill last year and won't be back."

Gravel and seashells crunched beneath the tires as Cass pulled into the lot. At least they didn't have to pay to park yet, as they would once the park officially opened for the season. "Well, if she does come back, ignore her. And don't hold any doors open for her."

Bee squirmed. He didn't have it in him to be rude to most people, even when they deserved it. He pointed out an empty spot. "Lot's pretty full for a Monday afternoon when school hasn't even let out yet."

Several cars and a couple of SUVs lined the lot, and a tour bus had parked crookedly against the sagging split-rail fence.

Cass slid her sunglasses off and squinted. "I didn't realize the tours had already started."

Bee gripped the seat backs and pulled himself forward until he was leaning between the two front seats. "Oh, didn't you hear?"

"Hear what?" If she didn't know better, Cass would have sworn Bee had scripted that exact moment to impart whatever dirt he was grinning like a Cheshire cat over for full dramatic effect. Who knew? Maybe he had.

"Fred DiCarlo is running ghost tours now."

"Ghost tours?" She studied the group of tourists and noticed they were lacking the usual designer brand khakis, loafers, and sundresses that probably cost more than Cass made in a month. And that was before you added the designer bags and cameras they all usually carried. This group was different, mostly wearing jeans or cargo shorts and T-shirts, and not a camera in sight.

"Yup. Swears the lighthouse is haunted." Bee poked her shoulder. "Hard to believe it took all these years to figure that out, huh? Especially when he's made it abundantly clear he doesn't believe in ghosts."

Stephanie laughed. "Hey, don't knock him, Bee. If he's bringing tourists to the island seeking ghosts, what better place to find them than Mystical Musings?"

Stephanie had a point. Mystical Musings would only benefit from tourists seeking to communicate with those who'd moved on.

Cass parked and turned off the engine.

"Supposedly, the old Madison Estate is part of the tour too. I think Fred worked out some kind of deal with the owner to have the guests stay at the B&B as part of a tour package." After a quick peek in the rearview mirror, Bee finger-combed his hair then stepped out of the car.

"Hmm . . . maybe you can talk to him, Cass, make a visit to the shop part of the tour, offer a commission for any customers he brings in." Stephanie climbed out of the car and stretched her arms over her head.

It wasn't a bad idea. If she confirmed Bee's gossip was actually true, maybe she'd give Fred a call, see if they could work something out. She started to shut the door, then thought better of it and reached in for her sunglasses. The glare off the water would be brutal this time of day.

At least, it would be if they actually reached the top of the lighthouse. Even strolls along the beach with Beast, which she took as often as possible between a harsh winter and a deluge of spring rain, couldn't prepare her for the climb up the circular staircase's hundred and thirty-seven iron steps. Her legs ached just thinking about it.

"You could always ask Amelia about the tours, if the gift shop isn't too crowded." Bee looked up at the lighthouse then back at Cass.

She grinned. If the appalled look on his face was any indication, his thoughts were running similar to her own.

"Ready?" Stephanie started across the lot without even glancing up.

Cass and Bee fell into step on either side of her.

"What do you want to do first? Walk the grounds? The museum? Stop into the gift shop to talk to Amelia?" Bee swallowed hard. "Or climb to the top?"

"The tour group just headed into the lighthouse, so why don't we stop at the gift shop first?" Stephanie said.

"Good idea." Climbing the lighthouse with a large group of people, every sound echoing through the entire place, was not as fun as having the space to themselves would be.

Bee shuddered. "Better a tour group than a school trip. I did that once when I first moved to Bay Island. Had to be a hundred kids, all screaming and excited. And they started up after I'd almost reached the top, so there was no escape. Don't get me wrong, I love kids, but never again. I developed a new appreciation for teachers that day."

Cass reached the keeper's house, which stood right beside the lighthouse, and held the gift shop door open.

Bee took over and ushered them both in ahead of him.

Cass's gaze immediately landed on a display of lighthouse

figures, the same ones she sold in her shop but priced a dollar lower. She'd have to lower her price as soon as she got back. She wouldn't go below their price, but she didn't want to be higher either.

"Good morning. Oh, well, afternoon, I guess now." Amelia DiCarlo hustled from behind the counter, then slowed when recognition hit. "Oh, sorry, I was preoccupied and didn't realize it was you guys. Tourist season seems to have started early this year."

"We saw the tour bus outside. Doesn't Fred usually wait until after Memorial Day to start up?" It didn't make much sense to pay guides before the season officially opened. The few tours that ran year-round could easily be handled by Fred or his one full-time employee.

Amelia sniffed. Her lower lip quivered, and tears shimmered in her eyes, but she simply nodded.

Cass glanced at Bee, but he just frowned and shook his head once. "Is everything okay, Amelia?"

"Oh, yes, fine." She waved off Cass's concern and forced a smile. "So, what can I help you with today? Are you going to climb to the top?"

Cass waited a moment but then let it drop. Whatever was bothering Amelia, she obviously didn't want to share. Cass would offer a reading, give the woman a chance to talk if she wanted to, but Amelia had never come into the shop in the past, and her husband, Fred, had made it clear on numerous occasions he didn't believe in anything beyond the here and now. Except when it could make him money, apparently. "Yes, and maybe tour the museum and the grounds for a bit."

"Sure thing. It's a beautiful day for it. Come on, and I'll ring you up." She headed toward the register. "You might want to start in the museum, since the tour group just headed up."

"We were hoping to run into Fred." Stephanie slung her purse off her shoulder and pulled out her wallet.

Bee laid a hand over hers. "My treat, remember?"

Amelia narrowed her eyes. "What do you want with him?"

"Thanks, Bee." Stephanie kissed his cheek. "Umm . . . oh, right. Is it true Fred is offering haunted tours now?"

Amelia gritted her teeth as she rang up their admission fees. "Uh-huh. Giving one right now, also training the tour guides he hired for the season on how to give the new tour, even those who were here last year. Apparently they need a refresher course."

Stephanie shot a quick glance from Cass to Bee while Amelia was looking down at the register making change.

Cass shrugged and Bee shook his head.

Since she'd already started, Stephanie plastered on a smile and continued. "We were hoping he'd consider adding Mystical Musings to the tour, give his customers a chance to stop in and shop, maybe have a reading. Do you think he'd be interested?"

She snorted. "If it don't have long legs and a short skirt, he probably ain't interested."

Uh-oh.

"Now, if you'll excuse me . . ." She handed Bee his change. "I have to go unlock the third floor for the group to get in."

"The third floor?" Bee asked.

The first floor of the old lighthouse keeper's house had been turned into the gift shop and museum, with offices and storage throughout the second floor, but Cass had always figured the third floor was an attic or more storage space. "What's on the third floor?"

"Used to be bedrooms up there, and one of Fred's supposed ghosts was staying up there when he got himself killed trying to find the treasure . . ."

Bee's ears perked right up, and he went from bored disinterest to fully focused in a fraction of a second. "Treasure?"

Cass shot him a scowl.

Amelia shrugged. "Darned if I know, some nonsense he was rambling on about. Ask me, I think he's just looking for an excuse to get the bedrooms opened up to him."

Though the words had been spoken with a casual shrug, there was no mistaking the pain in Amelia's eyes.

"Anyway, I gotta go. You guys, enjoy." She grabbed a set of keys from beneath the counter and sorted through them as she hurried across the gift shop, stuck the *Back in five* sign on the door, and walked out.

"Hey, Cass." Bee winked. "What do you say we sneak up to the third floor, and you ask the ghost where we can find that treasure?"

"Really, Bee?" Stephanie raised a skeptical brow. "I thought you didn't believe in ghosts?"

Chapter Three

Cass took her time strolling through the museum, enjoying the many exhibits. She could spend hours drifting through the past, exploring the history of Bay Island. The museum proudly displayed information about Gardiners Bay and its inhabitants, the local wildlife, many historical residences that could be found throughout Bay Island, and a variety of shipwrecks, rumors of which shifted as often as the tides.

"Hey, Cass. Check this out." Bee squinted and leaned closer to the plaque posted in front of an exhibit.

"What is it?"

He frowned and shook his head. "I'm not sure, but I think it might be talking about the buried treasure Fred wants to feature on the tour."

Cass and Stephanie crowded in on either side of him to study the plaque.

"Is this new?" Cass couldn't remember ever having seen the display before. Nor had she heard mention of the story.

"Yup," a man said from right behind them.

Bee squealed and jumped, knocking Cass to the side as he whirled to face the man who'd spoken.

"Hey . . ." Catching herself against the display case, Cass turned as well.

"Oh, for crying out loud . . ." Bee spread a hand against his chest with all the flair of a Hollywood diva. "What are you trying to do to me, Levi?"

The burly older man laughed out loud, ripped the mariner's cap from his nearly bald head—if you didn't count the few tufts of shocking orange hair that still clung for dear life—and slapped it against his leg. Laugh lines framed eyes the color of the greenest meadows and dappled with golden spots of sunshine. "Sorry, there, Bee. Didn't realize you hadn't seen me."

Bee huffed and fluffed his multicolored scarf. "Yeah, well . . ."

"Of course, if I had realized it, I wouldn't have changed a thing." He swiped tears from the corners of his eyes and fitted his cap back on. "Ah, that was priceless. Gotta admit, you're pretty spry there, old man."

Bee grinned. "Who you callin' old, old-timer?"

"I might be old, but I ain't dead yet, despite the fact you looked like you'd been spooked by a ghost." He tipped his cap toward Cass and Stephanie. "Ladies."

Fanning himself, probably in an effort to calm his racing nerves, Bee blew out a breath. "You should know better than to sneak up on people, Levi."

He folded his hands over the top of his dust mop's handle and crossed one leg over the other. "Hey, I said sorry. Besides, I didn't know anyone was in here when I came in to clean. I saw Amelia hurry out and figured it'd be a good time to get a few things done while it was empty. Not to worry, though, I have plenty to keep me occupied upstairs now that they're opening the third floor. I can do that first."

Bee waved him off. "Nah, don't change your routine on account of us. We're going to head up the lighthouse as soon as the tour group comes down, anyway."

Levi's smile faltered for an instant, his eyes darkening like molten lava pouring over the landscape. "Fred's up there?"

"Amelia said something about him retraining his tour guides to include a paranormal element." Cass waited for his reaction, paying more attention to his body language, the stiffening of his spine when she mentioned Amelia in particular, than the smile he beamed at her.

"Is that so?" He crooked a finger for Bee to come closer and looked around as if making sure he wouldn't be overheard.

All three of them leaned in.

"I'll tell you what, Bee. On account of me sneaking up on you and scarin' you so bad and all, I'll offer up some good gossip as a sort of, shall we say, sorry I'm not sorry."

Bee's eyes narrowed. "What do you want in exchange?"

"Nothing, this time, but if you ever hear anything juicy, I get dibs." He patted his chest.

"Fair enough." Bee stuck out his hand, and Levi shook it. "Let's have it."

"Okay, but this ain't the regular type gossip you'll hear down at the deli or the diner."

Bee's eyes widened, and he practically drooled over the news—

the same look Beast had the time Cass offered him half a steak she hadn't been hungry enough to finish.

Stephanie gave him a shove. "Down, boy."

Levi laughed. "Ah, let 'im be, missy. This here dirt's worth it."

"All right, let's have it." Bee rolled his hand for Levi to continue. "And I promise I won't forget where I heard it."

"Fair enough." Levi gestured toward the far corner of the room. A dim bulb flickered, casting shadows over whatever was displayed there. He pushed his dark glasses farther up his hooked nose. "You want to know more about the haunted tour Fred's touting? Go have yerselves a look-see at that display in the corner, the one tucked between Crustaceans of the Cove and Local Rocks. The one the local historical society insisted be included if Fred wanted their approval to declare the lighthouse haunted, since only one person ever died there, at least as far as anyone knows. Though there are rumors . . ."

Bee squinted across the room at the display. "I've never heard of anyone dying out here."

And if someone had, Bee would surely know about it.

"That's because it happened back in the late seventeen hundreds. The lighthouse keeper at the time, the first ever at the Bay Island Lighthouse soon after it was built, Samuel Garrison, was found beaten and bloody on those big rocks beneath the lighthouse."

"What happened to him?" Bee asked.

"No one knows. Some said he fell, others said he was pushed, and still others believed the tide battered him while he was searching for the treasure—"

Bee sucked in a breath. "Treasure?"

"Yup. And some, not as many, mind you, but some, swore he was murdered by the ghost of a pirate named Thomas who fell in love with Samuel's oldest daughter, Kitty." He gestured again toward the corner. "Go ahead, see for yourselves. Then let me know what you find out, because I have no doubt if anyone can dig up gossip from almost three hundred years ago, it's you, Bee."

Cass had to admit, the story had piqued her interest. "I don't know, Levi, but I think you missed your calling. Maybe you should ask Fred for a job as a tour guide."

He laughed, long and loud. "Honey, trust me when I tell you, I am not Fred's type. Now, I've gotta run and get a coupla things done upstairs before Fred's group shows up. I'll catch you guys later. You all have fun now."

He started toward the door.

"Hey, wait," Bee called after him. "Why is the display shoved in the corner over there where it's all but hidden from view? I'd think Fred would want everyone to know the story to prove his tours are historically accurate."

"See, that's the thing about Fred, he don't much care what's true, only what'll make him money. And finding that treasure, well now, that would be hitting the mother lode. And he most certainly don't want no one getting their hands on that journal. Thing is, I think he's angered someone's spirit, either Thomas or Samuel, not sure which, but I seen someone out on those rocks a coupla times now, dressed in those tight pants and frilly shirts they used to wear back in the day . . ."

Bee shivered. Apparently, the late-1700s pirate look offended his fashion designer senses, even in the midst of two-hundred-year-old gossip. "And you think it's a ghost?"

"Sure do." He nodded emphatically.

"When did you see it?"

Resting the handle of his dust mop against his knee, he lifted his cap and scratched his head. "Oh, a few times from up in the lighthouse when I was cleaning at night, but only in the past month or so, since they posted the display. Before that, I been here nigh on thirty years, and I never seen a thing."

"Levi."

Bee jumped and squealed, then whirled toward the door.

Levi dropped his hat when he spun to face Fred.

Fred DiCarlo stood in the doorway with his arms folded across his chest, a frown deepening his already stern features.

Cass couldn't call Bee's reaction dramatic this time, since he'd startled her just as badly.

Levi's expression hardened, his grip on the dust mop tightening, belying his easy tone. "Hello there, Fred."

Fred kept his gaze pinned on Levi. "Don't you have something to clean somewhere?"

"Yup."

"Then I suggest you stop playing tour guide and get to it."

Levi turned to Cass, Bee, and Stephanie, mock bowed, then winked before scooping up his hat and starting for the door. He kept eye contact with Fred as he crossed the room. When he reached him, he leaned closer and stage-whispered, "What's a matter there, Fred? Afraid someone's gonna figure out what you can't and beat you to the prize?"

Fred's gaze shot to Bee for a moment, then returned to Levi. "Not likely, and it definitely won't be you. You can take that to the bank."

Levi shrugged, fitted his cap back on and whistled as he moved off toward the stairs.

Fred stared after him but made no move to leave.

Stephanie nodded toward Fred and made a shooing gesture at Cass.

Bee nodded in agreement.

They weren't wrong. It would be foolish to waste the opportunity to talk to him when he was standing right there, only to have to hunt him down later to ask about the tour. Yet something told her she should just keep her mouth shut. Intuition? Something else?

Bee nudged her side with his elbow.

She cleared her throat.

Fred shook his head then turned to face her. "Did you want something?"

"Uh . . . well . . ."

"Spit it out. I ain't got all day."

Yup, should have gone with her gut, but since she'd already started, she may as well follow through. She offered her professional smile, hoping she pulled it off. "How are you, Fred? I haven't run into you in a while."

Bee turned his back on Fred and rolled his eyes.

"Been better, been worse. Is that all you wanted?"

"Actually, I heard you were running a paranormal tour this season, and I was wondering if you'd consider making Mystical Musings one of your stops. Of course, I'd be willing to—"

"That's not likely to happen. Why would I subject my clients to some charlatan snake oil salesman? Oh, wait, I mean sales*woman*."

Bee whirled, but Cass stepped in front of him before he could say anything.

Fred laughed. "I want them to come back, ya know."

Cass didn't bother being offended by the comment. Fred was known for making rude comments, then laughing them off as if he'd been joking. It was rare anyone laughed along with him. She also didn't bother discussing the generous commission she'd been prepared to offer.

"It was good seeing youse, now if you'll excuse me, I have people waiting." He walked out without another word.

"Why'd you stop me from saying something to him?" Bee offered an indignant huff.

"Because he's not worth it." She patted his arm. "But I appreciate the gesture. Thank you."

Bee nodded and kissed her cheek.

"So, other than Fred being his usual nasty self, what do you think, Bee?" Cass had no doubt he'd be at the library as soon as possible, digging through their extensive local history section, especially after Fred had snubbed Cass and issued what Bee would most likely view as a challenge to Levi, provided they'd been talking about searching for the treasure, which wasn't a given. That wouldn't matter to Bee.

Bee looked her right in the eye. "I think it's no coincidence that Amelia alluded to Fred fooling around with someone, not very tactfully, either, and Levi found a way to slip in that he wasn't Fred's type, implying that someone else was."

Cass stood dumbfounded. "That's what you got from that whole encounter?"

"Yup." He waved a finger in the air. "And if Fred is fooling around, trust me, it hasn't hit the rumor mill yet, or I would have heard about it."

Stephanie stared in the direction Levi and Fred had gone. "Or someone really dropped the ball this time, and good ole Levi wants to make sure the news hits. I definitely sensed some animosity between those two."

"And who better to tell than Bee to make sure that rumor gets circulating?" Cass turned toward the display Levi had indicated and crossed the room. "You can barely read it here under this light."

Bee took out his phone, turned on the flashlight, and directed its beam toward the display.

A worn book sat on a stand beneath a glass case. A card beside it read "Kitty Garrison's Journal—the life of a lighthouse keeper's daughter."

"It doesn't look like much." Bee crossed the rope barrier set up to keep patrons from getting too close, then leaned close to the glass and squinted.

"It looks like a diary." Cass tilted her head to try to read what was inside the book but to no avail.

Bee opened the case.

"What are you doing, Bee? You can't open that." Stephanie shot out a hand and pushed the small door closed.

"Well, then, how am I supposed to know what's in it?"

"Easy," Stephanie said. "You wait for Amelia to come back and ask her if she'll let you read it."

"Yeah, but your way, she might say no. At least my way I can just apologize after the fact. And then we would have seen the inside of the book, maybe gained valuable information on how to find the treasure." He grinned. "Much better to apologize later than to ask permission now."

"Is that what this is about, Bee?" Cass wouldn't mind having a peek in the book, either, but she wasn't about to upset Stephanie. "You want to find the treasure?"

"You bet I do."

And somehow Cass had a feeling Levi had counted on that when he'd shared the story. "Question is, if Fred is trying to find the treasure, what does Levi have to gain by making sure everyone under the sun—or at least those living on and probably visiting Bay Island—knows about it?"

Bee shrugged off her concern. "Maybe he doesn't want to see Fred find the treasure? Not that I can blame him. Fred DiCarlo is not a nice man."

"I suppose, but still." Cass looked in the direction Levi had gone.

Voices carried into the museum, and Bee deftly hopped the security rope, then propped a hand on his hip and leaned against the railing, possibly going for a nonchalant pose that ended up looking more like *I just got caught doing something I shouldn't have been doing.*

When the group headed past the museum entrance and up the stairs, presumably toward the third floor, Cass tugged Bee's arm. "Come on, we'll climb the lighthouse before it gets too late. We can always come back here afterward, if there's time, and talk to Amelia. Maybe she'll let you read some of the book once everyone's gone."

Bee stared longingly at the journal, then sighed. "Sure thing. Whatever you say, Mum."

They headed out of the museum and followed the concrete walkway toward the lighthouse. The salty sea breeze rustled the bushes lining the path. The mild wind carried the softest hint of a whisper, tantalizingly close, yet just out of reach.

Cass paused. An illusion created by the wind funneling along the walkway? It had to be. It's not like she was giving a reading, and that's the only time the voices called to her, assailed her as they competed for her attention. At least, that's the only time they'd reached out to her so far.

Stephanie looked over her shoulder. "Are you coming, Cass?"

Bee stopped and turned, then frowned. "Is something wrong?"

Shaking off whatever apprehension had stopped her, Cass moved on. "Sorry, daydreaming, I guess."

"It's a beautiful day. I bet you'll be able to see for miles." Stephanie dug through her bag and pulled out her phone.

"Oh, definitely." Bee pointed past the bushes and over the choppy waters of the bay. "Look, you can see the south fork of Long Island from here."

The height of the bluff the lighthouse stood on offered an amazing view across the bay. A foghorn sounded from somewhere in the distance, seagulls circled and dove, occasionally coming up with a prize, and the ferry chugged toward Long Island, only about half full from the looks of it.

They entered the tower and started up the circular staircase, the clang of their shoes against the iron steps echoing off the sandstone walls.

"Not what it seems . . ."

"What do you mean?" Cass studied Bee's back as he climbed a few steps ahead of her, though how he did it in his signature platform shoes was beyond her.

He paused and looked back at her over his shoulder. "Huh?"

"You said something, but I didn't quite catch—"

"*Stop.*" The man's voice seemed to come from all around her at once.

This time she'd been staring straight at Bee, and he'd been in the middle of saying something else when the male voice had interrupted him.

A woman's voice joined the man's. "*Why don't you . . .*"

A chorus of voices answered in unison.

Cass shook her head, willing the voices to retreat. "Nothing, Bee. Sorry, I thought you said something."

Though the scowl remained firmly imprinted on his features, Bee turned and resumed his trek up the stairs, seemingly content to ignore whatever was happening with her. Probably for the best, anyway. If he thought for one minute ghosts haunted the lighthouse, he'd probably plow both Cass and Stephanie over in his haste to leave.

"*Watch . . . go . . . stop . . . please . . .*" The voices continued unsolicited, demanding, insistent.

"What do you want?" Cass yelled and covered her ears.

Bee stopped again and looked back. "Are you sure you're all right?"

"Yes, please . . ." She lowered her hands, taking a firm grip on the railing to steady her shaking hands. "Just go."

Bee shook his head and picked up the pace.

Fear skittered along Cass's spine as she tried to open herself up, make sense of what the voices wanted from her. She focused intently on one voice, that of a man, more demanding that the rest, just a bit louder. "*. . . lighthouse . . . rocks . . . look . . . back . . .*"

Look back? Look back where? Did he mean literally? She glanced over her shoulder at Stephanie bringing up the rear. She seemed okay. Maybe figuratively? Look back. But at what? The past? The story of the lighthouse keeper, maybe. Is that what the voice was trying to tell her?

They stepped onto the observation deck, the wall of windows opening up an even more incredible view than offered from the bluff. She closed her eyes and concentrated.

"You know," Bee said, "you could try to block the voices out, ignore them. That's what I do when I don't feel like hearing what people are saying."

"Bee!" Stephanie's mouth dropped open.

He held up a hand, his eyes wide, as if just realizing what he'd said. "Other people, I mean. You know, when I don't want to hear what other people are saying. Never you two."

Stephanie pointed a finger past Cass at him. "That had better be what you meant, buddy."

Bee grinned and held up both hands in a gesture of surrender. "Of course that's what I meant."

"Uh-huh." Eyeing him out of the corner of her eye, Stephanie returned to admiring the view. She snapped a few pictures with her phone.

Cass tried to ignore the bickering. She massaged her temples. If she didn't relax, she wasn't going to get anything.

Bee continued offering advice. "And if ignoring the voices doesn't work, you can try doing what I do when I walk into the diner, or the deli, or Tony's Bakery when there is an undeniable undercurrent of excitement rippling through the air, and I know before I take another step there's really good gossip to be had."

"What's that?" At that point, she'd try anything to shut them up.

He turned his back to the view, leaning against the railing that would keep anyone from falling through the circular wall of windows. "Narrow them down one at a time, eliminating those that don't seem to know anything, those who are just hanging out trying to make sense of what's going on the same as you are, and continue to whittle away at them, ignoring those you dismiss in favor of those who seem to have knowledge, then focus in on them until you get the message."

Cass moved to the railing lining the circular platform and leaned her hands on it. Choppy waves battered the coastline, washing up onto the large boulders lining the bluff and beach, sea foam bubbling over between crevices.

"Lighthouse . . . away . . . back . . . push . . ."

She couldn't grab it. Something, though, so close. Like something just at the edge of her awareness, something she should be able to . . . She closed her eyes, allowing the voices to wash through her.

"Stay . . . back . . . stay away . . ."

Her eyes shot open. "I've got it. I know what the voices are trying to tell me."

Bee folded his arms over his chest, no doubt over any talk of the paranormal. "Oh, and what's that?"

Cass tried to swallow, her mouth gone to paste, and glanced from him to Stephanie and back again. "Stay away from the lighthouse."

Bee groaned and returned his attention to the view of the bay.

Stephanie studied her. "Do you think—"

Movement in her peripheral vision caught Cass's attention. Her gaze shifted to the third floor of the keeper's house just as someone tumbled out the window toward the rocks below.

A silhouette backed away from the window, barely noticeable, a shadow among shadows as it slid away into darkness. Was the vision real? Or was she witnessing some past tragedy that had played out time and time again over the past couple of centuries? Hadn't Levi said Samuel Garrison had been found dead on the rocks below the lighthouse, the very same jetty someone had just fallen from the keeper's house onto?

Muffled screams in the distance assured her the man lying on the rocks was real enough, but what of the silhouette she'd seen as the man fell?

Chapter Four

Sirens wailed in the distance as Cass ignored the walkway and hurried through the beach grass covering the dunes on the fastest route to whoever lay on the rocks below the keeper's house.

A small crowd had already gathered, screams and sobs shattering the peaceful afternoon.

Cass reached the boulders and started across the slick surfaces. While her flats were perfectly fine for climbing the lighthouse stairs, they did not work for trying to scramble across wet, slippery rocks. She kicked them off, her bare feet giving her better traction.

"Help him," Amelia screamed, leaning over whoever lay at such an unnatural angle. "Oh, please, you have to help him."

The lifeguard Bee had been talking about earlier, Quincy Yates, knelt over the victim, ignoring Amelia's pleas, counting out loud as he administered chest compressions. Though he knelt on a somewhat flat rock beside the victim, his feet were braced against the boulder behind him. Amelia's constant tugging on his arm threatened to topple him from his tentative perch.

Good, though, that he'd known not to move the victim.

Cass reached them and took over CPR while Quince jumped to his feet and struggled to keep Amelia back. Even though a quick assessment assured Cass there was no chance of reviving Fred DiCarlo, she would continue until someone official arrived to make the determination.

Bee clambered across the rocks toward her, his scowl a picture of sheer determination. "What do you need?"

She caught his gaze and discreetly shook her head once. "I'm okay here, Bee. Why don't you and Stephanie see if you can help Amelia."

"Ah, man . . ." He shoved a hand through his thick hair, then nodded and started backing up, leaving her and Fred with a semicircle of gawkers around them, some on the rocks, others standing on the beach just short of climbing onto the dangerous surfaces.

Cass leaned farther forward so her hair would fall over her face, continuing the compressions that were too late to help Fred, and whispered, "Are you still here?"

Though she'd never tried to reach a newly departed spirit, she couldn't shake the image of the silhouette framed in the window as Fred had fallen. Or had he jumped? Been pushed?

"If you can hear me, Fred . . ." Though the wind tearing across the jetty would certainly carry her hushed voice away from prying ears, she was still careful to keep the volume barely above a whisper. "Tell me what happened. I'll try to help if I can, but I'm not sure what I saw."

Except for the screams, sobs, and hushed murmurs of the living, she was met with only silence.

Rick, a volunteer EMT and owner of the local deli, rushed toward her as fast as he could carrying the equipment he needed. With Rick handling the call, Emma Nicholls, one of his employees and Bee's only true rival in the gossip department, would have rumors flinging fast and furious before the dinner rush ended.

Following the same quick assessment Cass had done, Rick looked up and shook his head. "I'll take over, Cass, thanks."

She sat back on her heels to catch her breath, and waited until Rick's partner reached them, then scooted out of the way to give them room to work.

Bee still had his hands full with Amelia, whose gaze was riveted on Fred over Bee's shoulder as he tried to move her back toward the keeper's house.

Stephanie stood beside him talking to Levi, who held his cap against his chest, twisting it into a knot.

Alone, for the moment anyway, Cass headed back up to the walkway by the lighthouse. She leaned against the sagging split-rail fence and squinted against the sun to look into the window she'd seen Fred fall from. Unlike the rest of the windows, which reflected the white puffy clouds gliding through the afternoon sky, that one lay in shadow, an open maw swallowing the light of the day. Who had opened it? Fred? For what purpose?

She replayed the vision again. Fred tumbling toward the rocks. A shadow moving inside the window. What had caught her attention? Fred's movement, or the movement of another? She didn't know, couldn't say for certain either way. Great.

Luke, her . . . something, though she wasn't quite sure what— their relationship seemed to be progressing comfortably since he'd taken a position with the Bay Island Police Department and moved to Bay Island—worked the scene with his partner, Stephanie's husband, Tank.

She enjoyed watching Luke in his element, could imagine his laid-back drawl, comforting when witnesses would be upset, uncertain, scared—*take your time, no rush, just tell me what y'all saw whenever you're ready*—bringing to mind lazy afternoons swinging on a front porch with a friend, where time spent equaled quality, not pressure. Luke's casual stance and easy Southern charm would make witnesses open up to him in a way Tank's harder veneer wouldn't encourage. It was no surprise that Luke was talking to witnesses while Tank hovered over Rick and Fred.

What did surprise Cass was Chief Rawlins's attendance at the scene. A tall, handsome woman with an imposing presence, she studied the scene, issued an occasional quiet order, and lingered on the sidelines, seemingly content to let Luke and Tank do their thing. So why was she there?

She glanced toward Cass, held her gaze, seemed to study her across the dunes. Her salt-and-pepper hair, pulled back into a tight bun, enhanced her long neck and sharp features. Her suit appeared custom-tailored to fit her slim build. The kind of woman who made Cass fidget when confronted with her authority.

Cass shifted from one foot to the other, looked over her shoulder to see if anyone was behind her. Nope. She was alone. Maybe the chief's presence wasn't as surprising as Cass had originally thought, given she had a good idea what would come next.

Chief Rawlins nodded once, then started toward Luke.

Frowning, Luke looked down at his notes, then approached Bee where he sat on a bench with his arm around Amelia and squatted in front of them.

Though Bee didn't always trust the police, and even still seemed a bit nervous around Tank, he'd seemingly taken an instant liking to Luke, trusted him in a way he didn't trust many people. Could be the thick, shaggy dark hair that always hung a bit too long over his collar, or those sometimes dark and stormy blue eyes framed by lashes that would make any woman green with envy, or that thick Southern drawl he sometimes laid on that could send heat rushing through you, but she had a feeling it had more to do with the fact that Detective Tall, Dark, and Steamy had an easy way about him that inspired confidence. He accepted people for who they were and didn't indulge in an ounce of judgment.

When Bee pointed toward Cass, Luke stood and turned toward her.

She lifted a hand to wave. Seemed her quiet moment was over.

He started to move in her direction, but Chief Rawlins stopped him. Cass could almost hear the accent that spoke of her roots in New Orleans, the same roots that allowed her a belief in the occult that other officers of the Bay Island Police Department didn't share. Including Luke and Tank.

It didn't take any psychic abilities to figure out what she wanted.

Cass closed her eyes and reveled in the feel of the bay breeze fluttering through her hair. She breathed deeply the scent of lilacs, their lavender blossoms in full bloom, then sneezed. Twice.

Reluctantly, she opened her eyes. Obviously, no time for a reprieve. She'd have to decide quickly what to share with Luke. Not that she'd ever keep anything from him, especially something related to a murder investigation, if that's what this was, but she had no way to be sure what had been real and what imagined. She'd certainly share the fact she'd seen Fred fall, but what of the shadow?

She and Luke seemed to be headed toward something nice together, something special, despite Cass's trust issues, thanks to her ex-husband and her ex-best friend, and despite the fact Luke didn't really accept that Cass could communicate with the dead. That was okay, though; Cass sometimes had a hard time believing it herself.

Bee accepted that she thought she could communicate with the beyond with an eye roll and a shake of his head, as if he'd convinced himself her intuition manifested itself as spirits she could hear. Until recently, she'd have agreed with him.

Stephanie had always believed Cass could communicate with the dead, ever since they'd been kids and Cass had earned money for college offering readings on the boardwalk, much to the dismay of the local sheriff's department.

Luke's shoulders slumped ever so slightly, and he nodded to the chief, then turned and headed toward Cass.

Though she couldn't be sure, she suspected Luke's less-than-enthusiastic approach had something to do with the chief's firm belief in the use of psychics, especially Cass, if past experience was any indication.

The firm set of Luke's jaw assured her she was right.

When he reached her, his stance was all business, notepad out, pen poised. His eyes, however, held only sympathy swimming in their depths. "Are you okay?"

Was she? Surprisingly so. "Yes, I'm fine, thank you."

"Okay, beautiful . . ."

A million butterflies sent her stomach all aflutter, and she marveled he could still have that effect on her.

"Seems I'm expected to make a request of you." He pursed his lips, and Cass had to resist the urge to slip into his arms. "An official request."

"Oh?" She raised a brow and waited, determined not to glance past him at Chief Rawlins. "And what's that?"

He shifted uncomfortably beneath her admittedly too-intense stare. "Chief Rawlins would like your input on this case. Of course, I'll question you about what you saw, your impressions, all the usual, but I've also been instructed to ask you about what your . . . ahem . . . *other* senses might have picked up."

Under the circumstances, she resisted her first instinct to tease him, as she might have in other, less dire, situations. "Thank you, Luke. I appreciate you asking, especially since I know it wasn't easy for you."

"Look, Cass, I understand —"

"But I'm afraid I can't help."

"How you feel, but . . . Wait." Luke's eyes narrowed. "You're saying no?"

"I'm sorry." It wasn't that she didn't want to help, but with the chaos going on in her mind, and her inability to sort through the messages trying to reach her, she was afraid she wouldn't do much good. And even worse than just not figuring anything out would be misinterpreting a message she was receiving, as she had with the lighthouse that afternoon, and having someone get hurt because of her. "I'm afraid I just can't help right now. I'm having some issues."

She didn't need to stand there and go into the whole thing with him when he had more important things to do than trying to understand her malfunctioning psychic powers . . . or maybe over-functioning powers . . . whatever.

"You mean your . . ." He rolled a hand as Bee often did when trying to describe abilities he didn't understand. "Whatever . . . is on the fritz?"

She didn't try to hold back the smile. "You could say that."

He contemplated her for a moment, then nodded and let it drop. Probably for the best. "Okay, then. Can you tell me what you saw?"

She started at the beginning, talked him through their visit with Amelia, then shared her short conversation with Fred.

"Bee told me what he said; don't take it to heart, Cass."

"I didn't. Everyone knows how Fred is. He thinks he's funny, but as long as . . ." She caught herself midsentence, remembering Fred was no longer with them. "I mean . . . uh."

"Don't worry about it. You're not the first person to mention his crass personality." Luke flipped a page in his notebook.

"Thanks." She didn't mean to be disrespectful, simply understood and accepted Fred's shortcomings. It wasn't like she'd run into him often.

"Bee said Amelia made veiled references that led him to believe Fred might have been involved with someone other than his wife." He frowned, his disapproval evident in his expression.

He should probably learn to school his features better, as Tank had. Though she couldn't quite picture Luke with the hardened expression Tank, who was really a big teddy bear, always wore.

"Did you get that impression?"

"Huh?" She pulled herself back to the conversation. "Oh. Yes, but it's really just gossip at this point. Levi also made a crack about not being Fred's type when I suggested he should get a job as a tour guide."

"Why did you suggest that?"

"He had Bee enthralled, telling him a story about a ghost and a treasure."

Luke groaned.

"Hey, you asked."

"You're right. I did." With a sigh, he jotted something on the pad. "So, go ahead and elaborate, but please tell me you don't think a ghost had anything to do with Fred's death."

"Levi said something about seeing a ghost out on the jetty a few times, digging around the rocks." Did she really believe it was a ghost he'd seen? "Could be he saw someone, a real flesh-and-blood someone, out there searching for the treasure. Maybe even Fred. Although I can't figure out why he'd be out there dressed as a pirate."

"A pirate?"

"Yup. At least, that's what Levi said. Who knows? Maybe Fred was immersing himself in the past while he searched." Though it sounded false even as she said it.

He nodded and scribbled, probably happy to have something substantial to focus on. "What else can you tell me?"

Now for the tricky part. "I saw Fred fall from the window."

His gaze shot to hers. "You actually saw him fall out the window? How sure are you that he fell? Any chance he could have jumped?"

"I didn't see the exact moment he exited the window." She closed her eyes and replayed the scene, which presented itself in more detail than Cass would have liked. Fred tumbling, over and over in her mind, a constant loop, just those few seconds immediately after he must have gone out, his body falling, tumbling, while he made no attempt to right himself, turn over so his head wouldn't hit, flail his arms as would be instinct. "I'm sorry, Luke."

He stuffed the pen through the spirals of the notebook and stuck it into his pocket. "Don't worry about it. You're not the only one. Unfortunately, no one seems to have seen the exact moment he went out."

When he reached for her, she stepped back, held a hand against his chest. "No, I mean I'm sorry I'm about to make your life more difficult."

He froze where he was, slowly lowered his hand. "What do you mean?"

"I can't be sure, but . . ." Something nagged at her, the silhouette, just a shadow among more shadows. Not a man. Not a ghost. At least, she didn't think so, and yet . . . something.

"Stay away from the lighthouse," the phantom voice whispered in her ear.

She scoffed. "It's a little too late for that, buddy."

"What?" Luke frowned.

"Nothing, sorry." She waved him off, not even realizing she'd spoken the words out loud. "Fred was too limp when he fell. He made no attempt to turn over, didn't flail his arms or legs . . . Even if he'd jumped, I would've expected him to at least stiffen up. But he didn't. His body plummeted to the rocks completely relaxed, as if he were unconscious."

As expected, his notebook came back out. "You think he was unconscious when he fell?"

"I do. I'm almost positive I saw a flash of red on his head as he was falling. I think he sustained the head injury before he went out the window."

"Okay." He nodded and jotted something down. "But that still doesn't mean he was murdered. It's possible he hit his head on something in the room, then got disoriented or blacked out and fell."

Now for the tricky part. "I don't think he was alone."

"Did you see someone else with him?" Luke flipped back a few pages, stopping a couple of times to scan something he'd written, then moving on. "According to all of the witnesses we've questioned, everyone else left the room, and he was left alone, said he had something to do but they were dismissed. And Bee and Stephanie both claimed they didn't see anyone else from the lighthouse."

"I can't be sure, but there was a shadow, a silhouette that backed away even as Fred fell."

Luke let out a harsh breath and ran a hand over the goatee he'd been sporting of late, then propped his hand on his hip and met her gaze with the intensity of a lion on the hunt. "How sure are you, Cass?"

"I'm positive I saw the shadow." The image replayed itself every time she closed her eyes, more ingrained than that of Fred falling. She cringed and went for it. "I'm just not sure it was a real person."

He stared at her for a long moment. Weighing her answer? Maybe. Either way, he'd have to investigate Fred's death as a homicide now, with everyone who'd been present a suspect, including whatever ghosts might be haunting the Bay Island Lighthouse. "Do me a favor?"

She nodded. "Of course."

"Keep that to yourself for now. Don't tell anyone, not even Bee or Stephanie, what you saw."

She nodded again and lowered her gaze.

"I mean it, Cass." Luke propped a finger beneath her chin and lifted her gaze to his. "If someone helped Fred out that window, there's no point painting a target on your back if the killer thinks you saw him or can identify him by any other means."

Chapter Five

Cass's feet sank into sand that still remained cool as she walked down the beach toward Mystical Musings. Soon enough the sun would make it too hot to walk barefoot unless you walked along the shoreline where the cool water would lap at your feet. But for now, she was content to walk on the dry sand, enjoying the cool early morning breeze and the beautiful pinks and lavenders of the sunrise.

She tossed a stick ahead of her down the mostly deserted beach, and Beast charged after it, his shaggy fur blowing behind him as he ran. She'd need to make a grooming appointment soon. No way was she bathing him again. Ever. But it had been a while since any mishap had her calling and begging the groomer for an emergency appointment.

Yikes! What was she thinking? Better not to tempt fate. A small surge of anxiety washed over her, and she shifted to less stressful thoughts.

Like murder.

By the time they'd finished at the lighthouse the day before, it hadn't made sense to go back to work, so she'd just picked up Beast—who, thankfully, hadn't done any real damage while she was gone—and headed home, ignoring Bee's pleas to go to the diner. The last thing she needed was to be smack in the middle of gossip central. The otherworldly voices beating at her were enough.

Beast returned with the stick and dropped it at her feet, then looked up at her, panting.

"Wow, boy. That's a first." Usually, he plopped down some-where and chewed on the stick until she caught up with him, took it, and threw it again. She weaved her fingers into the thick fur on his head as they walked. "Come on, let's get you some water and breakfast."

Reluctantly leaving the peace of the morning behind—who knew? Maybe, like Bee, ghosts liked to sleep in, granting her an early morning reprieve—Cass turned toward Mystical Musings. When she reached the back deck, she sat down on the top step, brushed off her feet, and put her sandals on. She couldn't help her gaze drifting to the lighthouse standing sentinel on its bluff, warning sailors of the danger posed by the rocks below. Too bad that warning hadn't helped Fred.

"Come, Beast." She stood and brushed the sand from her shorts, then unlocked the back door and went inside. She didn't bother locking it back up; few customers would venture into the shops from the beach at that time of the morning.

The chimes tinkled as she opened the door, and she took a moment just to stand and survey the shop. She inhaled deeply, the scents of incense, bath salts, lotions, and candles mingling together, enveloping her in comfort, easing some of the tension that had become her constant companion of late.

Since she hadn't cleaned up before closing the day before, she set to straightening what little had been left out of place. After wiping down the large round table beside the back window and the driftwood countertop that held her register, she straightened rows of stones and crystals that were already perfectly aligned, since her past had left her with a burning need for order.

Beast nudged her leg with his nose.

She laughed and petted his head. "Sorry, boy."

She went to the back room, with Beast trotting beside her, filled his water bowl then scooped dog food into his food bowl. When she turned from the counter with both bowls in hand, Beast plopped right down to sit and his tongue dropped out.

Herb Cox, the dog trainer Bee had finally goaded her into calling, had been right about making him sit before feeding him. Honestly, that had been the easiest training of all. Since he was always eager to eat, he'd figured out early on that he didn't eat until he sat.

"Good boy, Beast." She placed the bowls on the floor, cleaned the counter and took his leash and a bag with her to wait by the back door until he was done.

It didn't take long.

She took him for a brisk, all-business walk, then added a few new toys from a cabinet in the back room to his toy basket. She'd found if she changed the toys up now and then he got less bored and did less damage. After starting a pot of coffee and another of hot water for tea, she unlocked the front door and set about reducing the price of her souvenir lighthouse figures.

She'd almost finished when the chimes signaled a customer. She stood and stretched her back.

Beast picked his head up from where he sat chewing on a bone, studied the newcomer, then returned to his chewing. He'd developed a knack for knowing which customers would greet him with enthusiasm and which wouldn't be interested.

A tall woman, her darker skin tone contrasted beautifully by her white sundress, her midnight black hair slicked back into a tight bun, nodded toward her before folding her Maui Jim sunglasses and tucking them into her collar. "Good morning, dear."

Cass held out her hand to the new customer, who didn't look at all familiar. Since her striking beauty and commanding presence made her memorable, she was probably a tourist. "Good morning. I'm Cass Donovan."

"Simone Carlson." She shook Cass's hand with a firm grip, her accent holding a hint of the islands. "It's a pleasure to meet you."

"It's a pleasure to meet you too. Can I help you with anything, or would you just like to browse?"

The woman strolled through the shop as she spoke, taking her time with both. "As much as I'd love to look around and shop, I have to make the next ferry to the mainland. I just wanted to stop in to set up an appointment for a reading before I left."

"Of course." Cass started toward the counter to get her appointment book. "So, what brought you to Bay Island? Work? Pleasure?"

"A little of both, I hope." The woman fished a business card from her Michael Kors bag and handed it to Cass. Simone's name, phone number, and email address were embossed in gold ink on the black card. "I'm hoping to purchase Bay Island Tours."

"Bay Island Tours?" Fred's company had gone up for sale already? Or was this woman some kind of vulture who preyed on people while they were grieving in hopes of taking over a profitable business at a very reduced price? Her casual, relaxed manner would certainly inspire trust, soothe the aching soul of a grieving widow. Cass's spine stiffened instantly in Amelia's defense. "I wasn't aware it was for sale."

"Yes, I've been in discussions with the current owner for the past month. I was told they were trying to add a paranormal element, something I'd very much enjoy. Which, since I have neither the time nor the patience for game playing, brings me to the ulterior motive for my visit."

"Oh?" Cass opened her planner on the counter and grabbed a pen. "What's that?"

"I was hoping you'd agree to participating in my tours. I was going to wait until after my reading to discuss it with you, but I have to be honest . . ." She waved a hand around the shop with a flourish. "I loved the vibe the minute I walked in here, and I'd love to include your shop as one of my stops."

Cass's heart fluttered. That was exactly what she'd been hoping Fred would agree to. And yet . . . Guilt dampened some of the excitement. "I'm sorry, I don't know if you're aware, but Fred DiCarlo was killed yesterday."

"Oh, my." A delicate hand with long thin fingers and long maroon nails fluttered to her chest. "I'm sorry, I hadn't heard."

"I don't know if that changes your plans or your interest in a reading, but I—"

"Oh, no, not at all, dear." She set her bag on the counter and rummaged through its contents. "While that is quite unfortunate news, my discussions have not been with Mr. DiCarlo, they've been with the owner."

"Oh?" Caught off guard, Cass didn't have time to censor herself. "I thought Fred was the owner of the company?"

She pulled out her cell phone. "Oh, no. I've been discussing the acquisition of the tour company with Amelia DiCarlo."

"Amelia?" From what everyone had said, Fred had been excited about adding the ghost aspect of the tours. Why would Amelia have been selling the business? Bee was going to have a field day with this one. Finally, she might get to one-up him.

"Yes. She posted the business for sale last month, and we negotiated a very reasonable price." The woman scrolled through her phone as she spoke but still managed to keep her full attention on Cass.

Cass nodded, her mind racing. Had Fred known she planned to sell? Did she even have the authority to sell?

Luke had told Cass to keep quiet about seeing someone in the keeper's house window when Fred was killed but, surely, he'd be okay with her passing this tidbit on to Bee. Where it would take Cass some time to gather any information on the sale, if she could ever come up with any results, Bee would be on it and have answers in no time.

Simone looked at her watch and frowned. "Though this certainly does change things. I'm afraid I will have to stay on Bay Island a bit longer to pay a visit to Amelia and pay my respects, as would only be proper. Excuse me a moment, please."

Cass waited while she shot off a quick text.

"There. My assistant will take care of rescheduling my affairs. Now . . ." She returned her attention to Cass. "I was hoping to come in this weekend, but since it seems I'll be extending my stay, do you have tomorrow morning free?"

Cass flipped to the appropriate page in her book. "I can pretty much do whatever time you'd like."

"Hmm . . . I will be returning to the mainland later in the day, and I'd like to get an early start. Would it be possible to come in around six?"

Cass wouldn't typically open anywhere near that early, though she often walked the beach to the shop at sunrise when it was less crowded, then had breakfast with Bee and Stephanie before he went to bed and she and Stephanie went to work. But she wanted to talk to this woman, to find out why Amelia would have had the business up for sale without Fred's knowledge, or if Fred had known. And she would love the opportunity to be featured on a tour. "That would be perfect."

"Wonderful." She took a long look around the shop before sliding her sunglasses back on. "You wouldn't happen to know the history of this building, would you?"

"Uh . . . no, but I suppose I could look it up."

Simone waved a hand. "No bother, dear, I'll have someone take care of it. 'Til tomorrow, then."

Cass watched her climb into a black Porsche and gun the engine as she left the parking lot. Cass had liked the woman. Her easygoing way had cast an aura of peace and contentment. She just hoped Simone Carlson was legitimate and not some con artist who had her charming charade down pat.

A quick glance at the clock—barely ten thirty in the morning—

told her Bee, who often worked in his back room through the night to avoid interruptions, would have her head if she called.

She dialed anyway, then tapped her foot through four rings before he finally picked up.

"Is anyone else dead?" he mumbled.

"No, but . . ."

Bee hung up.

Great, now what? Stephanie had to work all day, and Cass really wanted to know what was going on with Amelia. The question of the business being for sale nagged at her, and no one could do research like Bee.

A familiar figure hurried across the lot toward Mystical Musings, and Cass grinned as she dialed Bee again.

It only took two rings this time. "If you want to remain friends—"

"Emma Nicholls is headed toward my shop as we speak," she blurted before he could hang up again. "If you'd rather me discuss the dirt I've got with her, by all means, go back to sleep."

She waited him out, humming a familiar tune she couldn't recall the name of. He'd never in a million years let Emma, his nemesis in the gossip department, get first dibs on whatever Cass had found out.

The sound of chimes carried through the phone to Bee. "You're bluffing."

"Am I?" She lifted the phone away from her ear but kept it where Bee would hear both her and Emma. "Good morning, Emma."

"Hey, Cass. How are you doing after that fiasco yesterday? I heard you tried to revive Fred."

"Okay!" Bee yelled.

"Excuse me one moment, please, Emma." She pressed the phone back against her ear. "I'm sorry, sir."

"Don't you give her one measly crumb." The sounds of Bee frantically rushing around to get dressed had her biting back laughter. "Ouch . . . Ugh . . . I'm on my way."

"That will be fine, sir, thank you. I'll see you then." She hung up and set the phone aside. "Sorry, Emma."

"Oh, no, please, don't worry about it. I didn't realize you were on the phone." Since Emma worked at the deli Rick owned, and Rick had been one of the first paramedics on the scene at the lighthouse, it was no surprise she already knew about Cass's attempts to save Fred.

Beast trotted over and sat, his rear end wagging frantically along with his tail.

"Good morning." Emma laughed and petted him. "You're a good boy, Beast."

"He is, isn't he?" Mostly. Cass rounded the counter. "Do you want coffee or tea? I have coffee cake this morning from Tony's. Gina dropped it off a little while ago, and it's still warm."

"Oh, mmm . . . that sounds amazing, but I'm shopping for a birthday gift for my mom, so would it be okay if we did that first, just in case you get busy?" To Beast's disappointment, Emma released him and lifted a peach-scented candle beneath her nose and sniffed. "Wow. That smells so good."

Cass offered Beast a treat from a jar beside the register, and he forgot all about Emma and ran off to either eat it or hide it somewhere. Hopefully, he wouldn't try to dig a hole through the wood floors again. As it was, she spent enough time on her hands and knees trying to fill in the scratches his claws left in the wood. "Do you have anything special in mind for your mom?"

"Not really." She chose a vanilla candle next. "This smells amazing too. My mom loves candles. She keeps tons of them in the fireplace and burns them while she curls up on the couch to read every night."

"I could put together a basket for you, with different scented candles."

"She'll love the basket of candles, but I was hoping to get her something a little more personal too. It's her fiftieth birthday, and she swears if she doesn't celebrate, the year won't count and she can stay in her forties." Emma laughed.

"Are you and your mom close?" Though she could already tell they were by the warmth in Emma's voice as she teased.

"Very. She is my best friend in the world."

The easy affection she spoke with gave Cass a quick pang of grief, the loss of her own mother a few years earlier still an open wound. "So, you need a gift that will make her realize that the past fifty years have been meaningful, make her happy to be where she is at this point in her life."

"Yes." Emma squealed and clasped her hands together. "Exactly. Do you have something like that?"

"I think I might have just the thing." Cass led Emma toward an octagonal glass display case in the center of the shop.

Emma browsed as she followed. "Oh, and I definitely want a gift certificate for a reading. She's been talking about coming in for one since you opened."

Cass smiled, thrilled with the idea of meeting Emma's mother. Despite Emma's passion for gossip, and the fact that Cass had to watch every word when they were together, Emma was one of those people who was just fun to be around. She always offered a smile and a kind word, and as much as she enjoyed gossiping, Cass had never heard her utter a mean word about anyone.

She unlocked the case and took out a small black velvet box with a necklace nestled inside, then handed it to Emma.

"Ooh, it's beautiful." She ran a finger over the delicate design, two interlocked rings, one slightly larger than the other, on a thin gold chain.

"The circles represent mother and daughter, and the design is an infinity symbol. It honors the infinite bond between the two of you, reminds her you are always linked, your love eternal."

"Oh, Cass." Tears shimmered in Emma's eyes. "It's perfect. Mom is going to love this."

A thrill coursed through her, the same thrill she always got when she was able to read the perfect gift someone needed and help them find that just right expression of their deepest feelings. "I'm so glad I could help. I'll wrap it up and put it in a basket with some candles."

"Wait. How much is it?" Emma started to turn the box over.

Cass plucked it out of her hand. "Don't worry. I promise it's affordable. And we'll ring the rest up one thing at a time, if you want, so you can see how it's adding up."

"That would be great, thank you."

Cass discreetly removed the price tag from the bottom of the box as she returned to the register. Emma was young, and everyone knew she'd given up a scholarship to go away to college in order to stay on Bay Island and work locally to help her mom out. She'd discount the items as far as she could without losing money to help Emma out.

When she'd finished ringing Emma up, she set a number of different-sized pillar candles in a basket amid pink tissue paper, then added the necklace, displayed in the open box, the gift certificate, which she only charged half price for, and wrapped the entire package in silver cellophane. She finished the package off with pink and silver ribbons. The scent of the candles permeated the wrapping, enveloping the entire package in the warm aroma of vanilla and peach.

"Thank you so much, Cass. Mom's going to love it." Emma leaned over the basket and inhaled deeply. "I guess what they say about you is true."

"Oh?" Cass's interest piqued. "And what's that?"

"That you have a knack for helping people choose the perfect gift."

Cass grinned. That was a reputation she could live with. "And now, how about that coffee cake?"

"You bet, thanks." Emma crossed to the back counter with Cass. Used to how Cass did things, Emma set out two mugs. "Coffee or tea?"

Cass laughed. "You serve coffee in the deli all day long; sit, relax. I'll take care of it. Coffee or tea?"

"Thanks, Cass. I'll have coffee, please." She flopped onto a couch in a small seating arrangement, slid off her sneakers and tucked one foot underneath her. "So, rumor has it you tried to revive Fred. That must have been hard."

Cass filled both mugs with coffee and set them on a tray. "I'm just sorry I couldn't save him."

"Did you know him?" She picked at the hem of her jeans, her gaze firmly fixed on a loose thread.

After adding cream and sugar to the tray, along with two plates of coffee cake, Cass set it on the low coffee table and took a chair across from Emma. "I knew him, but not well. I know Amelia better."

"Thank you." Emma turned to face the table but made no move to fix her coffee. "I knew him, sort of, because he came into the deli all the time."

Cass sensed she was working her way around to something, so she remained quiet as she added cream to her coffee and stirred longer than necessary.

Finally, Emma looked up at Cass. "There are other rumors going around too."

"Oh?" Her gut told her she wasn't going to like the other rumors, so did the chorus of voices whispering in her head. She ignored both. "What kind of rumors?"

"Look, Cass, I really came in to give you a heads-up, though I did also need a gift for my mom's birthday, and I'm so glad I did because it's absolutely perfect, but I figured I'd kill two birds with one stone, you know?" She twisted the hem of her T-shirt between her hands.

"It's okay, Emma." Whatever she had to say clearly held more importance than idle gossip, and Emma hadn't been entirely comfortable coming to Cass with it. "I understand, and I appreciate you coming directly to me rather than talking about it with anyone else."

"Thank you for that." She smiled. "At first, I thought about waiting for Bee to make the rounds and stop in the deli, since I knew he would with Fred dying and all, then quietly talking to him, because I know how tight the two of you are. But I didn't want to be overheard, and well, you know, when people see Bee and me with our heads together, they automatically eavesdrop. It's almost like an invitation."

The two biggest gossips on all of Bay Island, one day after a man fell to his death from the lighthouse—she could see where people might be interested in what they were talking about. Cass sipped her coffee and waited.

"So, anyway, I figured I'd come in and give you a warning."

She almost spit the coffee all over, managed to choke it down, and stared wide-eyed at Emma.

"You okay?"

Cass nodded. "A warning?"

"Well, people are saying you tried to revive Fred, but when you couldn't, you had a conversation with him instead." She looked so hopeful. "And he told you who killed him."

Cass hated to dash her dreams but, oh boy, that was not a rumor she could afford to have spreading. Apparently, she hadn't been as discreet as she'd thought. "I'm sorry, Emma, but I didn't have a conversation with him, and as far as I know, his cause of death hasn't been determined as of yet."

Her hopeful expression fell. "Really?"

"Nope, sorry." She could give her something, though, and, at the same time, somehow spread a rumor of her own, that Fred had absolutely not uttered one word to her. At least then, if it turned out he was murdered, she'd be out of the spotlight. "The spirits were restless that day, trying to warn me not to go to the lighthouse, but I had a hard time sorting out the message and received it too late. Even if Fred had tried to tell me anything, it would have been muffled by the constant barrage of voices."

"Really?" She perked right up then and dug into her coffee cake. "Don't you worry, I promise I'll make sure everyone in town knows you weren't able to get any message from Fred by the time the deli closes tonight."

Chapter Six

Bee barreled through the front door and skidded to a stop, huffing and puffing like he'd sprinted all the way there, just as Emma turned to leave with her gift basket.

Emma stopped short an instant before Bee would have plowed into her and smiled. "Oh, hey, Bee."

Beast barked once and charged him, but Bee stopped him in his tracks with a stern warning look Cass really needed to master.

"Emma." He nodded once and straightened his tunic-style shirt, which he'd apparently put on inside out in his hurry to make it out the door, unless, of course, seams and tags on the outside were a new fashion statement he was pursuing. "Good to see you."

"You too. I've gotta run, but I'm sure I'll see you at the deli later." She sidestepped him and glanced over her shoulder at Cass. "And don't you worry, I'll make sure the right rumors get circulating."

Bee watched her walk out the door then rounded on Cass. "What was that about? I told you I'd be here."

"I know, Bee, and I appreciate it—"

"Then what rumors is she talking about?" Red tinged his cheeks, though whether it was from his mad rush down there or his blood boiling over Emma's comment, Cass couldn't tell.

"Relax, Bee. Grab a bottle of water while I get Beast out, and then we'll sit and talk." After he'd had a few minutes to calm down and collect himself, which she didn't dare tell him to do, or she'd be in for the attitude of a lifetime.

When she returned with Beast, Bee was pacing the shop from one end to the other. He whirled toward her the instant the door opened. With a quick pet for Beast, he pinned her with a harsh stare. "Okay, Cass, while I appreciate that you didn't tell me to calm down, because you know that only makes things worse, it's time for you to explain what's going on."

"Sure thing. Have a seat." She gestured toward the back table.

He sighed but did as she'd asked, leaning his chair to tilt on the two back legs.

She sat across the table from him, looking out over the bay. "First off, it's not what you think. What Emma was talking about was something completely different from what I called you about."

Bee just stared at her and held up his hands, the chair wobbling precariously beneath his two-hundred or so pounds—all of it muscle, despite his lack of regular exercise, but still a lot for the two chair legs straining to keep him balanced. "Okay, enough with the drama. You don't see me being that cryptic when I deliver good gossip, do you?"

He was often more so, but she kept that to herself. She might have been offended at his attitude and snapped back, but she could read the underlying hurt that she'd asked Emma for help instead of him. He should know better, and the fact he didn't hurt more than annoyed her. Cass didn't trust easily, but she trusted Bee, and she expected his trust in return. "Emma came in to buy a gift for her mother's birthday, and while she was here, she told me rumors were spreading that I spoke to Fred at the crime scene and he told me who killed him."

"Oka—uh . . ." Bee's eyes went wide, and the chair dropped onto all fours with a loud thump and a creak of protest. "Are you serious?"

"That's what she said, so I have to assume it's right. Emma's information usually is."

Bee shook his head. "So, Fred was murdered."

Uh-oh. "No, I mean . . . uh . . ."

"Well, was he or wasn't he?"

Cass blew out a breath. And that's how rumors got started. "I don't know if it's true, just that it's a rumor, along with the fact that I talked to him."

"Did you?"

It seemed weird Bee was suddenly able to accept that not only were there ghosts, but Cass was able to chat them up on a whim. She ignored it. It wasn't an argument she had time for. "No, though I did try."

"Who was standing close to you when you tried?"

She closed her eyes. Though some people had ventured onto the rocks, most had stayed back on the sand. When she'd taken over chest compressions, Quincy had backed away and reached for Amelia to keep her from knocking Cass off the jetty. By the time more help had arrived, Bee had already moved Amelia back, and Quincy had returned to hover fairly close by. But had he ever moved away? "When you asked if I needed help, I told you to go to Amelia, remember?"

"Yes. She was trying to see over your shoulder, and I didn't want her to get a view of . . ." Bee rolled a hand. "Well, you know."

"Yes, but where was Quincy Yates?"

Bee squinted and scratched his head. "He was standing on the rocks in front of Amelia, whether intentionally trying to block her from seeing her husband or just trying to get a closer look at what was going on, I couldn't tell."

"Then he was probably closer than anyone else at the time." No matter how hard she tried to envision the scene, she couldn't see who'd been standing on the jetty when she'd bent over Fred. Either she hadn't seen then, in her rush to help Fred, or she couldn't remember. Either way, Quincy seemed the most likely candidate. "Do you think he could have overheard my attempt to reach Fred?"

"Possibly. I do remember him watching you try to revive him while I was trying to console Amelia, but then again, so was everyone." He snapped his fingers. "You know who else was hovering over you on the rocks?"

Cass shook her head, her mind still on Quincy. He was certainly strong enough to have hit Fred over the head and thrown him out the window. But then why try to revive him?

"That nasty tour guide he was dating last year, Piper Bonavich."

The name jerked Cass's focus from Quincy.

"She had her hand on Quince's shoulder to steady herself on the rocks while this year's fling, that new tour guide, Francesca Harding, stood nearby on the beach glaring at them."

Cass just stared at him.

He finger-combed his hair, his cheeks blazing red. "What?"

"Seriously? A man was dead, and you noticed all of that?"

Folding his arms across his chest, he snorted. "Well, in my defense, I didn't know he was dead at the time. Besides, it was hard to miss the tension zinging among the three of them."

As much as Bee distrusted the police, he'd missed his calling, because he'd have made a great detective. The guy didn't miss a single detail.

"Anyway." They'd strayed too far off topic. She needed to refocus, get back to the matter at hand. "If you remember, the spirits were restless that day, battering me so badly I didn't even understand the message to stay away. And that's exactly what I told Emma, the rumor she's promised to spread in place of the other, more dangerous one."

Bee sulked. "And you trusted her to do that more than me?"

Cass sighed, trying to curb some of her frustration. "It's not that I trusted her more, Bee, it's just that she came to me with that, and I had another, more important matter to discuss with you."

He raised a big bushy brow. "Nothing is more important than keeping you safe, Cass."

And just like that, the bubble of frustration surrounding her burst. She reached across the table to grip his hand. "Thank you for that, Bee. I can't tell you how much I appreciate it. But this is important and not something I could trust to just anyone."

He squeezed her hand, then released it and sat back. She might not have fully absolved herself in his eyes, but at least she was on her way. "A woman named Simone Carlson came into the shop earlier."

He frowned and shook his head, indicating he didn't know who she was.

"She's from out of town, says she's been in talks with the owner of Bay Island Tours for the past month negotiating a fair price."

"Fred was selling?" Bee asked.

Apparently, that rumor hadn't yet circulated. "That's just it, she said she was in talks with Amelia."

"Amelia?" Bee stood and started to pace, not the rushed pace he adopted when he was angry, but a smooth, steady, thoughtful pace. Bee in full concentration mode.

"Yup."

Beast fell into step beside Bee, keeping stride with him back and forth across the shop.

Bee absently laid a hand on the big dog's head. "Hmm . . ."

"That's it? Hmm . . . That's all you've got?" For all the drama, Cass had expected something more.

"No, just trying to think."

"Don't you find it just a little odd Amelia had the company up for sale before Fred even died?"

"I don't know." He paused and propped his hands on his hips. "Fred was adding the paranormal element; maybe he and Amelia had planned to sell, and they were adding it to jack up the price."

Stumped, Cass stared down at the table. "I hadn't thought of that."

"So, what'd you think?" Bee's voice held a note of skepticism she wanted to ignore. "Amelia knew he was going to die?"

It was Cass's turn to squirm under his sharp stare. That was exactly how it had seemed to her. "Wee-ell . . ."

"Seriously?"

An idea started to form, hesitant at first, hazy, then solidifying. "I don't know. It just seemed odd to me is all. Haven't you ever heard something that just didn't sit right in your gut? Not necessarily for any reason you could put your finger on?"

He flopped back onto the chair, leaned back, rubbed his hands over his face, and yawned. "I don't know. Maybe, I guess."

"And Amelia and Levi both suggested Fred might have had something going on the side." Had he been killed because of it? Very few people knew that answer. Probably only Fred and his killer. And since she couldn't talk to his killer . . . that only left one option.

Bee sat up straighter and scooted toward the edge of the chair. "They did both imply he was cheating, didn't they?"

"You were the one who pointed that out to me when we were there." And it was odd. Amelia had never seemed the type to air her dirty laundry in public. Then again, maybe they'd just happened in at a particularly vulnerable moment.

He was already nodding. "Yes, I did. I thought it weird at the time that they both mentioned it. Huh . . ."

"You were with Amelia right after it happened. How did she act?"

He gave up sitting and pacing and headed to the back counter for coffee, moving from one thing to the next in rapid-fire succession, like a kid who was afraid if he stayed still too long, he'd fall asleep. "I don't know. Upset, at least at first, probably more shocked than anything, but then she stopped crying and hardened her resolve. I figured she was just trying to wrap her head around what happened."

"And now?"

Bee took his time preparing his coffee, filled a new mug for Cass, and cut two slices of coffee cake. "Now, I'm not so sure. It seemed once she got over the initial shock, she pulled herself together better than I could have."

Since Bee tended to run toward the dramatic, they both knew that didn't mean much.

"But in the end, she seemed to think he jumped."

"Seriously?" That was the one option Cass hadn't explored.

He slid her second slice of cake for the day in front of her, set down her coffee mug, then brought his own coffee and cake to the table and sat. "Yeah, at least that's what she said. She also said maybe he couldn't live with the guilt anymore."

"What guilt?"

"She didn't elaborate, didn't even allude to his infidelity as she had earlier, but I assumed . . ." He took a bite of cake and moaned. "Oh, this is so good."

"It is, isn't it? Gina dropped a few by this morning." Gina was married to Tony of Tony's Bakery, and she often dropped off treats for Cass to serve her customers. It was a mutually beneficial arrangement, since Cass got to serve delicious, freshly baked treats, and Tony's got some exposure. Not that the bakery needed any more exposure, as the line often wrapped around the building, especially on Sundays, when they served cannoli balls.

Her stomach growled, but she ignored the cake in favor of the coffee that probably wouldn't slather ten pounds onto her thighs.

"So, what do you think happened?" Though she'd promised Luke she wouldn't talk about what she might or might not have seen, she hadn't promised she wouldn't ask anyone else what they thought.

"I honestly don't know. A few moments sooner, and everyone would have been in the room with him. A few moments later, and they'd all have been outside when he fell . . . or whatever . . ." He finished off his cake and pointed to hers with his fork. "Are you going to eat that?"

With a wistful sigh, she pushed the dish toward him.

"Thanks." He broke off a piece but didn't take the bite. "As it was, Fred had just dismissed the group of tour guides and, though they'd all scattered, no one had made it outside yet, so no one actually saw him go out the window. Unless . . ." He paused and waited, studying her.

Cass controlled any involuntary reaction. At least she hoped she did. Besides, she hadn't actually seen him go out the window, probably because she'd been watching the shadow behind him instead.

Bee pounced. "Cass . . . what aren't you telling me?"

She was saved from having to answer by the tinkle of wind chimes.

"Good morning." She stood to take care of the two women who'd entered. The sooner they left, the sooner she could work on trying to contact Fred.

Bee laid his fork down on the plate and caught her arm as she passed. "This conversation isn't over, not by a long shot, but when I finish my cake, I'll let you get back to work while I make the rounds and see what I can find out. And don't you worry. While I'm at it, I'll have a discreet talk with Quincy Yates."

Chapter Seven

Cass strolled across the diner parking lot with Bee and Stephanie, her mind a million miles away, trying to make sense of the constant, overwhelming chatter every time she tried to reach out to the beyond. After Bee had left, she'd tried to contact Fred, to no avail. Her attempts had left her with a pounding headache and nothing to show for her efforts.

When Bee had called and asked her to meet him and Stephanie at the diner, she'd almost declined, the desire to go home and snuggle with Beast for the night and forget about everything else a physical ache. But she didn't dare blow him off after the Emma fiasco that morning. As it was, she was on thin ice with him.

As they neared the door, a group of young women hurried up the stairs toward the front entrance.

Bee stepped ahead of Cass and started to reach for the door.

A young woman Cass probably would not have recognized had she not looked Bee up and down then sneered, stopped and waited for him to open the door.

Cass reached out and gripped his arm, then smirked at Piper Bonavich. "Hold on a sec, Bee."

He stepped away from the door and waited at her side while she rummaged through her purse for some imaginary thing that might have caused her to pause.

One of Piper's companions opened the door, and Piper shot Cass a dirty look before hurrying into the diner with her friends.

Stephanie laughed. "You do know that was really rude, right, Cass?"

She simply shrugged. Petty? Maybe. But she didn't care; no one got away with treating Bee like that.

Bee leaned down and kissed her cheek, then whispered in her ear, "You're forgiven."

A surge of warmth rushed through her, and most of the tension left her body. She hated being on the outs with Bee. It seemed nothing went right when they were angry with one another, or worse, when one of them hurt the other. But you couldn't be as close as she and Bee were without hurting each other now and then. The key was in accepting that everyone made mistakes, forgiving each other, and moving past them.

Bee opened the door, then mock bowed as they entered.

Unfortunately, since the place was packed, they couldn't even ask the hostess for a seat somewhere far away from the group. Instead, they ended up in the booth behind them. At least Piper's back was to them, so they wouldn't have to deal with her shooting them dirty looks throughout their meal.

Cass purposely slid into the booth on the side that would put her back to back with Piper. No sense letting Bee overhear any rude comments she might decide to make.

Stephanie sat beside her, leaving Bee the empty seat across from them.

Bee didn't bother opening his menu. "Do you guys know what you're having?"

With the dull ache in her head still lingering in the background, Cass didn't have much of an appetite.

"I'm just going to have grilled cheese with tomato and bacon, maybe fries," Stephanie said.

"That sounds good. I'll have the same thing." If the queasiness in her stomach abated long enough for her to eat. Exhaustion and stress definitely took their toll.

Bee stacked the menus together, then sat back while the busboy filled their water glasses. "How's everything going, Frankie?"

"Oh, not bad, Mr. Bee. You know how it is." Frankie, the owner's teenage son who'd just started bussing tables this season, leaned a hip against the side of Bee's seat. "Almost out of school for the year, and I can't wait to get out to the beach."

"I remember that feeling well," Bee agreed. "Do you have any plans for the summer, other than going to the beach?"

"Well, just between us . . ." He leaned closer. "I'm hoping to get Jess to go out with me, maybe take a tour of the lighthouse or something. If they ever open it again, that is."

"Hey, Frankie," his father yelled from behind the counter as he shook his head. "Let's keep it moving."

"Sorry, guys, gotta run." He started away, then turned back to Bee. "Maybe, if you run into Jess, you could, you know, put in a good word for me or something?"

Bee grinned. "You bet, Frankie."

He waited for Frankie to hurry off, then leaned across the table toward Cass. "See, even Frankie knows who to turn to when he needs help."

Cass sighed. So much for being forgiven. But the fact that he didn't dwell on it told her he didn't still harbor any hard feelings, but he also wasn't likely to let her forget too easily. Maybe he just wanted to make sure she didn't repeat the same mistake again.

Piper's group laughed out loud, really loud, drowning out anything else Bee might have said.

"Well . . ." Piper said, her tone somewhat more hushed but still loud enough for Cass to hear. "We're supposed to meet up tonight at the lighthouse, but I guess we'll see what happens. Can't very well take a chance of running into one of the cops crawling around all over the place up there."

"What about Amelia?" one of her companions asked.

"What about her? Do you really think —"

"Hi, guys." Their waitress, Elaina Stevens, stood at the side of their table. She winked at Bee. "Somehow, I expected to see you three tonight."

Bee shrugged. "You know how it is. Gotta keep up."

She laughed. Since she was born and raised on Bay Island, and also worked as a maid at the Bay Side Hotel, she knew exactly how it was. Big news brought busy nights. And any unexplained death topped the list of big news. "Aside from gossip, what can I get you tonight?"

While Bee placed their orders, adding a loaded bacon cheeseburger, fries, and coleslaw for himself, Cass tried to focus her attention back on Piper and her friends. No use. Bee's banter with Elaina drowned out anything more they might have had to say.

"I'll be back with your drinks in a minute." Elaina headed off, all smiles as she stopped at a few tables to see if anyone needed anything.

Bee leaned forward and folded his arms on the table, pitching his voice low. "Okay, so I made the rounds today."

Stephanie leaned in too. "And?"

"And it seems the rumors that Cass spoke to Fred after he was killed have slowed to a trickle," he grudgingly admitted. "Most of the people still discussing it are those who heard it late last night and early this morning."

"That's good, anyway." A little more tension seeped out of Cass's muscles, allowing her to relax a bit more. She tilted her head from side to side, trying to ease the stiffness that had settled in her neck, probably while she'd leaned back at an awkward angle trying to eavesdrop on Piper's conversation. How did Bee do that all the time?

"But . . ." Bee held up a finger and leaned even closer. "Rumors of Fred's infidelity are apparently running rampant."

"Oh, yeah?" Stephanie sat back to allow Elaina to place her diet soda on the table.

She put Cass's iced tea and Bee's cola down as well. "Can I get you anything else while you're waiting?"

"No, thanks." Bee waggled his eyebrows. "Unless you have any good dirt to pass on."

"Let's see. Obviously, you've heard about Fred's untimely death, since Cass tried to revive him, but have you heard he was supposedly cheating on Amelia?"

"Oh, yes." Bee pressed a hand against his chest. "That poor dear, as if it's not enough her husband's gone."

"I heard she's taking it pretty hard," Elaina said.

Cass's heart ached for her. She knew all too well what it was like to be the latest gossip fodder for Bay Island's rumor mill. Maybe she'd swing by her house and check in on her, see if she needed anything.

Bee's gasp pulled her attention back to the conversation.

"Seriously? Personally, I find it hard to believe he'd find one willing partner, never mind several." Bee seemed to agree with something Elaina had said that Cass must have missed.

"No kidding, but have you heard who his most recent conquest is supposed to have been?" Elaina looked around then leaned against the side of Cass's seat and discreetly hooked a thumb toward Piper's table and nodded knowingly. She leaned over under the guise of checking if the salt and pepper shakers were empty. "Supposedly, they were together last season while she was seeing Quincy Yates, and Quince was none too happy when he found out."

"Thanks, Elaina." Bee sipped his cola.

"Yup, gotta run, though, full house tonight." She hurried off before she got caught lingering too long in one spot.

"You said you were going to talk to Quince when you left the shop before. Did you ever find him?"

"Nope. I went to the Bay Island Tours office, but it was locked up tight, not a soul around. So I stopped in and hung around the hotel lobby for a bit, but none of the tour guides came in or went out while I was there." Bee swirled his straw in his drink.

"Are they staying at the hotel this year?" Usually, the tour guides grouped up and rented a house in town for the season.

"Nah, but I figured it was worth a try." His ice clinked against the sides of the glass in a steady rhythm. "I even walked down the beach and the boardwalk, figured maybe he headed out there since they couldn't work, but I didn't see him. I did run into Levi at the lighthouse, though. He was wandering the grounds."

"Did he have anything to say?" Levi would have his ear to the ground at the lighthouse, and he'd share whatever he learned with Bee in hopes of getting some juicy tidbits in return.

"Not really. I talked to him a little about the treasure and the journal documenting its supposed location, but he didn't really have anything new to offer."

"How did he seem?"

"Kind of lost really, like without going to work he didn't know what else to do with himself."

"Do you know when they're planning to open the lighthouse again?"

"No. Luke didn't mention it?"

Cass shook her head. She'd only spoken to Luke for a few minutes the night before, while she'd been getting ready for bed. "I haven't heard from him today."

"How about Tank?" Bee asked Stephanie. "Did he say anything?"

"Nothing. He came home last night after I'd gone to bed, and he was up and gone by the time I woke this morning." She shifted her attention to Cass. "What about you, Cass? Did you have any luck?"

"Luck with what?"

She rolled her eyes. "Oh, please, don't even tell me you didn't try to reach out to Fred when you had a few free minutes."

That was the thing about close friends, they often knew exactly what you'd do, sometimes before you'd even figured it out yourself. "I tried. But aside from a jumble of chattering voices, I didn't get anywhere."

"So, what now?" Bee sat back.

"What makes you think there's anything now? Maybe we just wait and see what the police investigation shows." Though the chances of that were slim.

Bee laughed, a little too loudly, drawing stares from more than one person. "Oh, please. I can see it in your eyes, Cass. And you said it yourself before. There's something about Fred's death that's calling to you, maybe not in the form of a voice you can hear, but also not something you can let go and walk away from."

How could she argue when he was right?

Chapter Eight

Cass overslept the next morning and ran out the door with one arm through her sweater sleeve and still hopping into one shoe, leaving Beast home with a promise to come back for him as soon as she was done. When she reached the shop at five after six, she found Simone Carlson sitting on a rocking chair on the front porch.

Cass locked her car, looked down to be sure she'd remembered to put on leggings, and ran up the steps. Great first impression she was making on a woman she hoped to do business with. "I am so sorry I'm late, Ms. Carlson."

"Simone, please." She stood and leisurely stretched her back. "And no problem. I assume you don't usually open at this time of the morning, and I appreciate you coming in so early to accommodate me."

"Of course." Cass unlocked the door and held it open for Simone to precede her. "Can I get you anything? Coffee? Tea?"

"No, thank you. I'm actually in a bit of a hurry today, so I won't take up much of your time."

Cass flipped on the lights but didn't bother to open the register. She'd do that after she went home for Beast and returned for the day. Gesturing toward the back corner, Cass stuffed her bag beneath the counter. "Have a seat at the table, and I'll be right with you."

"Thank you." Simone sat gracefully on the edge of a velvet-covered chair and crossed her legs, then smoothed her long skirt and folded her hands over her knee.

How could anyone in the world be that put together at six in the morning?

Cass ignored the flowing robe and coin belt she often wore for readings and reached for her crystal ball. At the last minute, she changed her mind and grabbed a stack of paper and the basket of colored pencils. While she'd originally thought to give Simone a more traditional reading, maybe put on a bit of a show with her gown and her crystal ball, something told her this woman might be more inclined toward a color reading. And, as much as Cass wanted to impress her enough to earn a spot on her tour, it was always more important to put her client's needs ahead of her own. Now if the spirits would just cooperate.

Cass lit a white candle and slid it to the edge of the table. She sat and straightened her small stack of white paper, took out a handful of colored pencils, confident she'd pull out the colors she needed and set them beside the paper. Once she had everything in order, she rolled the line of pencils back and forth.

Simone tilted her head and arched a perfectly sculpted brow as she studied the paper and pencils, but she remained silent.

"Okay . . ." With one deep, calming breath, Cass let her defenses fall and opened herself to whatever messages would come through.

The bombardment came immediately. Voices. All different accents, inflections, pitches, tones, all vying for her attention. Insistent. Demanding. Louder and louder, words and phrases tumbling over one another, surrounding her, sucking her into the abyss.

"Are you okay?"

Cass's eyes shot open, and she gasped. When had she closed her eyes?

The sun peeked over the horizon and shone through the back window, blinding her.

Simone sat forward, a scowl firmly etched onto her angular features. "Is everything all right?"

"Oh, uh . . . yes. I'm sorry, just trying to orient myself." She offered a small laugh, the best she could do under the circumstances, then got up and closed the blinds. "Are you ready to start?"

"Of course, thank you."

Okay. At least one of them was good to go. That was a step in the right direction.

Simone settled back in her seat, resting her elbows on the arms of the chair and steepling her fingers in front of her, her gaze on Cass intense. Silver flecks radiated from the depths of one dark green eye and one half-green, half-blue eye. Those tilted feline eyes, combined with her graceful, unhurried movements, reminded Cass of a cat lazing in a ray of sunshine.

A sense of peace flowed over Cass, unsettling under the circumstances.

She rolled the pencils back and forth. Maybe the color reading had been a bad idea. Perhaps losing herself in the depths of the crystal ball would have proven more soothing. Oh, well. Too late now. If she changed what she was doing, she might lose Simone's interest.

Bracing herself for the assault, Cass opened her mind.

The illusion of peace remained. No voices battled for her attention.

Cass lifted a pencil without bothering to look at the color and began scribbling back and forth, taking comfort in the familiarity of the repetitive motion, allowing the sound of pencil scratching against paper to ground her. When she finally looked down at the patch of color on the paper, she wasn't the least bit surprised at the color she'd chosen.

"Purple. A color often connected to power, nobility, spirituality." But which meaning pertained to Simone? All of them. "You are a powerful woman. Noble and strong, but not arrogant, as purple can sometimes indicate."

Simone smiled.

Cass opened herself further, searching for the truth about this woman. She found herself pressing the pencil harder against the paper, deepening the shade. "Your sense of spirituality is strong, as is your compassion and empathy."

Cass frowned and studied the blob she'd drawn. "Unless presented with chaos or disturbance. Trouble ruffles you, leaves you frustrated."

"True enough." Simone nodded once in agreement.

"... *there* ..." The softest whisper of sound intruded.

Cass returned the purple pencil to the line and chose another. She'd expected red to come next, a color of power and strength, passion even. Instead, she picked a turquoise pencil, a rare choice. "Turquoise. Not so surprising, really. A color whose blue undertones indicate peace, calm, and tranquility, combined with the balance and encouraging aspects of its green and the uplifting energy of yellow. A color that soothes the nerves. An interesting contrast and a good balance to the purple that leaves you ruffled in the face of disorder."

"... *killed me*."

Cass jumped, startled.

One voice only. A man.

She ignored him and returned her attention to Simone, then frowned as certainty flowed through her. "A choice, I think. The turquoise. A color that came from years of discipline in the face of crisis, despite that discipline being contrary to your nature."

Simone shifted forward, rested her forearms on the table, and clasped her hands.

Cass had obviously piqued her interest, but where to go from there?

"*. . . was push . . . pu . . . pushed . . .*"

Fred? Cass didn't dare say the name out loud, not under Simone's intense scrutiny. *Is that you?*

The woman sat perfectly still, didn't offer any of the tells her customers sometimes shared without realizing it, the twisting of a wedding ring that would tell her their problems lay with their spouses, fidgeting as if they'd lost something, smoothing hair or clothing in a gesture of self-consciousness, or, as in Luke's case, folding their arms across their chests in an effort to hold her off, to hide the truth from her. That hadn't worked out so well for Luke, since she'd obviously wormed her way past his defenses.

She shook off the distraction Luke always brought and focused instead on her pencils. Eventually, Cass would strike a chord with this woman, and she'd give some tidbit away. People always did.

"*Have to help me . . . have to find . . .*"

Trying to hear what the voice was saying, she grabbed another pencil, her hands shaking. Blue. "A color that soothes and relaxes, prevents chaos. It offers peace and tranquility. Inspires trust."

Was that the message she was supposed to be receiving? The urge to trust Simone washed over her. But why? Did it have something to do with her buying Fred's tour company? Maybe that her intentions were honest?

Did you know, Fred? Did you know Amelia was selling the company?

"*Pushed.*" Still only one voice. Strange. But maybe the others had figured out she couldn't help them and had given up.

Cass frowned and shook her head. Something . . . she could sense some knowledge hovering just out of her reach. She could almost grab it. But not quite. Did he mean he was pushed out the window? Pushed into selling his business? Was it even Fred she had connected with?

Eager to learn more, Cass grabbed another random color and began to scribble faster, with more urgency than before.

"Black. Hmm . . ." She tried to study Simone discreetly, tried to gage her reactions to put together a better picture of this woman. Black was a color of mystery, could indicate a shroud of secrecy. "An intimidating color, black. Strong, and yet . . ."

Simone tilted her head, her gaze fully focused on Cass, as if waiting for something. Her eyes narrowed.

"Protective. Instilling a sense of security. A shield, if you will." Cass's gaze clashed with Simone's. The black pencil clattered to the table. "It's you!"

She lifted a perfectly arched brow. "Excuse me?"

"The voices. The chaos . . ." Cass's heart skipped. "You're shielding me from them somehow, while allowing only one to enter."

"I am indeed." She grinned, the proverbial Cheshire cat. "And I have to say, I'm quite impressed you were able to figure it out."

"What?" Cass tried to shake off her confusion. "Why?"

"I am extremely adept at masking my abilities, even though most people are acutely unaware of any reality outside of their own."

The voices returned in full force, and Cass winced as she tried to ignore them and pick out Fred's once again.

"I was shielding not only you, but myself as well. I am surprised and delighted that you realized it."

"But I don't understand. How are you able to do that?" Because Cass needed to master that ability. In a hurry, if she hoped to be able to continue doing readings without being accosted by desperate spirits. "I'm able to block all of the voices or open myself to all of them. There doesn't seem to be an in-between, and I can't selectively allow some in while blocking others."

"Your psychic gifts, they are new to you?" Simone asked.

"Not really. At least, the gift itself isn't new. I've been able to read people for as long as I can remember, always had an intuitive way of knowing what people were thinking or searching for. I used it when I was younger to work on the boardwalk, offering readings to tourists. But I'd always chalked it up to good instincts, then later, when I received my psychology degree, to a mix of good intuition and training. It's only since I returned to Bay Island last year after my mother and father's deaths that I began to realize it was something more."

"Ah, yes. Not surprising. A tragic event often triggers not only latent abilities but also acceptance of abilities you already possessed but may not have fully understood."

While her parents' deaths may have been the catalyst that had started Cass second guessing where her knowledge came from, it was more likely finding Stephanie in danger with no hope other than Cass to save her that had precipitated her acceptance of this obvious connection to some other world.

"I think . . . yes, I agree there might have been an event that triggered this . . ." She waved a hand around her. "Whatever this is."

Simone reached across the table and laid a hand over Cass's. "This is a gift. A gift you've apparently been using most of your life. The only difference now is your awareness of how you receive your information."

"Yeah, well . . . I have to be honest, it's driving me crazy at the moment."

Simone laughed, a smooth sultry laugh that inspired a feeling of friendship and camaraderie. "Don't worry, you'll get the hang of it."

She certainly hoped so.

"And in the meantime . . ." She stood and rummaged through her bag, then pulled out a slim card holder, took out a business card, and handed it to Cass. Unlike the first one she'd given her, this card contained several phone numbers below her name, including her cell phone number. "You are welcome to call me any time, and I am looking forward to working together on the tours."

Thrilled with Simone's interest in pursuing their business arrangement, Cass shook her hand. "Thank you. I'm looking forward to working with you, as well."

Simone started toward the door.

"Oh, wait." Cass held up the paper she'd colored on. "Did you want to keep this?"

"You keep it, and when the chaos begins to overwhelm, focus on turquoise." She resumed her trek across the shop then paused and glanced over her shoulder. "Oh, and be sure to say hi to Fred for me."

Startled, Cass sucked in a breath.

Simone simply winked and sauntered out the door.

A range of emotions tore through Cass, the most prominent of which was confusion. Hmm . . . she'd have expected it to be excitement about the confirmation Mystical Musings would be included on the tour. Plus, the fact she had connected with Simone on some kind of personal level she didn't understand. Nothing like that had ever happened to her before.

She'd known Stephanie since they were kids, and when Cass had returned after seventeen years away, they'd resumed their friendship as if she'd never left. When she'd met Bee, she'd felt a sort of instant connection with him, the knowledge they'd be something to each other once they got to know each other. But the bond with Simone was different. Cass had never met anyone like her. She radiated a calm peace that slipped through you like a ray of sunshine on a frigid winter day. And on top of that, she seemed to understand Cass's abilities in a way Cass herself didn't.

Seemed the day was full of surprises, and the sun had barely even risen.

Cass stood and stretched, then went to the back counter for a cup of coffee. Darn. In her haste to begin Simone's reading, she'd forgotten to turn on the coffee maker. Since she'd readied it before she'd left last night, all she had to do was flip the switch. And wait. Which proved harder than she'd anticipated.

Simone's trick with the shield had been impressive.

While Cass seemed to be able to halt the flow of voices while she wasn't trying to do a reading, they were a constant presence when she was. The instant she opened her mind, a mad rush ensued, like shoppers plowing through the newly opened doors for the sale of the century on Black Friday. And, unlike Simone, she had no ability to let only one voice enter. She wouldn't even know where to start shielding someone else.

The scent of coffee wafted through the shop, its aroma enticing, comforting. Cass propped the back door open, inviting the sounds of the gently lapping waves and seagulls into the shop while the beach was empty and the worst of the day's heat hadn't started yet.

She opened the blinds, and the sun's rays poured into the shop, setting her crystal ball ablaze with the oranges and yellows of the sunrise. Cass retrieved the ball and set it on the table. It was much easier for her to use the crystal ball, rather than any other method, as a form of meditation.

She took her seat, pulled herself closer to the table, and focused, not really knowing what she intended to do until she stared into the crystal, letting her mind wander, opening herself. "Are you there, Fred?"

"*. . . told her . . . drifted . . . why? . . . I can't find . . . please . . . .*"

Cass tried to sort through the voices, as Bee had suggested. First, she tried to force all of the female voices to the background. She didn't need to listen to them right now if she wanted to try to reach Fred. Their stories would have to wait for later.

No luck.

She stared deeper into the crystal, concentrating, searching for its deepest secrets.

A flash of black, the darkest of shadows, flickered into view, and then disappeared. She leaned closer, searching . . . searching . . .

She ran a finger over the cool glass.

Again, the black swirl appeared, but this time she grabbed hold of it, tried to hang on to it when it would have disappeared. The black haze began to solidify, take on shape. The shape of a man encased in a square . . . no, a window. The lighthouse keeper's upstairs window. The silhouette split in two, one half standing strong, growing larger, the other tumbling into an endless abyss, whirling and spinning, not seeming to move any deeper yet unable to stop.

Cass focused on the image. Could she bring it clear? She narrowed her gaze, pouring every ounce of her concentration onto the silhouette hurtling toward jagged black peaks.

Come on, talk to me.

"*. . . ride . . . just want her to know . . . can't find . . . push . . . want . . . shove . . . Tony's . . .*" Probably a local, if he was referring to Tony's Bakery. But was it Fred? "*. . . jump . . . run . . . hide . . . push . . . Cass . . . push . . . Cass? . . . pushed —*"

A strong hand landed on her shoulder, ripping her from the vision.

Chapter Nine

Cass screamed and whirled toward the intruder.

Bee lurched back, bracing one hand on the table and the other against his chest.

Cass's chair tipped. She windmilled her arms, precariously balanced for just an instant before the chair went over and she sprawled onto the floor.

"For crying out loud, Cass, what are you trying to do to me?" Bee huffed.

"Seriously, Bee?" She sat up and took stock before making any attempt to stand. Everything seemed okay. She climbed to her feet with no help from the drama queen and brushed herself off. "What are you doing up already?"

"You mean still." He cocked a hip and fanned himself. "I haven't gone to bed yet. Could be that I finally got too stuffed making the rounds last night to keep eating, so I switched to coffee, which I continued to imbibe all night long, first at the diner, then at the convenience store, then back at the diner, which is open twenty-four seven for the season now, and finally at the deli just after they opened this morning."

What in the world was he talking about? Whatever it was, he was going to have to at least let her get a cup of coffee before she tried to sort it all out. "Do you want a glass of water?"

"No, thanks, I'm on my way to have breakfast. That's actually why I stopped by. I didn't know if you were still doing your reading, so I peeked in the door and you were in here alone, so I took a chance and came in to see if you wanted to go out to breakfast. Which, by the way, why were you in here all alone, lost in space somewhere with the door wide open? You're lucky it was only me who startled you." He finally took a breath and paused. "Oh, dear, are you okay? I'm so sorry. I don't know what's the matter with me. There's no excuse. I—"

"Stop." She held up a hand. "I haven't even had my first cup of coffee yet. You're going to have to slow down and give me a minute."

"Uh, sorry." Bee winced. "Are you really okay?"

"I'm fine." She moved to the counter and got her mug, then

filled it with coffee and added milk. "As to what I was doing here, I just finished Simone's reading."

He held up one beefy finger. "Speaking of, that's one of the things I wanted to talk to you about, and let me tell you, this information was not easy to come by. I had to work for it."

She suppressed a groan and corralled her patience. If she didn't show sufficient appreciation for his efforts, he wouldn't tell her anything. "Thank you, Bee. I really appreciate you working so hard to get the information I asked for."

He nodded and took a seat at the table.

Actually, she did appreciate Bee's efforts. Always. No matter what she asked for, whether it was of major importance or something trivial, Bee was always there for her. She set her mug down, then rounded the table and put her arms around Bee from behind, dropping a kiss on the top of his head.

Bee gripped her hands and held them. "Well, thank you, hon, but what was that for?"

She hugged him tight for another moment, then straightened and took her own seat. "Just for being you, Bee. For being such a good friend. For always having my back."

Splotches of red blossomed on his cheeks. "Well, don't forget that works both ways. I've never had anyone else I could depend on so fully. There's never a time you wouldn't come running if I called."

"No, there's not." Cass hadn't given that much thought before.

Everyone on Bay Island knew Bee, and most were quite fond of him. People seemed to trust him, to open up to him, even though they knew full well he was the biggest gossip going. It was also known he never said a malicious word about anyone or passed on information that might be sensitive or painful if it got out. And he was one of the most generous souls she'd ever met, often donating anonymously to good causes, or picking up a check or grocery bill when someone seemed to be in need. She'd once seen him leave a hundred-dollar tip for a waitress he knew who was heading off to college.

And he'd not only helped Tim Daughtry get into a fashion program at the school he'd wanted so badly to attend, he'd also hired him as an intern and had been mentoring him, even helping him to begin designing his own line. Cass had no doubt, when the time came, he'd reach out to his contacts to help Tim move forward.

But, despite all of that, he never seemed to get close to anyone, to open up fully and let anyone in. Except for Cass. And, to a certain degree, Stephanie, though his reticence around Tank made their relationship a little touchy at times.

"You do know how much I love you, right, Bee?"

"I do, Cass." He lowered his gaze. "As much as I love you."

Warmth embraced her. Not wanting to embarrass him further—Bee wasn't one to open up about his feelings that often—she sipped her coffee and switched topics to something he'd be more comfortable with. "So, what did you find out on your all-night coffee binge?"

He straightened in the chair and held up a hand with all the flair Cass was used to. "Okay, so, it seems your potential new business partner is not what she seems."

"I sure hope you mean that in a good way."

Bee frowned. "Why?"

She didn't dare mention her connection with Simone on a psychic level, not because she didn't trust him or didn't want his opinion or advice, but because it would make him uncomfortable. "After her reading this morning, she offered to include Mystical Musings as part of her tour package."

"Huh . . ."

"That's it? Huh?"

He scratched his head. "I guess that doesn't matter. It's not like you befriended the woman or anything, and business is business."

She'd let it go, for now. Once she knew what Bee had found out, she could decide where, if anywhere, to take her relationship with Simone.

"Anyway . . ." Bee bounced his leg up and down, vibrating with nervous energy—or an overdose of caffeine. She was going to have to feed him something. "As far as I could tell, Fred's company was never listed anywhere for sale, and I got quite a few people out of bed to confirm that."

Oh, boy. What had she unwittingly unleashed on the unsuspecting public?

"Not only that, but it seems Simone and Amelia go way back,

attended college together as well as being part of the same groups."

"What kind of groups?"

"Mostly historical type stuff. Apparently, they're both avid history buffs."

That made sense, since Amelia worked at the lighthouse gift shop and museum, and Fred's tours detailed the history of Bay Island. Probably just the sort of thing that would interest Simone. Then add the paranormal element. Considering Simone's obvious experience in that area, the tours would be perfect for her. "So, maybe Amelia just contacted her directly when they decided to sell, knowing she might have an interest."

"I thought the same thing, but then . . ." Bee wiggled closer to the edge of his seat, rested his forearms on the table, and leaned forward.

Cass braced herself for the doozy he was about to drop in her lap.

"But then I heard about Simone's husband." Bee paused.

Cass knew how to play the game. "What about him?"

"Seems Simone's husband disappeared under mysterious circumstances."

Shocked, Cass jerked back as if he'd slapped her.

He nodded sagely, sat back, and crossed one leg over the other. With his grand climax delivered, he was ready to discuss the aftermath.

"What do you mean, 'mysterious circumstances'? And who told you that?" Who on Bay Island would even know Simone? Never mind know the situation with her husband.

"Uh . . ." Bee yanked at his collar.

"Bee?" She pinned him with a stare.

"Oh, all right, I heard it from Emma in the deli this morning somewhere around my twenty-ninth cup of coffee. But I confirmed it with Tank."

"What?" And she'd thought the news about Simone was shocking. "Tank?"

"Yeah, well, I wanted to make sure it was accurate before I passed it on to you, so I stopped by the police station, thinking Luke might be there, but he wasn't available and Tank was, so, fueled by an overdose of caffeine, I told him what I'd heard, and that under the circumstances, since he was investigating Fred's death and all, that maybe it might be important information for him to have, so he looked it up, and sure enough it's true. Then he thanked me, shook my hand . . ." Bee grinned. "Held it a little longer than necessary, and warned me not to pass that around and to remind you that if you couldn't stay out of the investigation you should be very careful."

Cass just stared at him and tried to take all that in. "How in the world did you find all of this out in the middle of the night, while most of Bay Island slept?"

Though it had been a rhetorical question, mostly, Bee answered. "Oh, puh-lease, girl. Did you really expect anything less?"

She shook her head and marveled.

"Anyway, there's more. Supposedly, Andrew Carlson walked out the door one night to meet friends for a drink and never returned. Simone insisted he probably left her, said the marriage had been on the rocks for a while, but the police in New York City, where they were living, never found any indication that was true. He hasn't used a credit card, hasn't shown up on any kind of surveillance cameras anywhere they could find, and hasn't reached out to anyone, including, apparently, his longtime side piece."

"Hmm . . ."

"And, not only that, but there are rumors that his family and closest friends suspect he was murdered." Bee tapped his fingers against the table, over and over and over, the steady staccato threatening to drive Cass crazy.

"Why?"

Bee snorted and, mercifully, stopped the rhythmic *tap, tap, tap.* "Really, Cass? How much do you expect me to be able to find out in the dead of night?"

Touché. "So, where do we stand now?"

"Fred was killed under mysterious circumstances, and by all accounts he was cheating on his wife, while Amelia was in the process of selling his company to a friend of hers whose husband disappeared without a trace after she found out he was cheating on her."

"Is that all?"

"That's it in a nutshell." Bee flopped against the chair back and yawned. Seemed his caffeine rush was finally wearing off.

"Yeah, well, there's one more piece to that puzzle that could be a bit of a problem."

"Oh, what's that?"

Cass took a deep breath and blew it out slowly. "When Simone came in for a reading this morning, she was able to calm the voices for me, allowing only one to come through."

Bee shot up in his seat. "Are you saying she's psychic?"

Cass braced herself for Bee's outburst then nodded and squeezed her eyes shut. "And she thinks I talked to Fred."

Silence.

She slit one eye open and found Bee slumped in his chair, staring straight ahead, his thick eyebrows drawn together in a hairy V.

Before he could gather his wits enough to lay into her, Cass stood. "Come on, Bee. Let's get you something to eat so you can get home and get some sleep, and I can go get Beast."

"Sounds like a plan."

No doubt one that would allow him to ignore the otherworldly implications of her statement.

He pushed the chair back and stood then, knowing Cass's need for order, pushed the chair back in. "I'm starved. Where do you want to go? The diner?"

"May as well." Her stomach growled. She glanced at the driftwood clock over the front door. "Actually, I didn't realize how hungry I was. A breakfast skillet sounds good. Do you want to give Stephanie a call and see if she wants to meet us, while I set up Beast's food dishes so he can eat as soon as I pick him up and get back?"

Bee fished his phone out of his pocket while Cass headed for the back room, curtained off at the side of the shop.

Before he dialed, the wind chimes over the front door signaled a customer. Darn. If she'd have realized how much activity there was on Bay Island in the early morning hours, she'd have locked the doors. Lesson learned. Next time she decided to drift off into a vision, she wouldn't leave the door open so just anyone could walk in. A chill raced up her back.

"Oh, hey, Levi," Bee said. "What are you doing here?"

Cass filled Beast's food and water dishes and set them on the floor, washed her hands, then hurried out front. "Hi, Levi."

"Good morning, Cass." He reached to tip his mariner's cap, then realized he was holding it in his hand and grinned. "How are you doing?"

"I'm doing okay, how about you?"

"To be honest, I don't right know." He clutched his hat and a Bay Island Lighthouse souvenir bag tighter.

"Over Fred's death?" Bee laid a hand on his shoulder.

Levi looked up at him. "Heck of a thing, that. Ain't it?"

"It certainly is." Bee ushered him toward the table.

So much for breakfast.

"And now people are saying it might not have been an accident."

Rumors sure were soaring this morning, and she had to wonder if anyone on Bay Island had slept last night. And what, if any, Bee's role had been in churning the waters.

"I've heard that too." Pulling out a chair, Bee gestured for Levi to sit and, when he did, took the seat next to him. "But who would want to kill Fred?"

"Would you like some coffee?" Cass checked the pot. Enough to get started, but she'd have to make another pot when she returned with Beast.

Bee scowled at her. She'd interrupted him working his mojo.

Too bad. The least she could do was offer the man a cup of coffee before Bee started grilling him.

"No, thank you, though."

Cass sat across from them. Though she wanted to start her opening preparations, she didn't want to be rude to Levi, even though it seemed he'd really stopped in to see Bee.

Bee resumed where he'd left off. "I've heard the same rumors, but no one seems to have any indication who would have wanted to kill him . . ."

"Oh, I don't know about killing him, but Fred had pissed off a lot of people lately."

"Really?" Bee stopped just short of drooling. "Like whom?"

Levi sighed, rolling and unrolling the top of the paper bag with the Bay Island Lighthouse logo on the front. "Even before all of this happened, rumors had started to spread that Fred was having affairs with some of the tour guides, had been for a while."

"Really?" Bee feigned surprise.

That wasn't news, since Levi and Amelia had both hinted at it before Fred had died.

"Supposedly, he was foolin' around with that Piper girl, the one who was dating that beefy lifeguard last year. I really don't know what everyone sees in that one. Nothin' but snotty if you ask me." He shrugged. "To each his own, I guess."

Bee nodded in encouragement.

"So, the lifeguard found out about it—"

"Quincy Yates?" Bee asked.

"Yeah, that's the one. I don't know how he found out, but he confronted Fred the day before he was killed, right in the middle of the gift shop. In front of Amelia. Said Fred got away with it last year, because he didn't give a rat's . . ." His gaze shot to Cass and his blush shot clear over his head. "Uh, well, you know. Anyhow, said he had no real feelings for Piper, she weren't nothing more than a fling. But Fred had his sights set on Francesca Harding this time, who Quince had hooked up with a few months ago when they came to Bay Island for orientation, had already made more than one pass at her according to Quince."

"What was Quince doing here for orientation?"

"Apparently, he'd developed a yearning to become a tour guide. Ask me, I think he just wanted to stay close enough to keep an eye on Francesca, what with Fred sniffin' around and all. He might not have cared about Piper, but Francesca, he did have feelings for her. Told Fred to stay away from her, or else. And let me tell you, that man looks all easygoing and laid-back, but not so when he's angry. Scared me, and I wasn't even on the receiving end of his temper."

Cass's mind whirled. Could it have been Quincy Yates who'd shoved Fred out the window? Would he have had time to reach the body and start CPR if that had been the case? "When I reached Fred, Quincy Yates was already trying to save him."

Levi shrugged. "Just tellin' it like I saw it."

"You were there when they argued?" If she wasn't mistaken, Bee's tone held a note of envy.

"Yes, indeed. Saw it with my own eyes, and heard it with my own ears. And, let me tell you, Francesca, she stood there with her head down, looking embarrassed, but Piper had on a grin from ear to ear, just eatin' up the attention, that one."

That didn't surprise Cass.

"But the one I really felt bad for was Amelia." His jaw clenched. "She turned and ran out, left the gift shop with no one working in it, and had herself a good hard cry out on the jetty."

An ache formed in Cass's chest. She knew all too well what it felt like to suffer the pain of a cheating husband.

"Ah, well, I gotta run." Levi stood, leaving the paper bag on the table.

Bee and Cass stood as well.

"I was actually on my way up to the lighthouse and saw your car out front, Bee." He grinned. "And a beauty she is."

Bee grinned from ear to ear. That black Trans Am was his baby.

"Anyway, so I just stopped in to bring you this." He slid the bag across the table to Bee. "You seemed so interested the last time we spoke, and with Fred gone and the lighthouse closed I wasn't sure when you'd get to see it again. Who knows? Now that Fred's gone and Amelia's selling the tour company, they may even remove the display."

"What is it?" Bee opened the bag and peeked in, then pulled out a thick folder.

"The transcript of Kitty Garrison's journal. Fred had Amelia transcribe it because he was too impatient to spend time trying to make out the faded writing. I asked Amelia if she had it and if she'd mind lending it to you. She didn't. Said she hoped it might shed some light on the treasure he was searching for on the jetty all the time. Find out if it had anything to do with him winding up dead."

"Why didn't she give it to the police if she thought it might pertain to Fred's murder?" Cass looked over Bee's shoulder as he leafed through page after page.

"That's easy." Levi fitted his cap back on. "The police can't talk to ghosts."

Chapter Ten

Afraid she might never get out of Mystical Musings in time to eat breakfast and pick Beast up, Cass locked the doors the instant Levi walked out, and she and Bee headed for the diner.

Stephanie was already seated and waiting, and she waved when they walked in.

Good thing, too. If Cass had to linger next to the dessert case for longer than two seconds, she'd probably be having Linzer tarts for breakfast. Raspberry jam, powdered sugar. Saliva pooled in her mouth, and her stomach growled again.

No amount of walking down the beach would make up for that lapse of judgment. Of course, she could go back to the lighthouse and climb the stairs to the top a few dozen times.

Pressing a hand against her stomach to ease the traitorous hunger pangs, Cass ignored the case and strode toward Stephanie's booth.

She slid into the booth next to Stephanie and set her menu aside, trying, and failing, to think of anything other than the taste of a cookie melting on her tongue. "So, anything new and exciting?"

"Nah, just work, work, and more work." Stephanie groaned, then she brightened. "But, hey, I hear you had a chat with Fred."

Cass shot Bee, who was sitting across from her and suddenly engrossed in a menu he'd probably memorized, the evil eye.

Stephanie laughed. "It wasn't only him. Rumors abound this morning."

"Yeah, well." Cass pinned a sugar packet to the table with her finger and used her free hand to spin it around and around. Sooner or later those rumors would reach Luke and Tank. That was two complications she didn't need. Although, in all fairness, Luke had asked for her help. But he'd also asked her not to let anyone know she'd seen anything that would paint a target on her back. Of course, those would be the first rumors to spread. She raised her voice enough to be overheard but not enough to be obvious. "Rumors are wrong. I absolutely did not speak to Fred."

Not for lack of trying.

Bee peeked at her over the menu. When she didn't say anything, he closed the menu and set it aside, then folded his arms on the table. "You'll never guess who came into Cass's shop this morning."

Stephanie looked at her watch and frowned. "Already?"

"I had an early reading scheduled." Cass lowered her voice. No need to give the gossipmongers any more than she already had. "The woman who's buying the tour company came in for a reading. Turns out she has some psychic ability of her own, and she's definitely interested in adding Mystical Musings as a tour stop."

Stephanie's big brown eyes shone with anticipation. "That's awesome, Cass. That could mean a good bump in business for you, not only when tour groups come in, but if they generate repeat customers. Word of mouth is the best form of advertising. And it's free."

"Very true." The thought lifted her spirits. "Hey, I wonder if I could get her to agree to a group reading as part of the tour. I could add one, say, once a month or so, just for the tour group."

"You'd have to get her to add a night tour if you wanted to do that, so they could come in after you closed," Stephanie said.

"Or you could hire someone to man the counter while you take the tour group upstairs to do the group reading." Bee waggled his eyebrows.

He'd been advocating for her to hire help for a while now, ever since he'd hired his intern, Tim, for the summer, so he wouldn't have to get up early and go in to Dreamweaver Designs. Tim opened in the morning, made appointments for Bee with any clients who came in looking for custom work, and manned the shop until Bee got there. It gave Bee more time to work on designs and Tim valuable experience, plus a generous paycheck.

Cass suspected Bee's relentless suggestions for her to hire help had something to do with him wanting a friend to hang out with for the summer, since Cass opened the shop seven days a week through tourist season. "We'll see, Bee. If the tours generate enough of an income, maybe I could hire someone one day a week or something."

Stephanie fished a pen out of her bag and grabbed a napkin from the holder. "Yeah, but without hiring someone, you have no way to do an additional group reading. You can't be upstairs while the shop is open."

True. She couldn't leave the doors unlocked, even if she did empty the register, with no one to keep an eye on things. "Maybe it would be worth closing for an hour or two to accommodate the group?"

"Hmm . . ." Stephanie caught her bottom lip between her teeth and scribbled numbers on the napkin.

Since Cass had no clue what she was writing, she turned to Bee. "Do you think I could talk Simone into adding a late evening tour?"

He ran a finger slowly around the rim of his water cup. "I don't know. If you think about it from her standpoint, it doesn't make a lot of sense."

"Why not?"

"Well." He turned his paper place mat to face her and pointed to the two biggest local ads. "While the haunted aspect of the tour is intriguing, and would undoubtedly be even more so at night, especially after dark, the two lighthouses and the lighthouse museum that draw most people to a tour would already be closed."

"Hmm . . . I hadn't thought of that." Especially when one of the stories Fred had been trying to feature took place at the Bay Island Lighthouse.

Stephanie spun the napkin toward Cass and tapped a number she'd circled at the bottom with her pen. "If my calculations are accurate, which they should be since I handle your bookkeeping, that's what you'd need for the group reading to make it worth closing for an hour or two, assuming no one who tries to come in during the time you're closed comes back once you reopen."

Bee popped up and leaned over Cass's shoulder to look over the numbers with her. "And, really, you'd have to assume some people would come back. First off, you wouldn't schedule appointments for private readings during that time, so you wouldn't lose anything there."

"True." A spark of hope flared. This might be doable.

"And second, most people who come to see you know what they're coming for, and if you stick to a schedule, where you close at the same time every month for the readings, people will work around it." He returned to his seat. "So, all you'd really lose would be the people browsing the shops along the boardwalk."

"And once tourist season is over, I can open for the readings on Mondays or Wednesdays when I could close the shop for the day anyway. This could work." Her excitement grew. Simone's email address had been printed on the business card she'd given Cass. "Maybe I'll shoot Simone an email outlining my plan and see if she's interested."

"You might also suggest she talk to someone at the old Madison Estate." Bee sat back as the waitress approached. "Fred had a deal to have the guests stay there, and let me tell you, that is one creepy place, especially at night."

Bee shivered, and goose bumps popped up on his arms.

Cass didn't need the reminder. One weekend trapped in that place was enough for her.

"Good morning." A waitress Cass didn't recognize offered a bright smile. It seemed all of the businesses on Bay Island had already started using seasonal employees in anticipation of the heightened tourist influx once the schools let out. "What can I get for you this morning?"

Cass and Stephanie ordered breakfast skillets, while Bee ordered a hot roast beef sandwich, mashed potatoes, and coleslaw, since it was technically his dinnertime.

Once the waitress walked away, Bee looked around and leaned in closer.

Cass and Stephanie automatically did the same. "The other thing you haven't taken into consideration in your master plan with Simone is the possibility of her having some involvement in Fred's death."

Stephanie gasped and jerked upright, then looked around, leaned back in, and lowered her voice to a harsh whisper. "What are you talking about, Bee?"

Cass and Bee brought her up to speed on what he'd dug up during the night.

"And you really went into the police station and talked to Tank about it?" Of everything, that fact seemed to surprise—and please—Stephanie the most.

Bee sat back. "I really did."

The waitress hurried toward them with a tray of drinks. After depositing them on the table, she rushed off to take care of another table.

Cass looked around. "Actually, it's really crowded in here this morning."

Every table and booth was full; only three stools, not together, sat empty at the counter, and a small crowd had gathered in the vestibule, waiting for someone to leave.

Stephanie started to turn and bumped her elbow into Cass's arm. "Oh, sorry, Cass."

"Four."

"What?"

Stephanie and Bee both looked at her and frowned.

"Four."

With her friends staring right at her, it was obvious neither of them had spoken. "Oh, sorry. I thought one of you said something."

"I said I was sorry for bumping into you." Stephanie laid a hand on her arm. "Are you all right?"

"Four."

What in the world? The voice seemed feminine but deep, a woman, perhaps, though Cass didn't know what made her believe so, since the sound had come to her on the softest of breaths, no more than a wisp of smoke floating by and dissipating an instant later.

"Four."

Cass tried to grab hold of the sound, tried to follow when she couldn't grasp it. *Four what?*

Bee reached across the table and laid a hand on hers. "Hey. You okay?"

No use. Whatever had tried to reach out had disappeared.

"Uh . . . yeah . . . sorry."

"Really, Quince!" Piper Bonavich stood beside a booth a few seats from Cass, saving Cass from having to further elaborate on whatever that had been. Piper pointed an accusatory finger at the woman sitting next to Quince.

The young woman slid farther down in her seat, looking like she wanted to melt into the booth bench and disappear, though Cass couldn't see her expression, since she was sitting with her back to them.

She had a great view of Piper's face, though, and her cheeks were so red they bordered on purple, making her bright blue eyes stand out like lasers aimed at the poor young lifeguard.

Bee turned his back to the side of the booth so he could see what was going on, making no effort to disguise his interest. Instead, he settled more comfortably, resting his arm along the seatback to gawk at the scene unfolding.

"You stood me up to hang out with *her!*" Piper demanded.

"That's Francesca Harding, Quince's seasonal conquest," Bee whispered to them.

Obviously forgetting the need to be invisible, Francesca sat up and whirled on Quince. "What does she mean, stood her up? You told me things with her were over."

Quince tilted his head back and massaged his neck, ignoring Piper in favor of Francesca. "It's not what you think, babe."

"Oh, he didn't," Bee whispered. "Big mistake."

Piper yanked his shoulder then slapped him across the face.

"Oooh." Bee winced. "Told you it was a mistake, buddy. Never turn your back on an irate woman."

"You mean you weren't supposed to meet her?" Francesca shoved his shoulder, then flung a hand toward Piper.

"No." He held up his hands, looking at Francesca but trying to keep one wary eye on Piper. "It's not . . . I didn't . . . she wanted me to meet her out at the lighthouse, said she had to show me something important, but I told her no. When she demanded I come, I just walked away and she yelled after me that I'd better be there. That's all it was. I swear."

When he reached toward her, she slapped his hand away. "Get up."

"Huh?"

Piper smirked. "While I'll admit I am thoroughly enjoying this lovers' spat, I don't have time for it today. I need to talk to you, Quince. Outside. Now."

Quince propped his elbows on the table and cradled his head in his hands.

"Five bucks says he goes with Piper." Though Bee spoke quietly, his voice carried in the hushed diner.

"Shhh . . ." Cass put a finger to her lips.

"I said. Get. Up." Francesca shoved his shoulder.

Cass looked around, hoping someone would interrupt or, at least, get things moving again, but everyone stood mesmerized by the scene, waiting for whatever drama would come next.

"Francesca, please—" Quince pleaded, ignoring everything and everyone around him.

Francesca glared at him. "Now."

He continued to stare at her, mouth open, eyes wide.

She stood as best she could in the booth. "I won't ask again."

Cass held her breath, curious what Francesca intended to do if he didn't move.

Much to the dismay of the onlookers, Quince sighed and stood, then moved to let her pass.

Francesca stood and smoothed her knee-length skirt, lifted her chin, and stood toe to toe with Piper. "Just because you can't get over your schoolgirl crush does not mean he will go running out to meet you every time you crook your finger and bat your lashes. Sorry to be the one to tell you, but you're not all that."

"You tell her, girlfriend." Bee all but applauded.

Piper glared at him.

When Francesca sidestepped Piper and started to walk away, Piper grabbed her arm and spun her back to face her. "And you, miss high and mighty . . ."

"Talk about the pot calling the kettle black," Bee muttered.

Worried Bee would end up on the receiving end of Piper's ire, and not wanting to miss a word between the two women, Cass kicked him under the table.

"Ouch!" He scowled and rubbed his shin.

". . . have no idea what's going on or what you're interfering in. But, I promise you, you will be sorry if you don't back off."

Francesca shook her off with a sneer, then pressed a finger to Piper's chest. "Don't you dare threaten me."

"Oh, it's not a threat, honey. That's a promise." Piper smirked. "And I always keep my promises."

Apparently tired of the whole thing, or just mortified at the scene Piper had caused, Francesca glared at her another moment then turned and walked out, head held high, back straight, carrying herself with all the dignity she could muster.

Quince gripped Piper's elbow and ushered her toward the exit, his gaze firmly glued to the door Francesca had just fled through.

Chapter Eleven

Cass rolled down the window as she drove along the road beside the bay. The warm breeze whipped her hair, the rush of sound drowning out any voices that might try to intrude on her moment of peace. She couldn't get what Bee had said out of her mind, about Amelia thinking Fred might have jumped to his death. But no matter how many times she tried to embrace that scenario, it just didn't ring true for her.

She'd sent Bee home for some much-needed rest, and Stephanie had run off to attend a meeting with a client, leaving Cass with a bit of time alone before she had to open the shop. As she approached the turn to the lighthouse, she hit the brakes and the turn signal at the same time and took the turn just a little too fast. It couldn't hurt to take a ride up to the lighthouse and just walk around. Who knew? Maybe Fred would make an appearance if she showed up alone.

Except she wasn't alone. Four other cars sat in the lot, all empty, including Simone's Porsche. What would Simone be doing there so early? Maybe one of the other vehicles belonged to Amelia. If so, Cass could stop in and check on her, see how she was doing, which she'd planned on doing at some point anyway.

Plus, she could mention the idea of the group readings to Simone. If Simone planned to follow through with Fred's initial idea of having his guests stay at the Madison Estate, Cass might even be able to do a group reading in the ballroom there later in the evening after she closed Mystical Musings. That would save her having to close up during the day and risk losing customers. Who knew? Maybe Simone would even run the tours year-round.

Warming to the idea, Cass pulled between Simone's Porsche and a blue Blazer, then parked and turned off the ignition. Sitting for a moment, enjoying the bay breeze through the window, Cass tried to open her senses. "Are you still hanging around, Fred? It would be great if you could just tell me what happened. Sure would make this a whole lot easier. Don't get me wrong, but you didn't really strike me as the type to feel such tremendous guilt at hurting someone that you'd take your own life."

And there it was in a nutshell. Fred DiCarlo hadn't jumped to his death, because he'd never cared who he insulted or hurt, often stomping all over people's emotions for his own entertainment with no thought whatsoever. Which led her right back to the theory he'd had help out that window.

She turned the car back on long enough to roll up the window, then dropped her keys into her bag and headed for the keeper's cottage.

She pulled the door handle, half expecting it to be locked, but it opened easy enough and she walked into the foyer. "Hello? Amelia?"

Her voice echoed back through the high ceilings. No answer. Hmm . . . couldn't hurt to have a look around, see if she could find someone. With four cars in the lot, someone had to be somewhere, although they could also belong to people walking along the beach.

She moved into the gift shop. Her gaze landed on the full display of lighthouse figures. Either theirs weren't selling either or they'd been restocked. Tourist season would come soon enough, and hopefully sales would pick up. The figures weren't something most locals bought.

"Amelia?" She waited. Nothing. "Simone?"

She strolled through the room until she found herself in front of the display holding Kitty Garrison's journal. "What secrets did you share, Kitty? Whatever they were, my friend Bee will dig in and try to decipher them, I'm sure. Maybe you could help him out a little if there's something important we need to know."

A cool breeze blew across her back—and she tensed—followed by the sound of the air conditioner kicking on. She laughed at herself and moved on. A quick check of the other rooms on the first floor told her no one was around. She started up the stairs, Bee's voice arguing in her head that it was probably not a good idea to go snooping around. She ignored him. "Hello? Is anyone here?"

Still no answer. She reached the hallway at the top of the stairs and stopped. A door stood ajar, and she pushed it open and poked her head inside. "Anyone here? Amelia?"

Stacks of boxes filled the room, several open, some with packing slips on top. She peeked inside the box closest to the doorway. Lighthouse figures. Not the delicate ones from the gift shop that Cass also carried, but bigger, heavier versions of the Bay Island Lighthouse, more suitable for gardens or front yards. One of them had been shoved in the box upside down. Cass's need for order reared its ugly head, and she pulled the piece out to turn it over. She hefted it in her hand, a nice heavy piece that wouldn't blow over in a strong wind. Maybe she should consider stocking a few at Mystical Musings.

She studied the piece. It had a few of the rocks from the jetty with the lighthouse standing atop them. It really was a perfect replica, except for the sloppy paint job. It seemed some of the dark reddish-brown paint from the bricks had smudged across the white siding. Weird they'd let them go out like that. She pulled a second one from the box. Nope, that one was perfect, must have been just the one. Someone must have smudged it while it was still wet.

She stuck them both back into the box right side up, then searched for the packing slip and found it crumpled and stuffed between two figures. She pulled it out. The same company she ordered her figures from. She'd have to take a look and maybe order a box. She smoothed the page and folded it in half. Reddish-brown smudges, just like the one on the figure, marred the back of the page. Cass brought the page closer, her heart hammering against her ribs.

No. Not paint. Blood. Dried blood, as if someone had used the back of the page to wipe the blood from the figure, then crumpled it in a hurry and stuffed it all back into the box.

Bee's voice screamed at her to run. This time, she had every intention of listening. But take the page with her, or leave it and call Luke? Leave it. Bad enough her fingerprints were all over everything, no way should she remove the evidence. She stuffed the paper back into the box as close to how she'd found it as she could, then turned and fled down the hallway.

Sweat streamed down her hairline, and she fought the urge to wipe it away. Even though the blood had already dried and she couldn't see any on her hands, she knew all too well what contaminants could linger in dried blood.

The police had searched the keeper's house, though. How could they have missed something like that? Unless it hadn't been there then. Could the killer have hidden it, then returned it later? Possibly. But Luke and Tank could work it all out.

She hurried down the stairs, careful not to touch the railing or make any noise. By the time she hit the foyer floor, her hair was clinging to her neck and she was breathing hard. For all she knew, the killer could have just returned the items to the box and still be hanging around.

"Cass?"

She skidded to a stop a few feet from the front door and freedom and turned to face Amelia. "Amelia, hi. I was . . . uh . . . just looking for you."

Amelia frowned and looked up the stairs in the direction Cass had come from.

Simone moved up behind her from one of the open doorways off the foyer and lay a hand on Amelia's shoulder, her gaze intent on Cass. "You seem to be in an awful hurry."

Cass laughed as best she could under the circumstances. She already knew Simone possessed some level of psychic ability, one she had a good level of control over, but how much could she read from Cass? No way to know. Certainly her discomfort, that would be obvious. "I . . . oh, sorry, I . . . Do you by any chance have a bathroom I could use?"

Amelia shifted her gaze to Simone.

Simone held Cass's gaze in an unwavering stare, her focus seeming to bore directly through her. After a moment, the intensity relented. "Of course."

Amelia gestured toward a short hallway that led toward the back of the house. "Just down there."

"Thanks, I'll be right back." Cass hurried down the hall, grateful the bathroom door stood open when she reached it. She entered and shoved it shut with her foot, not bothering to turn the lock. Using her wrist, she turned on the hot water and pumped soap into her other hand.

While she lathered her hands, scrubbing off not only any remnants of blood but probably a few layers of skin as well, she studied herself in the mirror above the sink. Strands of her long hair clung to her face and neck, and she looked a bit pale, but other than that, she looked surprisingly normal. Whatever fear clutched her insides apparently didn't show in her expression. Okay. All she had to do was talk to Amelia and Simone, as she'd intended, and then hightail it out of there and call Luke. She could pull this off.

But what if Amelia and Simone had killed Fred? Amelia would most certainly have had access to the box of figures. But so would anyone who'd been present when Fred died. The box was open, sitting right by the doorway when you hit the second floor. Everyone who'd gone up to the third floor that day would have passed it on their way by. But how many could have gotten away with stashing the figure somewhere and then returning later to put it back? Amelia, for sure.

Cass rinsed her hands, dried them on paper towels, then used the paper towels to turn off the faucet and open the door before tossing them in the trash.

Bee's voice screamed in her mind, *"Run, run, run."*

She put an imaginary hand over his mouth, muffling the words. She'd have to remember to give that a try with the voices.

Simone and Amelia stood waiting in the foyer when she returned.

Darn. She should have thought to flush the toilet. Oh, well. Too late now. "Sorry about that. I should have gone before I left the diner."

Simone tilted her head.

Cass ignored her and focused on Amelia. "I just finished having breakfast with Bee and Stephanie, and I'm on my way to pick up Beast and head into the shop, but I had a few minutes and figured I'd swing past. When I saw all the cars in the lot, I was hoping you'd be here."

Amelia wrung her hands together. "Is this about Fred?"

"Oh." She should have realized Amelia might think she'd been able to contact Fred. "No, I'm sorry. I haven't had any luck contacting him. It was actually something Bee said that had me wanting to see you."

She nodded and lowered her gaze.

Cass reached out to her, rubbing a hand along her arm. "I'm sorry. I know this can't be easy for you."

"Thank you."

Simone handed Amelia a tissue. "So, what was it you heard that prompted you to seek out Amelia?"

"First, I wanted to see how she was holding up." She waited for Amelia to blow her nose a few times. "And then I wanted to ask your opinion on how Fred died. Bee seemed to think you were under the impression his death might have been self-inflicted."

Though that was irrelevant if what she'd found upstairs was what she thought it was. He certainly hadn't hit himself over the head then returned the weapon to the box before diving out the window.

Amelia shrugged. "I don't know what to think."

Simone put an arm around her and looked at Cass.

"While we appreciate you stopping by, this might not be the best time to talk. Amelia has been having a particularly rough morning." Simone started guiding Amelia toward the door, and Cass followed. "I tried to talk her out of coming here this morning, but she wouldn't be swayed. Said she needed to do something, couldn't just sit any longer."

"I understand."

Simone opened the front door.

Cass moved ahead of them into the doorway. "If there's anything I can do, please don't hesitate to reach out. And if I do find I'm able to contact Fred, I promise I'll let you know right away."

Amelia sniffed and rubbed her already swollen eyes. "Thank you."

Cass refrained from pulling out her phone as she started across the lot. No reason to make Simone any more suspicious than she might already be. And if either of them were guilty, she didn't want to give them time to stash the evidence before she could get help. She took a few deep breaths, trying to settle herself.

"Lighthouse . . . keeper . . . keep her? . . . lighthouse . . ."

She tried slapping a hand over an imaginary mouth, to no avail. The voices wouldn't subside, so she ignored them instead. More or less, since she found herself walking toward the lighthouse anyway.

A car started, and she glanced over her shoulder as Simone's Porsche headed out of the lot with two people in the front seat.

Cass whipped out her phone and called Luke. When he didn't answer, she left him a detailed message, then called Tank and did the same. She thought about calling nine-one-one, and if one of them didn't get back to her in the next few minutes, she would. In the meantime, she strolled along the walkway toward the jetty. Since there were still three other cars in the lot, she didn't want to leave until she'd made contact with someone about what she'd found in the upstairs room, though she couldn't exactly stand guard on the front porch, especially when she had no clue if a killer was still inside.

She kept her pace slow, occasionally looking back over her shoulder to see if there was any activity at the house. When she reached the lighthouse, she stood looking up at it. No way was she climbing to the top again, no matter what the voices told her, so what was she doing there?

She looked down at her phone. Still nothing. She checked her service and looked up the number for the Bay Island Police Department. If Luke and Tank were busy, maybe she could get ahold of Chief Rawlins. Leaving the lighthouse behind, she started back toward the keeper's house, this time walking on the beach rather than along the walkway. It was probably less conspicuous than walking back and forth along the walkway.

A man sat on the beach, his legs folded, elbows on his knees, head cradled in his hands. As she got closer, she recognized the clothes he'd been wearing in the diner a little while ago, along with the hair and build—there was no mistaking Quincy Yates. But what to do? She didn't know him, even though she knew who he was, so striking up a conversation—interrogation, whatever—might seem odd. Still, Bee didn't know him either, and he'd tried to track him down to have a chat, so she had to figure he'd approve.

"Excuse me," she said when she was within a few feet of him. "Aren't you Quincy Yates?"

He stood and brushed off his shorts. "Yeah."

"Hi." Cass extended a hand. "I'm Cass Donovan. I own Mystical Musings."

"I know who you are." He took her hand and shook it. "Thank you for taking over for me yesterday. With Fred."

"Oh, no problem. I'm just sorry I couldn't save him."

Quince looked out over the water, squinting against the harsh glare of the sun.

Okay. Now what? She wished Bee were there. He always had such easy way with people. "Did you know him well?"

He scoffed. "Too well."

"I'm sorry for your loss."

He finally turned to meet her gaze, his jaw clenched tight, fire blazing in his eyes. "Trust me, Fred DiCarlo's death is no loss."

Cass's cell phone rang, and she glanced at the screen. Luke. She had to answer.

"It was nice to meet you. Thanks again." Quince started back toward the parking lot.

Darn. She swiped her finger across the screen as she watched him go. She'd have to find him again later when she had more time. Speaking to Luke couldn't wait. Besides, if she didn't answer after leaving a message she might have found the murder weapon, he'd think she was in danger. "Hey, Luke."

Chapter Twelve

Cass picked Beast up from the house and walked back along the beach toward Mystical Musings. She'd have made it on time if she'd put him in the car and driven, but she enjoyed her time with him in the mornings, as did he. Why should they miss out on their time together just because the scene Piper had caused in the diner and Cass's trip to the lighthouse had held everything up? Besides, after she'd finished explaining what she'd found to Luke and promising up and down she wouldn't repeat anything, she'd driven down the boardwalk, and it had been fairly empty.

Beast jumped at a seagull as it dove low toward the water.

Even though she knew he just wanted to play, she had to wonder what he'd do if he ever actually caught one of the elusive creatures. Hopefully, she'd never find out.

Cass turned away from the shoreline and headed toward the boardwalk. "Come on, boy. We're late."

When he didn't fall into step beside her, she turned and looked over her shoulder.

Beast pranced into the water up to his chest.

Cass groaned. She'd just had to think it, hadn't she? Had to think he hadn't needed an emergency grooming appointment in a while. She had no one to blame but herself for this one. She ran toward him. "Beast, no."

He barked at the flock of birds.

"Beast. Come." She strode toward him, holding the leash's clip ready.

He turned and looked at her. Waited for her to wade into the water and reach him.

"Good boy." She bent over, intent on unburying the hook on his collar from the thick mane of fur surrounding his neck.

He undulated and danced out of the way, sending up a wave of water that even managed to soak her hair.

"You've got to be kidding me, Beast." She yanked up her leggings, waded farther into the ice-cold water, and tried the scowl that always seemed to work for Bee. "I do not have time for this today. I'm already running late. Now get over here."

He jumped, submerged, and came up wearing his happy face and shaking water everywhere.

She brushed water off her face, swiped an arm across her lips, but couldn't rid herself of the taste of salt. "Oh, come on, Beast."

He cocked his head, and she'd have sworn he smiled.

Okay, apparently whining wasn't going to work. She firmed her voice. "Beast, no."

He lowered the front of his body in acquiescence, or maybe ready to pounce.

Short, firm commands. That's what Herb Cox had drilled into her over and over, whenever she found time to show up for training classes. She took a deep breath, sucking more salt water into her mouth. Okay. She could do this. She backed to the edge of the water and stood her ground. "Beast. Come."

She slid the clip open with her thumb.

Hmm . . . Herb hadn't told her how long to face off with him before trying something else. "Beast. Come."

He bounced toward her, then away again, obviously not ready for playtime to be over. Then he barreled straight at her.

She braced herself an instant before he jumped.

But he stopped short, cocked his head, and looked up the beach toward Mystical Musings. Then he took off running, sending a surge of water over her leggings on his way by.

Oh, well, at least he's out of the water.

Brushing herself off as best she could, Cass hurried after him. Terrified he'd resume his playful disobedience and run out into the street, Cass refrained from calling to him again, opting instead to quietly follow him toward the shop.

When he reached the back deck, he hurried up the stairs and sat beside the back door. He glanced back at her, and his tongue dropped out the side of his mouth as he sat panting.

Now what?

She was already close to an hour late opening the shop, Beast was not only fully soaked but loaded with sand from his mad dash up the beach to the shop, and Cass was pretty much soaked from head to toe. She tried to spit out some of the wet sand that had somehow made its way into her mouth. Wiping her mouth with her arm didn't help, since that was also covered in sand.

She reached Beast and clipped his leash to his collar, then simply stared at him.

He slumped and lowered his head, peering up at her from beneath his lashes.

At least he understood he'd done something wrong. No sense reprimanding him after the fact, since he wouldn't understand. She sighed and petted his head.

Now she just had to figure out how to fix this mess.

Cass gripped Beast's collar, unclipped his leash, and wrapped it through the deck railing before securing it once more. "It's only for a couple of minutes, Beast. I promise. I just have to grab a couple of towels."

She opened her soaked bag and pulled out her key ring, then tried to wipe the gritty coating of sand off on her shirt. No use. Giving up, she unlocked the back door and pushed it open, then froze.

"Oh, hey, Cass. Took you long enough." Bee looked up from whatever he was sitting at the table reading. The instant his gaze landed on her, his mouth fell open, and his hand fluttered to his throat. "Heavens to Betsy, girl, you look like something the cat just dragged in."

She glared at him. "Ha ha."

He glanced out the large back window at Beast curled in the shade beneath the overhang, apparently exhausted from his morning romp in the bay. Bee's lips curved upward.

She pointed a finger. "Don't you dare."

His shoulders started to shake.

"Bee . . ."

And, with that, the dam burst. He laughed so hard he had to clutch his stomach, sucking in ragged breaths in an effort to gain some semblance of control. "Oh, owww . . ."

Cass ignored him and marched toward the counter, her dignity in tatters. She dialed the groomer and prayed someone would pick up. "Come on, come on, come on . . ."

Nicole answered on the sixth ring. "Hey, Cass, it's been a while."

"Well, he made up for it this morning." She pressed a hand against her ear and tried to ignore Bee's hysterics in the background.

"How bad?" To Nicole's credit, though Cass could hear the

humor in her tone and had no doubt she and Bee would share a good laugh over it later, Nicole kept her voice steady. Of course, she was probably, in Bee's words, laughing her keaster off on the inside.

"He's soaking wet and his fur is loaded with enough sand to fill a child's sandbox."

"Oh, no." Her voice hitched. "Umm . . ."

Good cover.

"Where are you?"

"I just got to Mystical Musings, and I haven't even opened yet."

"All right. Sit tight, I'll be there to pick him up in a few minutes."

Relief rushed through her. "Oh, thank you, Nicole. You have no idea how much I appreciate it."

"Of course I do, Cass, or I wouldn't offer. I'm on my way." She said goodbye and hung up.

Cass whirled on Bee.

He held up a hand. "I'm sorry, Cass, I can't . . ."

Propping her hands on her hips, she tapped her foot while she waited for him to get a grip. "I thought you were going home to bed. What are you even doing here?"

"I couldn't help myself." He sucked in a few more breaths, wiped the tears that had trickled down his cheeks, then patted the stack of papers in front of him. "I came back here to pick up the folder Levi brought me and started skimming through the transcripts from Kitty's journal and just had to read them."

She glanced at Beast, still happily sleeping on the back porch.

"So, why are you doing it in my shop, instead of your own? Or even better, why aren't you curled up in bed with them?"

"Oh, Cass." He waved a hand. "Don't be like that. I wanted to share my discovery with you, and I knew you'd be here soon, so I let myself in."

Interest piqued, she peered over his shoulder at the pages, though she did rethink having given him a key. "What discovery?"

He shrugged. "How do I know? I haven't discovered it yet."

The wind chimes above the front door clinked, and a couple walked in.

"Besides, if I get tired, I can always crash on your couch in the back room." He wiggled his fingers, shooing her toward her customers.

Just what she needed, Bee snoring up a storm while she was trying to work. She sighed. "Do me a favor, Bee, and keep an eye on Beast until I finish up here?"

"Sure thing." With customers in the shop, Bee's attitude changed. All business, he shifted his chair so he could see out the back window and still peruse the journal.

The woman appeared older, her hair styled meticulously with enough hairspray to burn a new hole through the ozone layer, makeup so thick it gave her face a permanently pinched look, and a designer sundress covered in brightly colored hibiscus flowers. Diamonds the size of key fobs hung from both ears.

The gentleman accompanying her wore jeans, a sport jacket over a plain white T-shirt, and an apologetic expression.

"Good morning." Cass started to smooth her hair as she approached the couple, but only succeeded in getting her fingers tangled in the rat's nest that had somehow managed to get full of water, sea salt, and sand. She smiled, and heat crept up her cheeks. "Sorry, a mishap with my dog."

Bee snickered, then sighed and shook his head.

Cass ignored him. Or, at least, she tried to. "What brings you in this morning? Are you looking for something special, or did you just want to browse?"

Cass very much hoped it was the latter, so she could excuse herself, go to the back room, and make some attempt to freshen up. The drying salt tightened her skin, and the sand in her clothing had begun to itch. Soon after inheriting Beast, she'd started leaving a change of clothes in the back room. If only she could escape for two minutes.

The woman reached out to Cass across the counter and gave her hand and energetic pump. "Actually, we are in desperate need of your help."

Of course you are.

"If I told Stanley once yesterday, I told him a thousand times, don't take your wallet with you. Put your cash in your pocket with your driver's license, and leave your wallet in the safe back at the hotel." She plopped a purse the size of a small suitcase on the driftwood countertop. "It's not like I don't have enough credit cards in here if we see something we want. But did he listen? No. Of course not. And now he's gone and lost his wallet."

Of course he did.

Bee kept his head buried in the journal, a little too interested in Cass's opinion, but kept glancing at Beast through the window, so she went with grateful instead of annoyed.

Cass checked the clock. Nicole should be there any minute.

". . . and that nice maid at the Bay Side Hotel suggested you might be able to help him find it. Not that I believe in psychics, mind you. Personally, I think they're all a bunch of quacks, but at this point I'll try anything. We have tickets to a Broadway show next weekend, and did he take them out of the wallet like I told him? Of course not. So now, not only are we out all of our credit cards, ID, and cash, he went and lost our tickets too. And, let me tell you, those tickets were not easy to come by."

Bee lowered his head even farther and massaged his temples, his arm conveniently blocking his face from view if the woman ever paused long enough to notice him.

"Well?" she demanded.

Cass jerked her attention back to the woman. "Uh."

Stanley rolled his eyes and stuck his hands in his pockets.

Cass's heart went out to him. No wonder he hadn't listened to her about the wallet. Or the tickets. If this was normal for his wife, he'd probably tuned her out somewhere soon after she'd said I do.

"If you'd like to take a seat and make yourselves comfortable, I'll be happy to see if I can help." Cass gestured toward the back table. "Can I offer you something to drink?"

"No, thank you." The woman turned her back on Cass and Stanley and strode across the shop.

He leaned over and blocked his mouth with his hand. "Her name's Loretta. She hasn't told you, but she'll be insulted as all get-out if you don't remember it later."

Bee looked over, caught sight of Loretta striding toward him, and straightened up immediately, his expression frozen somewhere between deer-in-the-headlights and you've-got-to-be-kidding-me.

Stanley coughed and followed his wife.

Nicole stuck her head in the back door. "Hey, Cass. I'm taking him now."

Grateful for the distraction, Cass ran to say goodbye to Beast and to ask Nicole to feed him once she'd given him his bath, which she easily agreed to. Cass would have to remember an even bigger tip than usual when she picked him up.

With Beast taken care of and Bee frowning over whatever he was reading, Cass took a seat at the table. Not her normal seat, because Loretta had already claimed that one.

It's going to be a long day.

Cass took a deep breath, cleared her mind, and turned her attention to Stanley. "Okay, Stanley, can you tell me where you last remember having your wallet?"

Bee gasped.

All eyes turned to him.

"Oh, sorry." He pointed to his pages, offered a sheepish smile, waved them off, and went back to his reading.

Scratch that. It's already been a long day, and it's not even noon yet.

"I'm sorry about that. As I was saying." Cass cleared her throat and looked straight at Stanley, trying to focus his attention away from Bee and back on her. "When is the last time you can recall seeing your wallet?"

"He most certainly didn't have it when we got to the wine shop this morning. I stood there waiting for him to take it out and pay, and he just kept patting his pockets and looking confused." Loretta crossed her legs, propped her elbow on the table, and rested a finger against her cheek.

Cass shifted her chair to face Stanley, keeping her profile to Loretta. "It would help if you could tell me exactly what you remember, Stanley."

He turned his chair to face her and clasped his hands between his knees. "Last I saw it, it was on the nightstand beside the bed at the hotel. Next thing I knew, it was gone."

"If you'd have listened to me and put it in the safe, we'd know where it was now," Loretta said.

"Oh, no, he didn't." Bee fanned himself with his silk scarf, gaze riveted on his pages.

Loretta gave him a sideways glance.

Cass pounced while she was sidetracked. "Please, try to focus on me, Stanley. When did you see your wallet?"

He rolled his lips in and tilted his head.

Cass waited him out.

Loretta sucked in a breath to say something.

Bee put his pages down, leaned closer to her, and whispered, "Cass can hear the voices better if it's quiet," then winked at Loretta, shot Cass a thumbs-up, and went back to reading.

With a harrumph, Loretta clamped her lips closed.

Stanley scratched his head. "Put it on the nightstand when I got back to the hotel last night. It was gone when I got up."

"Oh, don't be ridiculous, Stanley. It didn't just get up and walk out on its own."

"Nope." He clasped and unclasped his hands.

"Pushed."

You have got to be kidding me today. A dull throb started across the top of her head.

"I saw that wallet on the nightstand when you were in the shower. I remember thinking it shouldn't be there; you were going to lose it."

"Lighthouse, pushed, slid, more, now, tell, find, lost . . ."

Cass pressed her hands against her ears and squeezed her eyes closed.

"Well, I never," Loretta huffed.

"Oh, no way." Bee set the papers down and leaned over them, his scarf pulled up over his mouth.

"Move, move, move . . . Lighthouse. Go. Pushed. Lighthouse."

Ahhhhh . . . If you just tell me where that darned wallet is, I'll go to the lighthouse the instant I lock the doors.

Cass sighed, fully intent on apologizing to Loretta, when a vision slammed through her.

A hand holding a brown leather wallet, hovering beside a lamp, long crimson nails tapping against the leather, *tap, tap, tap.* Pause. *Tap, tap, tap.* Pause.

Her gaze shot to Loretta. "Did you pick the wallet up when you found it on the nightstand?"

"What?"

"Stanley's wallet. You said you saw it on the nightstand. Did you lift it up? Hold it in your hand?" A quick glance at her hands confirmed the long red nails.

She frowned. "Actually, I think I did. I remember I was going to yell at him about it, but he was showering, so I picked it up to confront him when he came out."

"And did you?"

"Did I what?"

"Did you confront him?"

"No, my daughter called, and I talked to her and the grandkids for a bit, that whole FaceTime thing they have now, you know, makes it easy to keep in touch—"

"Were you holding the wallet while you spoke to them?" Cass tried to gently steer her back on topic, but her head was beginning to throb, and she just needed Loretta to go.

Poor Stanley just sat staring in wonder.

"Of course, I wasn't holding the wallet. How ridiculous would I look talking to them while standing there clutching a man's wallet?"

Cass counted to ten in her head. "Were you holding the wallet when the phone rang?"

"I already told you I was. I was waiting for Stanley to get out so I could—" Her mouth dropped open into a big O. She dug through her purse and pulled out the brown leather wallet.

Stanley smirked.

Cass sat back and blew out a breath.

"See." Bee nudged Loretta with an elbow. "I told you she needed quiet for the voices to get through."

"Oh. I. Um." Loretta turned on Stanley. "See what you did? If you hadn't left that danged wallet on the nightstand, none of this would have happened."

Chapter Thirteen

As soon as Cass ushered Loretta and poor Stanley out the door, she returned to the table, dropped into her own chair, folded her arms on the table, and rested her head. "I need a shower."

"Whining, Cass, really?" Bee didn't bother to look up from his pages. "Not very becoming."

"I don't care. I'm having a bad day." And it had barely even started.

"There, there, sweetie." Bee patted her shoulder. "Maybe this will help."

She turned her head to look at him but lacked the energy to pick it up. "What's that?"

He lifted the stack of papers he'd been so engrossed in and held them out to Cass. "This journal is fascinating."

"As evidenced by all the drama while I was trying to help a customer."

"Drama? What drama?"

Since she couldn't tell for sure if the innocent routine was real or a ploy, Cass kept the eye roll in her imagination. She wanted to hear what had him so hooked, and if he was annoyed with her, he'd make her find out for herself. She didn't have the energy for that. "I don't have time to read it all, so why don't you give me the highlights?"

"Okay." Bee settled more comfortably, crossing his legs and turning toward her to hook one arm over the chair back. He left the pages on the table. "This really is such a tragic story. If it's portrayed correctly, it would make an intriguing story for a tour."

Cass sat up, her curiosity aroused.

"The journal belonged to Kitty Garrison. Her father, Samuel, was the original Bay Island lighthouse keeper, and Kitty lived in the keeper's house with him, his wife, Eleanor, and a scattering of sisters whose names I don't remember, of which she was the oldest."

"Does it say how old Kitty was when she wrote it?" Cass got up and got a brush from her bag. Since it seemed like Bee was just getting warmed up, she had a feeling it was going to be a long story, and no way was she greeting another customer in her current state.

Bee got up and followed her to the back room, carrying the

transcription with him. "No, and it's not dated either, but the writing sounds young, though kind of mature. I'd guess no later than late teens, early twenties at the oldest."

Cass raised a brow at him. "How'd you come to that conclusion?"

He shrugged and flipped through the pages he'd bookmarked with Post-it notes. "She never mentions school, though the entries start during the autumn months and go through the winter. Yet, she doesn't seem to have much experience with boys, mentions that she hasn't ever met someone she connected with like she does Thomas."

"Thomas is the pirate?"

"Mm-hmm." He shifted through the bookmarked pages.

Cass took one look in the mirror above the bathroom sink, braced herself, and yanked the brush through the tangled, sticky mess. As much as she'd love to wash it, she couldn't be sure when another customer might come in, and after staying closed so long when Fred had died and then again this morning, she didn't want to close up again, even if only for a few minutes. She added buying leave-in conditioner to her mental to-do list. "Does it say how they met?"

"It does. And it is so romantic." He ran his finger along a couple of lines. "She describes a terrible storm. From her description and the time of year, I'd say possibly a hurricane or, at the least, a nor'easter."

Cass shook sand out of her hair. Great, now she was going to have to vacuum. Tears leaked from the corners of her eyes, but she finally managed to get the brush through and smooth her hair.

"I'm going to go out of order here, give you a little background that Kitty didn't write down until later, after Thomas was able to share what had happened, but it's helpful to know ahead of time." Bee stared at her a moment, held up a finger, and disappeared into the shop. When he returned, he held out the sash she sometimes wore to cover her hair.

"That bad, huh?"

"Ehh."

She took the sash and tied it around her head. Better. Taking advantage of Bee having left the doorway clear, she hurried to the row of cabinets in the back room and pulled out black leggings and a black long-sleeved tunic-style shirt. At least the purple sash added a pop of color.

Bee perched on the edge of the couch with the papers on the table in front of him. He leaned over and rested his elbows on his knees. "Thomas's ship's captain apparently tried to land out by Montauk Point somewhere, but they were getting battered too badly, the ship taking on water, much of the crew sick, some already dead. They'd missed the Point, but made it into Gardiners Bay, but the ship went down, anyway. When Samuel Garrison went out to check the lighthouse, to be sure it stayed lit during the height of the storm, he found Thomas mostly dead on the jetty. He took him in, and Eleanor and Kitty nursed him back to health."

A chill pricked the back of Cass's neck.

"Kitty sat by his side, ever the loyal nurse, and when she wasn't tending to his needs, she read to him, often holding his hand and offering both comfort and strength. She fell in love over the tragic tale of Romeo and Juliet." Bee paused and pressed a hand to his chest, then shook his head and kept going. "It took months but, eventually, Thomas regained consciousness and began to heal. When he did, he fell fast and hard for his young caretaker."

"Aww, what a sweet story." Cass bent and picked up Beast's bowls, since Nicole was going to feed him. "Did they end up getting married?"

"Oh, no. When Samuel Garrison found out what was going on, he blew a gasket, refused to allow the relationship to continue."

Cass paused, midway to the sink. "Oh, no, how sad."

"Indeed." He held up a finger. "And it gets worse. Thomas told Kitty about a treasure supposedly buried out by the lighthouse, said he could find it based on what his captain had said, and it would be his, since everyone else who'd been aboard the ship had perished in the storm. So, as soon as he recovered enough of his strength, Thomas began searching. During the days, while Kitty did her chores and tended to all of her younger sisters, Thomas hunted for the treasure that would allow him to provide for his bride once they ran away together."

Cass dumped the food into the garbage pail, dumped the water down the drain, and washed the bowls. When she was done, she cleaned out the sink, washed her hands, and grabbed a Diet Pepsi for her and one for Bee. She handed him his soda, then leaned a shoulder against the doorjamb, holding her clothes, ready to bolt for the bathroom as soon as he finished the story.

"Thanks," Bee said absently as he leafed through a few more pages. "Each night, after everyone went to bed, the two met under the stars, despite the freezing cold temperatures—and you know how cold it gets out by the lighthouse on winter nights."

Cass shivered. Just the thought of the wind tearing across the open expanse of beach and jetty was enough to chill her right down to her bones. Add the ice-cold spray of the water hitting the rocks, and it could be pretty brutal.

"Okay." Bee flipped ahead to another bookmarked section. "So far, at this point, Thomas has disappeared. He left Kitty one night with a kiss and a promise he'd locate the treasure and dig it up that very night, then return for her. They planned to elope the following night."

"Does she say what happened to him?" Cass couldn't help getting lost in the past. Bee was right; it would make an interesting ghost tour story.

"Supposedly, Kitty heard rumors that her father had found out about their plans and either run Thomas off or killed him. But she didn't believe it. Even though her father was being difficult, she'd held on to the hope that he'd come around once he realized how much they loved each other, and once Thomas found the treasure and could take care of his new bride. But, until this point, Thomas hasn't returned."

"Does he ever?"

Bee shrugged and set the pages aside. "I don't know. I haven't read that far yet."

"Bee, if you expect me to believe for one minute that you didn't skip ahead to the end of that transcript to see if he returned, forget it. I know you too well."

"Well, when you put it like that." He huffed in mock indignation, then grinned. "Of course I did."

"No." Cass feigned shock. "Really?"

"Knock if off, you, or I won't finish the story."

No way would Cass have time to read that entire transcript, and she found she really wanted to know what had happened to the two young lovers. "Sorry, Bee."

He winked. "I had a feeling you would be."

"Ha ha." She took a quick peek out the front window. Though a few people walked along the boardwalk, none seemed to be heading her way. Even so, she needed to get cleaned up before anyone did. She was not waiting on another customer until she changed her clothes. "Finish up. I am working, you know."

He waved a hand. "Yeah, yeah, so am I."

"Oh, really? How do you figure that?"

"I'm creating brilliant gowns in my mind." He tapped his temple and winked. "Ingenious, really."

"There's one problem with that, Bee."

"Only one?"

"Yup. You can't multitask to save your life."

"Yeah." He laughed. "There is that."

"So, keep going."

Bee yawned and slid farther back on the couch, settling in more comfortably.

She needed to hurry him along before he fell asleep. Although if he did fall asleep, she could escape and change her clothes. On the other hand, she wouldn't know what happened to Thomas and Kitty.

"Oh, fine. Thomas never returned. But rumors started, about a pirate ghost seen out on the jetty at night, searching for something. Then, one day, Samuel went out to check on the lighthouse and didn't return in a timely fashion. When her mom sent poor Kitty out to look for him and call him for dinner, Kitty discovered his body, battered and bloody, on the rocks beneath the lighthouse.

"Despite her alienation from her dad over the way he'd acted with Thomas, she was devastated by his death. And then the rumors kept flying, rumors of the ghost pirate seen out there around the time Samuel died. Kitty started to wonder if Thomas had come back for her, maybe fought with Samuel over her and killed him by accident, then ran off and was too ashamed to return for her." He opened his soda and took a sip.

"So, every night, no matter the weather, Kitty took to sitting out on the rocks waiting for Thomas to come home. She spent hours out there every single night, hoping he'd see her and know she awaited his return."

"Did he ever come back?"

"Nope." He flipped through the last few dozen pages. "Eventually, she stopped posting regular entries in the journal. Then there's nothing but a few sporadic updates every year or two saying that he hadn't returned and she'd never stopped waiting, along with a quick recap of how she'd spent her time."

"She never moved on and married anyone else?" Cass ached for the poor young woman who'd spent her life waiting for her lover to return. "She had to have realized at some point he wasn't coming back."

"Apparently not. Or, if she did, she just couldn't move past it. She didn't date, didn't marry, never had children, cared for her mother and several of her sisters through their deaths. At the end, though, she seems to have accepted his death."

"That's so sad." Cass shivered again, placed the cold soda can down on the counter, and hugged the small stack of clothes against her.

"Here, listen to this." He took a page from the bottom of the pile and placed it on top, then straightened the stack, took another sip of his drink, cleared his throat, and started to read from the page. "As I look out over the vast expanse of the sea, awaiting my beloved's return, a chill takes me, despite the sun's heat and the warmth of the rocks I sit upon. A whisper of a breeze touches my cheek, and I lean into Thomas's caress. It won't be long now, before I once again return to my true love's embrace.'"

Bee sniffed and clutched the page to his chest. "And that's it. Her last entry."

"Wow." Cass couldn't imagine loving someone so much that you'd spend your entire life just sitting and waiting for their return.

Bee dropped the transcript onto the coffee table and went for a tissue to blow his nose. "You do realize, though, that if the rumors were right, and Samuel did kill Thomas that night, the treasure was never found, right?"

Cass had to work for a second to switch gears. "You think that's what Fred was trying to do? Find the treasure?"

"I think it's a good possibility." He leaned back against the counter, crossed one ankle over the other, and folded his arms across his chest. "And guess what else?"

Cass got a sinking feeling in her gut. "What?"

"I think, based on what Thomas told Kitty and she shared in her journal, I can find the treasure."

"Bee . . ." The last thing Bee needed to be doing was searching for a buried pirate treasure, especially when the last person that may or may not have been searching for the same treasure had just turned up dead under suspicious circumstances. "It's not safe out there for you to be digging around."

"Don't worry. I'll be careful." His eyes lit up with anticipation.

She knew that look all too well. It came over Beast whenever she held up a piece of bacon.

The chimes above the front door signaled the end of their conversation. It also meant she didn't have time to change. She dropped the clothes onto the counter and peeked through the curtains.

An older woman entered and headed straight for the counter, her stride determined, as was the set of her jaw.

"I'll be with you in just a minute, ma'am."

The woman glanced at the clock over the door, then nodded once at Cass, her mouth set in a grim line.

Great. Just what she needed, another difficult customer.

Bee shoved away from the counter. "Hey, Cass, would you do me a favor?"

"Sure." There was nothing she wouldn't do for Bee. "What do you need?"

He held the curtain aside for her, then followed her back to the shop's main room. "Would you go out to the lighthouse with me later and take a look around? I'm not going to do anything stupid, but I'd really love to —"

"Sure, Bee, I'll go with you." And keep her word to whatever voice had shown her the vision that had allowed her to find Stanley's wallet.

"Wait?" He stopped short. "You will?"

"Sure. Maybe Stephanie will take a ride too." Since she'd be more receptive to the idea of trying to contact whatever spirit had requested Cass's presence. Who knew? Maybe it would turn out to be Thomas himself, and she could ask him what had happened the night he disappeared. Or it could be Samuel. Though, if he had killed his daughter's lover, he'd probably not be as forthcoming. "I actually made a promise to meet someone out there tonight, anyway."

"Really?" He studied her from the corner of his eye. "Who?"

She fluttered her lashes and offered her sweetest smile. "Trust me, Bee, you do not want to know."

Chapter Fourteen

Cass straightened the sash covering her hair, still sticky with sand and salt, and plastered on a smile. "Good morning, ma'am. I'm Cass."

"I certainly hope so, or I came all this way for nothing." The woman plopped an expensive-looking tote on the counter and opened it, then stuffed her hand in and yanked out a small white ball of fur.

"This—"

One end of the fur ball opened up, baring a set of tiny razor-sharp teeth, and nipped the woman's hand. Then it turned its attention to Cass, growling and snarling and baring what looked to be two needle-like fangs amid the teeth.

Cass lurched back. What had this woman brought into her shop?

She glanced at Bee, who stood mesmerized beside the back counter and made no move to come any closer. A lot of help he was going to be.

"Henrietta, no," the woman commanded.

The adorable but vicious little demon-dog nipped her wrist.

She plopped him onto the driftwood countertop, let go, and patted her stylish gray updo. "Can you see what the problem is?"

"Um." An image from the movie *Gremlins,* which she hadn't seen since she was a kid, popped into her mind.

Bee snickered from across the room.

The woman stared at her.

"What's this little . . ." A bunch of names rocketed through her head. "Cutie's name?"

"It's Henrietta, dear, as if I didn't just say that."

"Oh. Right." And with that, she promptly ran out of conversation starters.

Henrietta paced from one end of the counter to the other and back again, peering over the edge each time she reached one. She stopped long enough to scratch her neck, digging in good beneath her collar, then once more resumed her pacing.

Cass prayed the little beast wouldn't find her way down.

Bee dropped onto one of the chairs at the table and propped his feet up on another, his thoughts apparently running along the same line as her own. Though he held the transcript pages in front of him, his gaze never left the animal.

Cass searched the woman's gaze, hoping for some tell as to why she was standing in Cass's shop with what Cass assumed was some kind of miniature dog breed. When none was forthcoming, she studied the dog.

Small. All white fur, smooth and silky. A leather, gem-encrusted collar circled her neck with a tag hanging front and center. The dog was obviously well cared for, so what was the problem?

Cass was the last person anyone would come to for dog-rearing advice, as evidenced by the smirk Bee currently sported. "Is this behavior unusual?"

"Oh, yes." The woman fished a small package of tissues from her bag, wiped tears from the corners of her eyes, and blew her nose. Then she took a clean tissue and wiped the small trickle of blood that had started from the bite mark on her wrist. "I don't know what to do. I'm beside myself. Henrietta is usually so well behaved, has the utmost perfect manners—as well she should, after the astronomical amount of money I spent on all the best trainers. I have always been able to take her anywhere, but since we've arrived on Bay Island, she's been this . . . this . . . monster."

Henrietta continued to pace, head down, peering up at her surroundings from beneath a white veil of fur that had fallen in front of her eyes.

"Have you tried calling one of her trainers to see if they can offer advice? Some trainers offer that as part of the training package." At least, Herb did. She should know. His number was on speed dial right below the groomer.

A sudden realization hit Cass. What would happen if Beast got this out of control? She tried to blow it off; Beast was too kind to ever act this way, but didn't Henrietta's owner seem shocked by her behavior as well? Henrietta had already nipped the woman twice, had drawn blood the second time. Cass made a mental note to contact Herb right away for a training session. "Okay, first things first. What is your name, ma'am?"

"I'm sorry. I'm Helen Monroe." She reached across the counter, keeping a wary eye on the dog, and shook Cass's hand.

"It's nice to meet you. Now." Cass took a deep shuddering

breath and willed her erratic heart rate to slow. "What are you hoping I can do for you?"

"Everyone in town talks about how wonderful you are, how caring and kind. They also say you possess actual psychic abilities."

Uh-oh. Cass had a sinking feeling she knew where this was going. Not sure what to say, she remained quiet.

"Well, I've heard of pet psychics, so I figure you can talk to Henrietta and figure out what's wrong with her."

Bee laughed out loud, no doubt imagining an image of Cass as she'd looked after Beast had taken off for a frolic in the bay that very morning.

Henrietta spread her front legs wide, crouched low, stared at Bee, and growled deep in her throat.

Bee rocked onto the chair's back legs and folded his hands across his stomach.

Searching for a way to explain to Helen that she wasn't that kind of a psychic, Cass stepped a little too close to Henrietta.

The dog whirled on her faster than Cass would have thought possible and lunged.

Cass managed to dance out of the way just in time to avoid getting bit. Thanks to Beast's penchant for knocking things over when he got excited, Cass's reflexes had improved since she'd gotten him.

Bee dropped the chair back onto all four legs and sat forward. All former signs of amusement fled in the instant the dog had turned on her.

Her heart swelled. Her savior. Always ready to jump to her defense.

"It's okay, Bee." She read people for a living, and she could usually tell what Beast needed, if he was hungry or wanted to play or go for a walk or snuggle. How different could this be? She turned to Helen. "I'll be honest, I've never tried anything like this before, but I'm willing to give it a shot."

"Wait." Bee held up a hand. "What?"

Helen breathed a sigh of relief, and her rigid posture slumped a bit. "Oh, thank you."

"And if I can't help you, I can give you the name of a great trainer right here on Bay Island."

"Thank you. Yes, that would be perfect, though I'm confident if I can figure out what's bothering Henrietta, and give her what she wants, the problem will be solved."

Cass refrained from saying too much; giving Henrietta what she wants might very well *be* the problem.

Bee cleared his throat but remained silent.

Cass studied the dog, careful to stay well out of striking distance. "You said she's been like this since you arrived on Bay Island?"

"Yes." Helen frowned. "Not barking and growling all the time, but agitated. She paces, sleeps very restlessly, barks at people. She's usually very friendly, loves the attention people shower on her."

"Is this your first visit to Bay Island?"

"Oh, no. We've been coming here for about three years now. And Henrietta always loves it. She's such a tiny, polite little thing that I'm able to take her wherever I go."

Hard to tell.

Bay Island was very pet-friendly, and Cass often took Beast places with her, but because of his size, some places were off-limits, while smaller dogs would pretty much be allowed anywhere that didn't serve food. "And she was fine last time you came?"

"Yes."

"Did you stay in the same place?"

"Oh, yes, that adorable little bed-and-breakfast down at the end of the boardwalk." She gestured over her shoulder.

Cass knew the place. It sat right at the end of the boardwalk with access to the beach. A peaceful place, far enough out of town to be quiet most of the time. "How was she on the ferry?"

"Sweet as pie."

You'd never guess that from watching her pace, but Cass believed the owner was being completely honest and not wearing blinders where Henrietta was concerned—much as Cass had initially when it had come to getting Beast trained.

"Do you think you can help her?" She took out another tissue, twisted it into a ball.

"When did you first notice the change in her behavior?"

"Hmm." She scowled as she looked back into the past. "I guess, I'd say after we got the car off the ferry and headed into town."

"When was that?"

"Two days ago."

"What did you do while you were waiting for the car to be unloaded?"

"I don't know." She lifted her hands to the sides and sighed. "Walked around, I guess."

"Please, humor me." The last thing she wanted to do was frustrate Helen even further, but without knowing where she was headed, she had to fish around for somewhere to start. "Since Henrietta can't speak for herself, I have to depend on you to speak for her."

The wind chimes over the door sounded, and Luke walked in. Seeing her with a customer, he waved and headed for the back corner where Bee sat.

"Yes, yes. Of course. I'm sorry." Pressing the tattered tissue against her eyes, she sucked in a deep, shaky breath. "I'm just frazzled by all of this."

"Don't worry. I understand." If anyone understood frustration with a pet, it was Cass.

Helen took a moment to compose herself, then started off with new determination. "Okay. We got off the ferry and walked around down by the pier, shopped a little, picked up the treats Henrietta likes from that cute little shop down there."

Allergies, maybe? "She's had the treats before?"

"Oh, yes, all the time."

"Did you feed her anything new?"

"No. Nothing."

So much for that theory. "Okay, so what'd you do after the pet shop?"

"I stopped in the bookstore and picked up a couple of things to read while at the beach then went to the car."

"And you went straight to the bed-and-breakfast from there?"

She frowned. "Yes. Um. I stuffed Henrietta's old collar into the pet shop bag and reached for her, and she shied away. She'd never done that before, but I figured maybe I'd just startled her."

Cass held up a hand. "Wait. Why did you take off her collar?"

"Oh." Helen beamed. "Because I got her this new one with her birthstones on it. Isn't it beautiful?"

Cass studied the red stones studding the collar. "She was born in January?"

"Yes." Helen's smile slipped. "How did you know?"

Cass started to reach for the collar.

Henrietta backed away with a growl, and Cass yanked her hand back.

"It's okay, girl. I'm not going to hurt you," she soothed. "January's birthstone is garnet. In ancient times, some believed gazing at a red garnet could lead to passion or anger. Not that she can see the stones, but they are encircling her neck. Where's her old collar?"

Helen pulled out a collar ringed with pink stones.

"Ah, rose quartz, a much better choice for Henrietta, I think. Would you mind changing it?"

"Seriously?" Helen studied her for a moment.

Luke and Bee both sat up straighter, suspending their conversation to watch her.

"Please, humor me?"

Helen shrugged but did as Cass asked. Unbuckling the new collar, while dodging nips, she petted Henrietta's head and uttered soothing nonsense sounds. She handed the collar to Cass and hooked the old one into place.

Cass studied the collar, running her fingers over the stones.

Henrietta sat and watched her, head tilted.

"Is that any better, girl?" Cass asked.

Henrietta licked her lips and slid her back end out until she was laying on the counter. She propped her head on her front legs.

"I don't believe it." Helen stared back and forth between Cass and Henrietta.

Cass turned the collar over and over in her hands, studying Henrietta and waiting for any sign of agitation. "Is it okay if I pet you now?"

The little dog's ears perked up, and she lifted her head.

Taking her time, so as not to startle Henrietta, Cass reached out a hand and petted her silky head.

Henrietta tilted her head into Cass's hand and all but purred.

"There you go. That's so much better, isn't it?"

Henrietta rolled onto her back and bared her belly for Cass to pet.

Laughing, she continued to pet a much different animal than had first come out of Helen's bag. "You really are a good girl, aren't you."

Helen's mouth opened and closed a few times. "Huh. Unbelievable."

Cass started to set the collar aside, and something sharp poked her finger. "Ouch."

A small spot of blood blossomed, and she grabbed a tissue to blot it.

"What happened?" Helen asked.

Bee and Luke both stood.

Cass pulled the collar closer and studied its surface. She turned it over and ran a finger slowly along the inside. A jagged point caught her finger. "It's broken here. See?"

Helen took the collar from her and inspected the damage where the underneath part of the buckle had broken apart, leaving a sharp edge. "You think it was poking her?"

"From where it's broken, I'd say there's a good chance it's been digging into her, maybe not all the time, but at least when she moved certain ways."

"Oh, my poor baby. Mommy's so sorry I didn't realize you were hurting." Helen scooped Henrietta up and snuggled her close. Then she lowered her to the counter and dug through the fur around her neck searching for damage. She held the fur parted for Cass to see the scratches crisscrossing her neck. "Do you think it'll be okay?"

"I think so, but I can give you the number of a great vet if you'd like to have her checked out and see if she needs antibiotics or anything." Cass dug out the doc's card and handed it to Helen. It wasn't like Cass needed it, since she had the vet's number on speed dial right ahead of the groomer and Herb Cox, thanks to Beast's fondness for eating things he shouldn't.

"Oh, thank you." Helen punched the number into her phone but stopped short of hitting Send, then dropped the card into her bag.

Cass pulled one of Beast's treats from the bin she kept beneath the counter and broke it into pieces for Henrietta. She put the pieces on a paper towel and set them in front of her and petted her head. "You're a good girl, right, Henrietta? You were just hurting."

"Oh, my. I don't know how I can ever thank you." Helen rummaged through the bottomless bag and whipped out a small stack of bills.

Cass held up a hand in protest. "There's no charge for today. I'm just glad I was able to help her."

"Oh, thank you, thank you, thank you. I am so grateful. I will be sure to recommend you to everyone I know."

"Thank you so much. Recommendations are always appreciated." Cass handed Helen one of her business cards from a small holder beside the register. "And if you wouldn't mind, could you let me know what the vet says and how Henrietta's doing a little later?"

"Of course, thank you." Cass's card went into the bottomless bag with everything else. "You know what? While I'm here, could I make an appointment to come in for a reading? If you're this good with animals, I can't imagine how you are with people."

Bee's mouth fell open.

A smile tugged at Cass when she imagined walking over to him, propping a finger beneath his chin, and pushing his mouth closed. Definitely not with a customer in the shop, though. Next time. If there was a next time. Bee had a remarkable knack for being right about people, and Cass's track record with training an animal was admittedly less than stellar. Though in her defense, Beast was the first pet she'd ever owned, so there had to be a learning curve.

Cass sighed, pulled out her appointment book, and opened it. "I'd love to do a reading for you. How long will you be here?"

The door opened again, and Tank walked in. Seeing Luke and Bee at the table, he waved to Cass in greeting and crossed the shop to join them.

Helen laid her hand over Cass's. "Oh, look at how happy she is. You truly are a miracle worker."

"*Four . . . take him . . . four . . . him . . . four . . .*" The woman's voice came out of nowhere, her fear palpable, shattering any shield that might have been protecting Cass from the onslaught. "*Take him . . . must . . . four, four, four.*"

Myriad other voices competed for attention but none as insistent as that one.

A tremor tore through Cass. Him? Was the dog in danger? Helen didn't seem abusive toward it. If anything, she doted excessively. Besides, Henrietta was female. Nothing to do with her then. Someone else had garnered this spirit's fear. Someone who might be in danger. Him?

She studied Bee, Luke, and Tank. Could one of them be in trouble?

"Are you okay?" Helen held Henrietta close.

"Oh. Yes. Sorry. I just zoned out for a minute." With her hands shaking, Cass booked an appointment for Helen to come in for her reading. She also handed her a pamphlet with information about her next group reading over the weekend. "I'd love to see you there."

"I'll definitely be there. Thank you again, Cass."

"I'm just glad I could help." She petted Henrietta again. "You be a good girl now, and I hope you feel better, little one."

Henrietta tilted her head into Cass's hand and licked her wrist.

As Helen walked out, Luke, Tank and Bee approached the counter.

Bee looked after Helen and Henrietta. "You know, that was really impressive."

"Thanks, Bee, but it was really just intuition." She hadn't dared open herself up, not that it had stopped someone from getting through. A woman. And she was terrified.

"Yeah, well, you might want to give some of that intuition a try next time Beast decides to take a dip in the bay."

The fact that Tank and Luke laughed cued her in that Bee had already shared the morning's unfortunate incident with the two.

"Help him . . . take him . . . help him . . ."

Needing something to do, lest any of the trio realize how badly she was trembling, Cass pulled out a bottle of cleaner, her hands slick with sweat, and sprayed it over the counter. She wiped it down with paper towels, brushing the crumbs from Henrietta's snack into the garbage pail, all the while hoping the two detectives and her closest friend, who normally didn't miss a thing, didn't notice how badly shaken she was.

"Are you all right, Cass?" Concern shone from the depths of Luke's deep blue eyes, the intensity of which could normally set her ablaze in an instant.

Right now, she just wanted all three of them to leave so she could figure out who was trying to contact her and why. "I am, thank you."

"Okay, good. First, I have to tell you we had no luck finding anything at the house this morning." He studied her another

115

moment to be sure she understood what he was talking about. Apparently, someone had moved the figure between the time Cass had left, which he'd told her to do immediately, and the time the police had arrived.

Then he dropped the folded newspaper he'd had tucked under his arm onto the counter and tapped the front page with one finger. "Maybe you'd like to explain this."

Chapter Fifteen

Cass read the headline, *Voices Assail Local Psychic as Man Plunges to His Death*, three times before she finally looked up at Luke. "Oh. Uh."

"You do remember that conversation we had about not painting a target on your back, right?" He folded his arms across his chest, obviously waiting for an answer Cass didn't have. "The one where you promised you wouldn't say anything to anyone about what you saw up there?"

What could she say? Instead of answering what she viewed as a rhetorical question, Cass skimmed the article.

"Did you get to the good part yet?" Bee propped a hand on one hip and leaned against the counter.

Cass tried not to squirm beneath the three pairs of eyes weighing on her as she read. "According to local resident Emma Nicholls . . ."

Oh, boy.

"Local psychic Cass Donovan, who later tried to revive the victim, suffered under a barrage of voices in the minutes before Fred DiCarlo was pushed to his death." She gasped and her gaze shot to Luke. "Pushed? It was confirmed?"

He swiped a hand over his goatee. "The ME confirmed Fred had an antemortem injury to the back of his head, consistent with being hit with a blunt object. Since most of his injuries were sustained on the front of his head and body, we're assuming that one came before he went out the window."

Cass blew out a breath. She'd suspected as much, especially after finding what she was pretty sure had to be the murder weapon, but having it confirmed threw her for a loop. "Speculation has it, Fred may have confided who attacked him even as Miss Donovan worked to save him."

She lowered the paper to the counter. "Oh, no way. I never said anything like that."

"Hello . . ." Bee tapped the page. "That's why it says speculation. This way you can't sue him."

She ignored Bee. Even though he wasn't asking what she'd seen at the lighthouse and had kept from him in front of Luke and Tank, he was glaring daggers at her. As soon as the other two walked out, she had no doubt she'd get ambushed. Which wouldn't matter to her as much if the look beneath the glare wasn't filled with so much hurt that she hadn't trusted him.

Dealing with Luke's rising anger was easier than knowing she'd hurt Bee's feelings. "Look, Luke, all I asked Emma to do was make sure people knew I didn't talk to Fred."

"Yeah, well, how'd that work out for you?" Bee snorted and muttered, "That's what happens when you send an amateur to do the job of a professional."

As if the article wasn't bad enough, it was accompanied by a photo of Cass bent over Fred. Though she knew full well she was in the process of administering CPR at the time, the photo had captured her profile, frowning as she hovered over him, looking to all the world like they'd been having a serious conversation. "Where did the picture come from?"

Luke shrugged. "It doesn't really matter. The fact is, now who-ever killed Fred DiCarlo thinks you may be able to point him out."

Great. The exact scenario they'd been hoping to avoid.

Bee strode toward the door.

"Hey, Bee. Wait. Where are you going?" She needed Luke and Tank to leave so she could talk to him, explain that she hadn't even been sure she'd seen anything.

He whirled back to face her. "I'm going to see if I can undo the damage this has caused and, hopefully, keep you from getting killed."

"Bee . . ."

He shook his head and walked out.

Tank laid a hand on her arm. "Look, Cass—"

"... stop him ... take ... lighthouse ... four ... take him ... four ... treasure ... tide ... take him ... four ..."

The litany continued, two distinct voices, a man and a woman, the woman's pleas filled with fear. "Kitty and Thomas?"

"What?" Tank gently shook her arm. "Have you heard a word I've said?"

"Oh, uh. I'm sorry, Tank."

He stepped back.

"Cass, you do realize how serious this is, right?" Luke frowned at her.

"Yes, thank you, I do." *Take him? Lighthouse? Treasure?* Did the spirits want her to take Bee to the lighthouse to look for the treasure? Were they hoping it would be found at long last? Or were they warning her away? As they had last time. "I promise I'll be careful."

"Yeah, well, zoning out like that isn't exactly careful," Luke said. *Touché.*

She offered a shaky smile. "I promise I'll try to do better."

"Try hard."

"You weren't able to find the lighthouse figure I told you about?"

"No. Nothing. The entire box was gone."

"I'm sorry, I should have waited."

"No, you shouldn't have, especially since the killer obviously returned to remove them, had probably been in the process when you walked in." He kissed her cheek. "I've gotta run. I'll see you later on."

"Sure. See ya."

"You know they both just worry about you, right?" Tank leaned in and kissed her cheek.

"Take him!"

Cass gasped and grabbed Tank's hand.

"Four . . . four . . . four . . ."

"Tank, listen to me, please. I know you don't really understand or believe in what I do—"

"It's not that I—"

"No, it's okay, really. I understand, and I appreciate that you always support me despite your feelings." She squeezed his hand. "But you have to listen this time. There's something going on. I can't explain what—I'm not even sure myself—but I keep getting a frantic plea from a terrified woman begging me to 'take him' and then repeating the number four, it seems like three times. At least, I think it's the number four. I guess it could be saying 'take him for something,' but it doesn't feel right in my gut. You know what I mean?"

Tank seemed to chew that over for a few minutes before finally nodding. "I might not understand the rest of it, but gut instincts I do understand. And either way, I trust you. So, why are you telling me this?"

A surge of relief washed over her. Her own? She couldn't be certain. "I'm not sure, but I've been hearing a jumble of voices lately, two of which have begun to stand out among the others. When it just happened a few minutes ago, I thought the voices were somehow related and telling me to take Bee to the lighthouse to search for the treasure—"

"Cass—" His tone held a note of warning.

"No, it's okay." She waved him off. "Then, just now, when you touched me, the woman's voice said 'take him' again and repeated the number four three times."

He shrugged. "So, what do you think it means?"

"That's just it. I don't know." And she should be able to latch on to more. If the other voices would just leave her alone to concentrate, she might be able to figure it out. Because she had a feeling it was important. And that time was running out. "But it's happened a number of times now, and I realized I only hear that woman's voice when either you or Stephanie is around, especially when either of you touch me in any way."

His demeanor shifted immediately as he stiffened and went into protective mode. "What does it have to do with Stephanie?"

"I'm not sure it has anything to do with either of you, but I'm afraid it does, and I'm afraid one of you may be in danger. Since the voice is saying 'take him,' I am assuming it's you."

His posture relaxed and he nodded. "Okay, Cass. I'll keep it in mind."

"For real, Tank? You're not just humoring me?"

He studied her for a moment and smoothed a hand over his buzzed hair. "You know what, Cass? I don't claim to understand what you do, or to believe in anything paranormal, but I can't deny your instincts are spot-on most of the time. Thank you for reaching out to me, especially when you didn't even know if you'd end up getting laughed at, or worse, ignored. I promise I'll be careful and try to be aware of any situations where those phrases might be meaningful. Thank you for trusting me enough to talk to me."

She rounded the counter and hugged him. The voices remained deafeningly silent. "Thank you for trusting me enough to set your disbelief aside."

"Aww, Cass." He rubbed a hand up and down her back. "I'd never turn away a friend's offer to help."

"I'll call Stephanie and talk to her as soon as you leave." If she could make sure Stephanie wasn't alone any more than necessary, maybe she could keep her safe.

"Thank you. I appreciate that. And she does believe in what you do, with every last ounce of trust she has, so I know she'll listen." He grinned. "But I'll still call her or stop by in a little while to make sure she does. And if you figure out anything else, give a yell."

"You've got it."

When Tank left, she finished straightening up the counter and headed to the back room to finally change her clothes. The instant she picked the pile of clothes up, the chimes alerted her to a customer. She tossed the clothes onto the couch, with a little more force than necessary. "Ugh."

When she walked out to the front, Bee stood in the middle of the shop, hands on his hips, disapproving expression on his face. "Do you call this being careful? Going into the back room, when Beast's not even here, and leaving the doors unlocked?"

"Oh." *Oops.* "I hadn't thought of that."

She'd grown so used to having Beast with her at the shop, she hadn't realized she'd come to rely on him for protection. Not that he had a vicious bone in his body, but people were generally wary of dogs that weighed in at close to a hundred and fifty pounds. Seemed Beast's protective streak ran as strong as that of the other men in her life. "Look, Bee, I just want you to know I'm sorry for not saying anything about the shadow I saw in the window."

"It's okay. Don't worry about it." He crossed the room and kissed the top of her head. "Luke caught up with me and explained that he'd asked you not to, said you weren't even sure you saw anything. He also didn't want witnesses coming forward at a later date thinking they remembered something based on anything you might have said. I can understand that."

"Thanks, Bee." And she'd have to remember a giant thank-you to Luke later for making him understand. With everything else on the fritz already, the last thing she needed was to be on the outs with Bee. He was her rock.

"Of course." He shooed her toward the back room. "Now, hurry along and change those clothes so we can pick Beast up before the groomer closes and head out to the lighthouse. I've got me a treasure to find."

Chapter Sixteen

The sun dipped below the horizon just as Cass pulled into the lighthouse parking lot.

Beast poked his head between the seats to see why they were slowing down.

"Sit back, Beast." She ruffled his mane quickly then, remembering Herb's warning about rewarding him when he wasn't doing what she'd asked, dropped her hand back onto the steering wheel. "Sit back, now, Beast."

His tongue dropped out and he crouched lower to peer out the windshield beneath the rearview mirror. He barked once.

"Hey." Stephanie, who sat in the passenger seat, turned toward him and rubbed her ear. "Watch where you're barking there, buddy."

Beast licked her cheek.

Though Stephanie had taken what warning Cass could offer well enough, she'd been kind of quiet since they'd spoken, no doubt worried about her husband, who was a detective on an active murder investigation.

"Come on, boy. Sit back with me." Bee gripped Beast's collar and pulled him back to sit beside him on the backseat. "Between the seats is the last place you want to be when your mama's driving."

"Ha ha, Bee."

He smirked into the rearview mirror at her.

"You okay, Steph?"

She looked out the window. "I am. I can't help worrying about Tank, but really, what's different? I always worry about him. I'm not gonna lie, I can understand that birth mother's hesitation to place her baby with us."

"Oh, Stephanie." Cass rubbed her arm. "Tank is going to make a great father. And you'll be an amazing mother. And, the honest truth is, something can happen to anyone. None of us is going to live forever."

"I am." Bee grinned.

Stephanie laughed and patted Cass's hand. "You're right, Cass. Come on. If Beast wags his tail any harder, he's going to go right through the back window."

"Hey, wait till you see his new trick." If he'd do it in front of an audience.

Bee lifted a brow. "Does it involve getting you all messed up again?"

Indignant, Cass stared him down in the mirror. "Actually, it doesn't."

He pouted. "Too bad."

"Cass, look out!" Stephanie braced her hands against the dashboard.

Cass threw her arm across the gap between the seats to keep Beast from flying forward, slammed on the brakes, and skidded to a stop in the gravel and seashell-covered lot. "What's wrong?"

"I don't know." Stephanie shoved the passenger door open and hopped out. But then she simply stood, staring toward the lighthouse, using her hand to shield her eyes from the last rays of the setting sun.

Cass got out and went around the car, gravel and pieces of broken seashells crunching beneath her feet, then stood next to her. "Did you see something?"

"I did, but I'm not sure what it was. A flash of white that looked like it was headed toward the car and then nothing." She continued to block her eyes from the sun as she scanned the beach and jetty. "With the sun setting, it's difficult to see across the jetty, but I got a flash of movement just as we rounded the curve into the lot. I thought something was going to run out in front of you."

"Hey," Bee yelled out the back window. "Do you want me to put Beast on his leash?"

The parking lot stood empty but for Cass's car. And, despite whatever Stephanie saw, the beach and grounds seemed quiet. Even if Stephanie had seen an animal of some sort, Bay Island had no natural predators that could harm a hundred-forty-pound Leonberger. Except maybe deer ticks, but she'd already had him vaccinated against Lyme disease since they walked along the beach so often and he loved a good romp in the dunes. "Nah, don't worry about it. He'll be okay. But bring it with you, just in case."

Bee contorted himself out of the backseat and stood.

Beast bounded out behind him then and trotted at his side.

"Is everything okay?" Bee stared out over the bay toward Long Island.

"I think so. Stephanie thought she saw something." Pinks, blues and lavenders painted the sky in beautiful pastel shades, and a soft warm breeze ruffled her hair. The perfect night.

"Must have been my imagination." Stephanie shrugged it off.

Cass closed her eyes, breathing in deeply the briny scent of the sea. She braced herself against the barrage of voices and opened her mind. *Okay, I'm here. Now what?*

"*. . . let them know . . . cold here . . . not to worry . . . four . . . take him . . . four . . . four . . . afraid.*"

Cass latched on to the last word. *Afraid.* A chill rushed through her as the woman's fear seeped into her, penetrating all the way to her bones. Her eyes shot open and she scanned the beach, then shivered.

"Hey, you okay?" Bee frowned at her.

She shook off whatever had gripped her. Whatever spirit had lured her to the lighthouse had been a man. Of that she was certain. So, whose fear had crossed into this world to seek her out, and did it have anything to do with the past or Fred's death? Or was it, as she expected, something to do with Stephanie, who was once again standing next to her when the woman's voice appeared.

Bee handed her Beast's leash and crossed the lawn, then walked through the dunes and jogged across the beach, to the jetty.

Stephanie and Cass followed with Beast happily prancing beside them, sniffing around the fence, the shrubbery, the flowers. Since inside the lighthouse was one of the few places pets weren't technically allowed, for their own protection, he'd never been there before, so everything was new and exciting.

When Bee started climbing the boulders that made up the jetty, Beast barked.

"Beast, stay." With the memory of Beast's rebellion against authority this morning fresh in her mind, and not wanting to take a chance of Beast trying to follow Bee onto the rocks and getting hurt or falling into the bay, Cass clipped the leash to his collar. "Hey, Bee. What are you doing?"

He scrambled across the jagged stones to a large flat rock in the center. Then he sat, folded his legs, and stared out at the bay. "I'll bet this is where she sat waiting."

Stephanie looked back and forth between him and Cass as if he'd lost his mind. "Who sat waiting?"

"Kitty Garrison." Though they'd brought Stephanie up to speed on the ride over, she still didn't seem to grasp the full impact the story had had on Bee. Plus, her mind was now fully occupied with concern for her husband. Cass couldn't blame her. Her own mind was pretty caught up on that too.

"Oh, right." Stephanie nodded.

"Could you hold him while I go get Bee?" Cass held Beast's leash out to her. "I heard the voice again when I got out of the car and stood beside you, and I need a few minutes without you next to me so I can see if the voice continues. Who knows? Maybe I'm wrong about it having to do with you and Tank. Maybe it's a coincidence that one or the other of you happened to be standing very close to or touching me each time I heard it."

But she already knew she wasn't wrong. Mostly. No matter how badly she wanted to be.

"Sure. Come on, Beast. Let's take a walk while your mama makes sure Bee is okay." She headed for the beach.

Cass climbed onto the jetty, wary of the slick surfaces of the rocks. When she reached Bee, she sat down next to him, tucked her legs beneath her, and took his hand. "You okay?"

"If it was me, I'd have sat right here. That way, I'd be sure to see any ships making their way toward the island from the ocean." He sighed.

"You do realize whatever happened it's been over for a long time, right?"

He squeezed her hand. "You know I don't really believe you speak to the dead, right?"

"Um . . . I guess." She had no idea what had brought that on or where he was going with it, so she simply agreed and let him get around to it in his own way.

"I actually don't even know if I believe there's anything beyond this world." He ran his thumb back and forth over her fingers. "Sometimes, though, like now, I'd really like to believe there is, and that she and Thomas are finally in each other's arms and at peace."

"Aww, Bee." Cass rested her head on his shoulder, gripped his arm with her fee hand, and looked out over the water. Bee had the unique ability to put himself in someone else's shoes, to feel what they would certainly be feeling, to understand their pain. If more people shared his empathic abilities, the world would be a much nicer place. What could she possibly say to him that would ease his pain? "I know it's not always easy to believe in something you can't see. And I can't see into another world or anything like that, but I do feel a connection. And I do believe there's an afterlife, with every ounce of my being. That being said, I'm very sure Kitty and Thomas finally found their happily ever after."

He peered down at her. "Sure because someone told you? Or sure in a general sense?"

She started to answer, then paused. The sun's parting rays fell over them, cocooning them in warmth. Something skittered across the water's surface, bouncing along, splashing up a small spray as it went, before dropping beneath the surface. A seagull's cry carried to her on the soft breeze, and a sense of peace enveloped her. She kissed Bee's cheek. "I know for sure they are at peace."

A smile lit his eyes a second before it reached his lips. "Thanks, Cass."

"Any time." She held him close a little longer, just enjoying the moment, then stood when she saw Stephanie and Beast heading back down the beach toward them. "Come on. Let's get out of here before it gets any darker."

"Sure." He stood and brushed off his pants, then started across the rocks after Cass. "Hey, what happened to whomever you were supposed to meet out here?"

Cass paused and opened herself once again. Though the usual bombardment assailed her, she couldn't pick out any one particular voice that seemed more insistent than the rest. And the frightened woman remained silent. She tried to shrug it off. "I don't know. I was so sure I was supposed to come out here for some reason, but I guess maybe I was wrong."

Her foot slid from beneath her, and she started to fall.

Bee grabbed her arm and steadied her. "Be careful."

"Thank you."

She slowed a little so as not to tumble into the bay, scanning the horizon for any sign of the spirit who'd helped out with Stanley, listening for the man who'd been trying to tell her something about the lighthouse and the treasure.

"Oh, oww," Bee yelled.

Cass stopped and turned. "What happened?"

"I slipped." With one foot stuck between two rocks and the other knee precariously balanced on another rock, Bee held on for dear life.

Cass lunged for him and gripped his hand. "Can you pull your foot up, or is it stuck?"

"No. I think I can pull it up, but I'm trying to reach something."

"Reach what, Bee?" Cass tried to haul him up, but he shook her off. "Come on, Bee. It's getting dark and we have to get off these rocks before it does. Are you hurt?"

"My ankle is killing me, but there's something down here."

"Define something?" Cass had visions of some kind of sea creature grabbing Bee's leg and pulling him down. "Is it alive?"

"No. Just give me a minute." He braced his hands against the rocks on either side of him and wiggled his leg back and forth to free his foot from the gap between the rocks. Once he was free, he laid down on his stomach and reached down into the hole. After fishing around for a minute, he came up with what looked like a bunch of rags.

"What is that?" Hardly the treasure he'd been expecting.

"I have no idea, but here, take it so I can get out of this." He shoved the pile at Cass, then scrambled to his feet, favoring the one that had gotten caught.

Cass tossed the bundle onto the sand and reached for him, helping him climb across the rocks and work his way back down toward the beach.

Though he favored his right ankle and winced now and then, the pain didn't seem to be too bad. Hopefully, just a sprain.

When they reached a flat rock, Cass stopped. "Why don't you sit here and let me take a look at your ankle?"

Bee stopped and sat. He blew out a breath and pulled his ankle close to him.

Cass moved his hands aside and pulled off one of his signature platform shoes. "I don't know why you insist on wearing these high shoes."

"Listen, girlfriend, I love you to death, but do I question your fashion choices?" He lifted a brow at the leggings and tunic top she now wore, her tangled hair pulled into a sloppy knot since she'd removed the sash before leaving the shop.

"Fair enough." She examined his ankle.

"Is everything okay?" Stephanie called from the beach at the edge of the jetty.

"I think so." She felt around his ankle. No bruising. Little swelling. Definitely not as bad as she'd feared. "Does that hurt at all?"

"Actually." He frowned and rolled his ankle. Full range of motion. "I think it's fine. Once I get off these rocks and onto a flat surface, I'll see how it feels."

"Do me a favor, though? Please take your other shoe off and walk barefoot 'til we're off the rocks and sand?" She handed him his shoe. "No sense asking to roll that ankle again, especially before we can get it iced."

"Yes, Mommy." He winked at Cass and pulled off the other shoe. When he started to stand, he dropped one shoe into a crevice between the rocks. "Oh, great."

"I'll get it." Cass started toward him.

"No, you stay where you are. I've got it." He set the other shoe aside, knelt down, and leaned over. After a moment of reaching into the crevice, he sat back on his heels. "Is there a stick laying around?"

"Oh, right. That reminds me, I wanted to show you Beast's new trick." And he'd better be sufficiently impressed. If, of course, Beast would cooperate and retrieve the stick again. Hmm. Maybe she oughta try it a few more times alone with him before inviting an audience.

Bee glared at her.

"Oh, sorry." She searched the area for a stick but didn't find anything.

"I'll run and get the tire iron from the trunk." Stephanie held her hand out for the keys, which Cass tossed to her, then she ran off with Beast and returned a couple of minutes later with the long metal rod, bent on one end, that served as a jack handle and tire iron.

Cass took it from her and handed it to Bee. "Do you want me to try it."

"No, I've got it." He continued to study the gap, tilting his head in one direction then the other. "But I think there's something else down here."

Cass moved up behind him and looked over his shoulder. The

crevice was only about six inches wide and maybe a foot long. She could see Bee's shoe laying on it's side in the damp sand. "What do you mean? I don't see anything."

Bee pulled out his phone and shined the flashlight down into the hole and to the right, beneath a gap under the large rock beside them. "See that?"

Another bundle of cloth peeked out from beneath the other rock.

Bee leaned over onto the rock to give Cass a better view, and it tipped beneath him.

Cass grabbed his shirt. "You okay?"

"Yeah, yeah. Just didn't expect it to move."

"You know, it looks like it was moved recently, doesn't it?" All of the other rocks sat pretty steadily against one another in a chaotic rocky pile. This one rocked with Bee's weight.

"Could be the tide loosened it." Bee lay on his side, shined the light into the hole, and reached in with the tire iron.

"You think? I don't know. Maybe if it was the ocean or an inlet crashing through here, but I don't think the bay waters would loosen something like that, even during a storm."

"And we haven't had any really bad storms lately, anyway." Bee fished his shoe out and handed it to Cass.

She tossed it and the other one onto the beach along with his socks. "Need a hand up?"

"Give me a sec. I want to see if I can grab this." Bee set his phone aside then reached into the gap with the tire iron once more. "What the heck?"

"Is something wrong?"

"I don't know, but whatever I just moved is too heavy to be just cloth." He set the tire iron down and shined his flashlight into the hole.

"Anything?"

"Oh, my . . ." He yanked his hand back and dropped the phone onto the rock as he rolled over to the edge and gagged.

Chapter Seventeen

Cass laid a hand on his shoulder. "Are you all right?"

He sobbed and shook his head.

Cass grabbed the cracked phone and shone the light into the hole to see what Bee had fished out.

A hand and arm stuck out into the gap from beneath the loosened rock. Cass reached in and gripped the wrist, automatically searching for a pulse. "Oh, man. Bee! Help me now!"

"I can't, Cass. I'm—"

"She's not dead, Bee."

"What?" He staggered to his feet. "You're sure?"

Stephanie already had her phone out and was speaking rapidly as she ran toward the parking lot.

"We have to get this rock off her." Though the pulse was faint, just the barest flutter, it was there. As long as there was any chance they could save her, there wasn't time to wait for help or preserve the crime scene.

Bee came up behind her. "Move, Cass. Let go."

Cass released the hold she hadn't realized she still had on the woman's arm and scrambled out of the way.

Bee braced his feet against two rocks and wedged his hands beneath the enormous boulder.

"Don't try to pick it up, Bee, just tilt it back when I say go. If you drop it, it'll crush her." Cass hurried across the rock to Bee's other side and reached down into the crack.

"Why hasn't it already?" he grunted.

"It looks like some of the sand washed out from beneath the rocks." She reached under the rock and felt around until she hit cool flesh, then slid her hand around the woman's ankle. She wouldn't have long to get her moved out of the way before Bee would have to let go of the rock, though she hated not being able to assess her before moving her.

"Ready, Cass?"

"Okay, when I say go, just lift enough for me to pull her out."

Stephanie slid in the sand and flopped onto her stomach on the rocks beside Cass. She reached beneath the rock and grabbed hold of the woman's other ankle.

Cass braced her free hand against a rock for leverage. "One, two, three, go."

Bee heaved the boulder up and over, just a few inches, but enough to allow them to pull the woman toward them. Cass reached into the gap to cradle her head as best she could as Stephanie adjusted her grip to hold both ankles and continued to pull.

"Get her on the sand." Cass hooked her arms beneath the woman's armpits, and together they carried her and dropped her onto the sand, less gently than Cass would have liked, but time was too short. She had to hurry if there was any chance of saving her, no matter how slim it might be.

"Stephanie, get someone and find out how long until they get here, then pass this on." Cass felt for a pulse. "Pulse is thready, breathing labored."

Bee fell to his knees at her side. "Is she alive?"

"Barely."

Stephanie spoke rapidly into the phone, relaying the information as Cass assessed her.

"Victim is female, approximately . . ."

"Ah, man." Bee shoved his hands into his hair. "Cass, it's Piper."

Every harsh thought she'd had about the woman disappeared as she worked to save her. No one deserved to end up like this. Tears streamed down her cheeks, blurred her vision.

Bee reached over and wiped them, then he gripped Piper's hand. "Hang on, Piper. We've got you."

Cass assessed her head injuries. Several cuts and contusions, one severe gash. "I need something to use as a bandage."

Bee stripped off his shirt and held it out to her.

She grabbed it and applied pressure to the worst of the head wounds.

"I think she stopped breathing, Cass," Stephanie sobbed.

"Bee, hold this."

He pressed the shirt against Piper's head.

Cass tried to get a pulse. Nothing. She started chest compressions. Piper had to live. She just had to. Cass had given all of this up, because she hadn't been able to deal with holding someone's life in her hands after she'd so miserably failed a patient who had trusted her. She couldn't lose another one. She wouldn't. "Come on, Piper. Just hold on a little bit longer."

"You have to hurry," Stephanie screamed into the phone. "She's not breathing."

Sirens finally wailed in the distance, coming closer. Not fast enough. Cass continued compressions. She paused and felt for a pulse. "I have a pulse. It's weak, but it's there."

Rick and Luke barreled across the sand and slid to a stop as they reached her. Rick started pulling out equipment. He applied leads and hooked up the EKG.

"I've got her, Cass, thanks." His partner, Jamie, a woman Cass had seen around town, took her place.

Cass fell back in the sand and scrambled out of the way to give them room, then she pulled her knees to her chest as the scene unfolded around her in some sort of surreal slow motion. She cradled her head in her hands, her gaze riveted on Piper.

Stephanie sobbed softly.

Cass's heart pounded hard enough to rock her back and forth, bringing a wave of nausea. "Stephanie, where's Beast?"

"He's good, Cass. He's okay. I had to let go of him to help you pull her out, so I put him in the car with the windows cracked and the air conditioner running so he wouldn't get hit when the emergency vehicles started pulling in."

"All right." She nodded, numb. "Okay."

Bee knelt on the beach a few yards away, crying softly.

Luke bent over him, his hand resting on Bee's shoulder, soothing, comforting.

She folded her arms on her knees and rested her head, took a few deep breaths. Beast was safe. Stephanie was sitting next to her fine. Bee was upset, but Luke was with him. And the paramedics were tending to Piper. Everything was as right as it could be. Maybe she'd been wrong about the woman's voice. Maybe it had been Piper's fear she'd been feeling. Or Kitty's. Maybe the voice had been urging her to take Bee to the lighthouse. Except—

She jerked upright. "Where's Tank?"

Stephanie sniffed and pointed toward the ambulance, where Tank stood with Chief Rawlins. "I'm going to go get Beast now."

Cass nodded. "Thank you."

Okay. She had to calm down. She closed her eyes and inhaled deeply. Counted to ten. Willed her heart to slow down.

"Cass?" Chief Rawlins crouched beside her a few moments later. "Are you doing okay?"

"I'm okay, thanks." The weight of responsibility weighed on her, the fear of having failed someone who needed her churning in her gut. "Is Piper okay?"

"She's breathing, and her heart rate has leveled out." Chief Rawlins held out a hand to help her up.

Cass accepted it and stood, then watched as the paramedics loaded the stretcher into the ambulance they'd managed to pull onto the walkway to get closer to the beach.

"Can you tell me what happened? What brought you out to the lighthouse in the first place?"

All Cass could do was help the police find whoever had done this to her; it was up to the paramedics and doctors to save Piper now. "Bee was reading Kitty Garrison's journal, and he wanted to come out here and see if he could find the treasure. So, I took a ride with him."

She nodded and flipped through a couple of pages in a small notebook. "We talked to Bee."

"Is he okay?" She should be there for him. Should have gone to get Beast herself instead of Stephanie having to do it. She'd just needed a moment, but now guilt tugged at her.

The chief glanced over to where Bee still sat with Luke. "He's as good as could be expected."

Cass brushed the sand from her pants.

"But he did mention you wanting to meet someone out here. Can you tell me who it was, please?" Though the chief had been kind enough to phrase it as a question, she left no doubt it was a demand.

"It wasn't a someone." Since Chief Rawlins seemed to believe strongly in Cass's abilities, way more than even Cass did, she answered honestly. "I've been hearing voices. A lot of them, and I haven't been able to sort through them, but one in particular kept saying something about the lighthouse."

"Have you heard it before?"

"Yes. I think, anyway. The day Fred was killed, I believe the same voice was telling me to stay away from the lighthouse, only I didn't realize that at the time. I only kept catching lighthouse, so I came out here."

"Can you tell me anything else?" She stuffed the notebook into her jacket pocket.

"Not really. There's been a woman's voice also, very frightened."

"Could it have been Piper?"

"No, I don't think so anyway." Until then, at least, Cass had never been contacted by someone who was still alive. Besides, she'd heard the voice before Piper had gone missing. "For some reason, I thought it had something to do with Tank or Stephanie, since it seems to call to me when either of them is around."

"But you can't make any sense of what it's trying to communicate?"

"No. I'm sorry. I just hear 'take him' and the number four, amid a jumble of other voices. And I feel immense fear. I thought maybe it meant to take Bee to the lighthouse today, but I'm not sure, and it doesn't feel right."

The chief nodded and studied her. "You know, Cass, I've worked with psychics before, both those who had incredible talent and those who conned whomever they could to make a buck. You haven't given me any indication you're a con artist, you seem to care deeply about those you're trying to help, and yet, you don't really seem to take your gift seriously. If you truly want to help people, I'd suggest embracing your talent, working to hone your skills. I truly believe you have the ability, if the desire is there as well."

Cass worked to swallow past the lump in her throat.

"If you think of anything else, just give a call." She walked away without saying anything else. She didn't need to.

Cass forced back tears. All she wanted to do in that moment was hug Beast, go home, and hide away. Instead, she went to Bee. "Are you all right?"

He nodded.

Luke held a plastic evidence bag containing the clothing Bee had found.

Cass pointed to the bag. "Does that have anything to do with what happened to Piper?"

"We don't know yet." Luke kissed Cass's cheek and rubbed a hand up and down her arm, leaving a trail of warmth behind. "How are you doing?"

"I'm okay." Despite a reality check from Chief Rawlins.

He nodded. "Bee said you witnessed an argument between Piper and Quincy Yates and his new girlfriend, Francesca Harding."

"Yes. And then when I was here earlier, Quincy was sitting on the beach right over there." She pointed to where she'd seen him.

"Did he say anything?"

"I only spoke to him for a moment. He thanked me for taking over CPR for him, and I told him I was sorry for his loss, but he didn't seem the least bit broken up over Fred."

"What else can you tell me?"

She shrugged, trying to remember anything that might prove important. "He was sitting alone with his head down, as if the weight of the world balanced on his shoulders, but when he stood, his clothes were clean, no dirt or blood spots I noticed. I didn't notice if his hands were dirty, but they didn't stand out to me as they might have if they were."

Luke nodded and jotted everything down, then pointed toward the jetty. "Bee was just about to show me where he found these clothes. Then we'll send them to someone to authenticate."

"Why? What are they?" Though she tried to focus, her mind kept leaping back to Piper. Surely, if they lost her, someone would contact Chief Rawlins or Luke immediately.

"They seem to be pirate garb. Definitely not stuck between two rocks since the seventeen hundreds, so I'm thinking a costume of some sort, even though they appear old. We'll get in touch with someone from the historical society, though, to see if they've had anything go missing from the museum."

"Would you mind if I take a look?" Bee sniffed and wiped his cheeks with the palms of his hands.

Luke shrugged, pulled a pair of gloves from his pocket, and handed them to Bee. Then he slid his own glove on, opened the bag, and handed Bee the first garment, what might once have been a white shirt with full sleeves and ruffles decorating the front and cuffs, tattered and torn, stained with blotches of brown.

Bee held up the garment and looked in the collar. "No tag, but if you look here, you can see where it was cut out."

Though stitch marks were still visible, no part of the tag remained.

Bee tugged on the shirt a bit. "It's definitely not authentic."

Luke frowned. "How can you tell?"

"An authentic pirate shirt should be made of canvas, leather, wool, linen, cotton, maybe even sheepskin, but this one contains spandex, which wasn't invented until the mid-nineteen hundreds, somewhere around nineteen fifty-nine or sixty, if I'm not mistaken." He sniffed the garment, then scrunched up his nose. "Plus, despite the briny salty odor from being stuffed between the rocks, and the barely perceptible smell of sweat, you can still detect the tiniest whiff of the tea that was used to create the vintage look."

Luke yanked out his notepad and started scribbling notes.

"Do you think this could belong to the mysterious pirate ghost Levi swears he saw out on the jetty?" Because a real-life person dressed as a pirate made a whole lot more sense.

Luke flipped a page. "What pirate ghost?"

"Levi said he saw a pirate ghost out on the jetty a few times over the past month, said it had spooked him." Could be someone trying to scare people off while he searched for the treasure.

Bee handed the shirt back to Luke and held up a pair of breeches. "Well, someone was definitely playing dress-up."

"Maybe Fred was searching for the treasure and wanted to scare off anyone who might show too much of an interest." She couldn't remember if Levi had mentioned seeing the "ghost" after Fred had been killed.

Bee folded the breeches and placed them back into the bag then scratched his head. "Thing is, Fred was pretty average sized. Not that it matters, I guess, since pirate shirts tended toward loose and flowy, anyway, but even allowing for the baggier style of the day, those breeches would have been falling off of him. Those things would fit me."

Which meant whoever had worn them would have to be better than six feet tall and pretty well built. Cass's gaze shot to Bee. "They'd fit Quincy Yates."

Quincy Yates, who'd argued with Piper in the diner and who'd been sitting only a few yards from where they'd just found Piper earlier in the day. And Piper, who, according to gossip, was cheating on Quince with Fred last season. Had Quince been angry enough to kill Fred over it and then try to kill Piper?

Chapter Eighteen

Cass petted Beast's head, hugged him, then opened the door for him to get into the car.

"So." Bee sat on the edge of the backseat with the door open, shook the sand out of his socks, and pulled them on.

"How's your ankle?"

"It's a little sore, but it'll be fine." He bent forward and massaged his back. "My back's gonna ache for a while, though."

"Do you want a couple of ibuprofen?" She started to reach for her bag.

He waved her off. "It'll be fine."

"Stephanie said she'd be here in a couple minutes. She just wanted to talk to Tank."

Once he got his shoes back on, Bee folded himself into the backseat and peered out the windshield toward the lighthouse. "Now what?"

A shadow drew Cass's vision to the window Fred had fallen from. Had something moved? "I'm going to want to take a walk through the keeper's house when there aren't so many people around."

The last thing she needed with abilities on the fritz was an audience.

Bee chewed on a thumbnail. "You want to come back tonight, after everyone's gone?"

"I don't know. Maybe." Doubt plagued her. Even though the chief's comment that she needed to take her gift seriously had stung, she hadn't been wrong. Cass loved what she did, loved that she could help people find something they'd lost or find peace or forgiveness from a loved one who'd passed on. But the avoidance of true responsibility had come at a price.

"Do you think Piper will be okay?" Bee stared at her in the rearview mirror, searching her gaze for the truth.

She turned to face him, took his hand in hers. "I hope she will, but either way, Bee, you saved her, at least gave her a fighting chance."

He swallowed hard and nodded, then lowered his gaze.

"You're a hero, Bee."

"Then why do I feel so guilty?"

"About what?"

"Don't get me wrong." He sagged against the seat back. "I never wished harm on that girl."

"Of course you didn't. I would never think you could wish harm on anyone." Bee was one of the kindest, most sensitive people she knew.

"Yeah, well, I did enjoy seeing Francesca put her in her place."

Cass chose her words carefully, torn between wanting to comfort Bee and her own feelings of guilt. "Bee, just because something horrible happened to Piper, something no one deserves, something you never would have wanted to see happen, doesn't mean she was a nice person. Hopefully, she'll make a full recovery, and maybe the experience will change her, make her treat people with respect and kindness."

He sniffed and nodded without looking fully convinced.

"And the fact that you went out of your way to save her, are still concerned for her welfare despite the way she treated you, speaks volumes for the kind of person you are."

He offered a shaky smile and patted her hand. "Thanks, Cass."

"Any time." Now if she could just alleviate her own guilt. Hmm. Perhaps she could. Chief Rawlins had said she needed to master her abilities. At the moment, that meant somehow shielding some of the voices while allowing others in. And she had a good idea of who could help her with that.

"Here comes Stephanie." Bee put his seat belt on.

Stephanie opened the passenger-side door and sat in the passenger seat. "Thanks for waiting."

"No problem." Cass started the car and turned on the headlights. "Did Tank say anything?"

"They're looking for Quince."

"They're going to arrest him?" Bee asked.

"Right now, he's just considered a person of interest. They just want to question him and Francesca."

Bee unclipped his belt and leaned between the seats. "Cass, would you mind running by Mystical Musings?"

Cass shifted into reverse, then turned and looked behind her to make sure she had enough room to back up amid all the emergency vehicles scattered throughout the lot. "Sure, why?"

"I left Kitty's journal there, and I wanted to finish reading it tonight."

"No problem." She inched back just enough to get out of her spot, then headed toward the boardwalk. If she was stopping by the shop anyway, she could pick up Simone's business card, the one that contained her cell phone number as well. At least then she could call her first thing in the morning, before she headed into the shop.

Bee tapped Cass's shoulder. "Do you want to go to the keeper's house tonight?"

"For what?" Stephanie asked.

"I just want to walk around, see if I can sense anything." And check out the room Fred fell from, see if she could tap into any lingering trace of energy.

"How do you plan to get in?" Bee quirked a brow.

"We are not breaking in. Period." Stephanie's order left no room to argue.

Understandable, really. The last thing she needed in the middle of trying to adopt a baby was a B and E charge. Though, chances were Tank and Luke wouldn't let it go that far even if they did get caught. Probably.

Stephanie searched through her bag and pulled out a pack of gum. She offered Bee and Cass each a piece before popping her own into her mouth, dropping the pack back into her bag and pulling out her phone. "Why don't you just ask Chief Rawlins to open it up for you?"

Cass shrugged as she unwrapped her gum. "I guess we could do it that way."

Bee pouted. "Fine. But you have to admit, it's more fun the other way."

"I'll call Tank and ask him to meet us out there." Stephanie unlocked her phone to make the call. "What time do you think?"

"I have to stop at Mystical Musings for Bee to pick up his transcript, and I can feed Beast there and take him for a walk. Plus, I want to spend a little time with him. I never did get to show you how he brings a stick back when you throw it now."

Bee laughed. "I'll believe that when I see it."

"He did, right, Beast?"

Beast barked, and some of the tension filling the car eased.

"Then I want to try to do another reading for you, if you're up for it, Stephanie." It still troubled Cass that she hadn't been able to tell Stephanie anything about her adoption plans. Plus, she wanted to see if the woman's voice returned while she was reading Stephanie. Even if it meant suffering the rest of the voices as well. The thought of waiting until after she could ask Simone about shielding flittered through her mind, but she shoved it right back out. She needed to figure out if the woman's fear she'd been feeling had had something to do with Piper or if Tank or Stephanie could still be in danger. No way could that wait.

"Sure." She shrugged, her lack of enthusiasm digging at Cass, a reminder she'd failed her the past few times she'd tried.

By the time she did all that, plus got something to eat, it would probably be close to midnight. "Maybe it could wait until tomorrow. Why don't we play it by ear?"

"Sounds good," Bee said. "What do you want to do for dinner?"

"I don't know. The barbeque place just opened for the season, but it's probably mobbed, if it's even still open by the time we're ready to go eat." Cass pulled into the parking lot, let Beast out of the car, and hurried up the boardwalk to unlock Mystical Musings.

"If it's okay with you guys, I'm not really in the mood for a crowd tonight. For once, I don't want to hear the gossip or have to explain what happened out there today." Bee held the door open for them to precede him. "Do you want me to lock it?"

"Nah, leave it open. I'm not opening the register or anything, but if a customer comes in to schedule a reading, I could do that." Cass dumped her bag beneath the counter and headed to the back to fill Beast's bowls.

Bee followed. "If you want, I could order pizza or something and just have it delivered here."

"That would be perfect." Cass had no burning desire to listen to the gossip either.

"Then I'll make myself scarce and read the rest of Kitty's journal while you do Stephanie's reading."

"Great, Bee. Thank you." She put Beast's bowls down and got a plastic bag, then leaned against the counter and waited for him to finish eating. "Where's Stephanie?"

Bee hooked a thumb over his shoulder. "Tank called, and she

stopped out front to answer."

When Beast was done, he headed right for the back door, and Cass followed.

Bee stopped by the table, collected the transcript pages he'd left there, and looked around. "Did you see the folder these were in?"

"Oh, yeah, I put it in the drawer under the coffeepot."

Leaving Bee alone with Kitty, Cass wandered down the beach toward the shoreline. Spotlights still lit the jetty by the lighthouse, and she wondered if they'd found Quince. He seemed a logical suspect, since he had left the diner with Piper under less-than-ideal circumstances and was sitting on the beach very near the crime scene. Plus, Bee was right. He was tall and well built and could easily fit the pirate costume they'd found by the jetty. But why would he be searching for the treasure? Unless he wasn't searching for the treasure at all. What if he'd left other women out on the jetty and used the pirate costume to scare people off?

She was going to have to call Luke.

When Beast finished doing his business, Cass cleaned up and found a long, thin stick. She tossed it down the beach, and Beast bolted after it.

When he reached it, he picked it up and turned toward her. Then plunked down in the sand and started chewing it to pieces. So much for the bath he'd just had.

Bee laughed out loud from the deck of Mystical Musings. "Great new trick, Cass."

"Ha ha." She called for Beast to come. "He's probably just tired now."

"Uh-huh. Anyway, come on in. I called and ordered the pizza, and it should be here any time now."

"Thanks, Bee."

Since Beast made no move to get up, she went to him and clipped the leash to his collar. "Way to make me look bad in front of Bee."

He licked her chin.

She laughed and snuggled him. "Don't worry, I still love you anyway."

With Beast taken care of and happily ripping the stuffing out of a toy, Cass grabbed three Diet Pepsis from the fridge and put them on the table with paper plates, napkins, and a knife. She hadn't eaten since breakfast and she was starved. "Pizza was a good idea, Bee."

"Yup. And we didn't even have to go get it."

True enough, though the fact Bee was avoiding people and gossip had Cass a little concerned. If it went on too long, she'd have to talk to him.

Stephanie walked in the front door, took a seat at the table, and opened her soda. "Thanks."

"Sure. Is everything okay with Tank?" Cass sat too.

Bee stacked the folder on top of the transcribed pages he'd been reading and set them aside so he could sit down to eat before retiring to the back room so she and Stephanie would have some privacy for the reading.

"He said he'd let you into the keeper's house either tonight or tomorrow morning, whichever works for you."

She really wanted to go home to bed, but she would probably only lay awake anyway. It might be better to just get the lighthouse over with. At least that would be one less thing on her mind. "And he was okay with that?"

"Define okay." Stephanie smiled. "Not exactly, but since Chief Rawlins cleared it, he didn't have much of a choice."

That would have to be good enough. "Did he say how Piper is doing?"

Bee sucked in a breath and held it.

"She's holding her own."

He blew out the breath he'd been holding.

Stephanie sobered and leaned forward. "He also said they have a good idea where the photo of you that was leaked to the paper came from."

"Oh?"

"Piper's phone was in her pocket, and she had several pictures of you leaning over Fred trying to revive him."

Cass wasn't sure how to feel. On the one hand, she wanted to be offended at the invasion of her privacy. On the other, it was hard to be angry with someone who had suffered whatever had happened to Piper. So she took the coward's way out. She'd think about it some other time.

"So, now what?" Bee lifted the folder from the top of the pages and tapped it up and down on the table.

"Now we eat pizza and go back out to the keeper's house to take a peek. If you want to come with me, that is. You don't have to." She would definitely understand if Bee wanted to take a pass.

He tipped the folder on one edge, propped a finger on the top corner, and twirled it around, seemingly mesmerized by the spinning motion.

"I'll take a ride with you," Stephanie offered. "Then I'll get a ride home with Tank if he's able to leave. Are you taking Beast or leaving him here?"

"I don't know. Maybe Bee would rather stay here and keep an eye on him for me."

She hoped she was offering him an out that would still make him know how much she appreciated him.

A knock at the door gave him another few minutes to make up his mind.

Determined not to make him feel pressured, Cass got up and answered the door. She paid for the pies, added a generous tip, and returned to the table with two pizzas. "Really, Bee? Two pies? Did you invite company I don't know about?"

"That's okay, wait 'til you open them up. One of them has everything on it. Well, except anchovies, of course. I had a feeling I'd feel the need to stress eat. Better to have too much under those circumstances than too little."

"Not really, Bee." Though the tantalizing aroma drifting out of the still-closed pizza boxes made her wonder if maybe he was right.

He shrugged and tossed the folder aside. It slid off the table and onto the floor, and Bee bent to retrieve it. "Huh. Will ya look at that?"

"What?" Cass opened one of the boxes and the scent of peppers, onions, and sausage wafted out, making her mouth water. Okay. One slice of everything.

Bee stood and dropped what looked like a grainy black-and-white surveillance photo onto the table, then pointed to something in the middle. "What do you suppose is in that package Amelia and Levi appear to be exchanging?"

Chapter Nineteen

Cass and Stephanie both leaned over for a closer view.

The two people pictured were definitely Amelia and Levi. Amelia was looking over her shoulder directly toward the camera, and Levi was looking at her, but there was no mistaking his profile. The hooked nose was a dead giveaway. Between them, they held what looked to be a folded-over manila envelope.

Cass lifted the photo for a closer look, then handed it to Bee. "Can you tell which of them is handing the other the package?"

Bee held the photo closer to him and squinted. "I can't tell."

Stephanie looked over his shoulder. "Me neither."

"Where did you find that, Bee?"

He handed the photo back to Cass and opened the folder that had held the transcribed journal pages. He pulled each of the pockets open, looked inside, then turned the folder upside down and shook it out. "It's empty. The only thing I can figure is that the photo was in one of the pockets and fell out when I dropped it."

"But why would Levi have given you the transcript with this in the pocket?" Cass rechecked the folder she'd already seen was empty. "It doesn't make sense."

"Unless he didn't know it was in there." Bee flipped through the papers he'd left on the table, checking the backs of the pages as well as the fronts. "He said this was Fred's copy, that Fred had asked Amelia to transcribe it because he didn't want to bother reading the journal."

"You think Fred stuck that in there, and neither Levi nor Amelia knew?" Stephanie asked.

Cass shook her head. "I have no idea what to think."

"I wish I could tell what was in the envelope." After once more studying the photo, Bee set it aside and sat. "Maybe it's the journal? Or the pages?"

Despite closer examination, Cass couldn't make out anything more. No writing on the envelope. No markings at all. "If it's the size of a standard manila envelope, it's folded, so it's not the transcribed pages. It wouldn't be big enough to hold the sheets of printer paper, and the stack is too thick to fold."

Bee put slices of everything pizza on plates for each of them. "It could have been the journal, though. That was a pretty small leather-bound book."

"Could be." Cass turned the photo over to see if there was a date or time stamp on the back. Nothing. She set the photo aside and took a bite of her pizza. Grease dripped off the back edge of the slice, over her hand, and onto her plate. She grabbed a napkin and wiped her hand.

"Oh, man, this is really good." Bee wiped his mouth. "Sal must have been working tonight. He always makes the crust nice and thin."

Cass couldn't argue. She took another bite. The pizza was extra good tonight, thin crust, lots of cheese and toppings, and the sauce just right. Either Sal had made it or stress eating made it taste so much better. She reminded herself if she wanted a second slice it had to be plain, then bit in again and savored the moment.

"Okay." Stephanie gestured toward the photo with her slice still in hand. "Let's say, for argument's sake, that Levi didn't know the photo was in there when he gave the folder to Bee. Let's even say his sharing the journal was legitimate and he was just being nice because Bee had seemed interested and didn't have any ulterior motive."

"I would agree with that," Bee said. "Since we both share an interest in gossip—and what is history, after all, but gossip from the past? He might have been intrigued enough to want to share the information, especially since he said he was afraid the journal display was going to be removed."

"But why would they remove it after Fred's death? He's the one who apparently didn't have an interest in being historically accurate. The Historical Society wanted it displayed."

"So why would anyone remove it?" Cass finished off her slice, wiped her hands and mouth and took a drink of her soda. "Even if Simone was slated to buy the tour company, I'd imagine she'd want to include any related history she could find."

Bee reached into the box for a second slice, offered it to Cass, then deposited it on his own plate when she shook her head. "What makes you say that?"

"It lends credibility to the ghost stories when the history surrounding them is accurate. Plus, when she was here, after she decided to include Mystical Musings on the tour, she asked if I knew the history of the building. Why worry about that if she had no interest in including history as part of the tour?"

"Hmm . . ." Bee took a bite, frowning as he chewed and then swallowed. "That makes a lot of sense. If she'd planned on including the history of Mystical Musings, she'd want to include everything she could about the lighthouse's history too. And Kitty and Thomas's story is quite intriguing. And leaves room for not one but two ghosts. Three if you count Samuel along with Thomas and Kitty."

"She might even get away with bringing in some of the crew who died when the ship went down." If it were Cass running the tour, she'd move that display front and center, so it would be seen as soon as you walked into the museum. Maybe even have some of the transcribed pages made into plaques and posted, so her guests could read some of the story's highlights.

"Okay, hear me out before you disagree." Stephanie tossed her napkin onto her empty plate. "Let's say Levi did have an ulterior motive for giving Bee the transcripts. What could it have been? Keeping in mind, he also said he's seen a ghost out on the jetty several times."

Bee set his slice down with only one bite taken out of it. "You mean if he had something to do with Fred's death?"

"Well, I'm not saying he did, but think about it. Someone was hanging around the jetty dressed as a pirate. Looking for treasure? Who knows? But still, what better way to spread the rumor that a ghost is haunting the lighthouse than to pique Bee's interest? Maybe that would even convince people the ghost had something to do with Fred's death, either by giving him a shove or maybe scaring him into falling."

Bee stared down at his plate. "Do you really think he'd do something like that?"

Stephanie twirled her soda around in the condensation puddle on her coaster. "Not really, but that photo sure does look like a surveillance shot, and if it is, Fred had to have tucked it away in the folder for a reason. To confront the two about whatever was going on?"

Maybe. Cass shrugged. "Maybe the envelope was a payoff, and

Amelia paid Levi to give the transcript to Bee so suspicion wouldn't fall on her after Fred was killed."

Bee waved the thought away. "I don't think Amelia would have killed Fred. I don't think she had the strength to do it, personally."

"You could be right, but still." Stephanie's phone rang, and she dug through her purse, then silenced it and set it aside. "It's something to think about. I still wonder why Piper wanted to meet with Quince at the lighthouse so badly. Do you think she could have stumbled onto whatever was going on between Amelia and Levi?"

"If" — Bee held up a finger — "anything was going on."

Stephanie was right, though, it was something to think about. They had to consider Piper might have been silenced because she knew something and not just because she was mean.

"So, what about Quince and Francesca? You don't think either of them had anything to do with Fred's death?" Because, at that moment, Luke and Tank were probably interrogating them both. "I wanted you to try to talk to Quince, Bee, but right now, he's either hiding somewhere or in police custody, so we won't be able to get near him anyway. We're headed to the lighthouse, though, and Levi is the custodian out there, so maybe we ought to have a chat with him."

"You mean ask him about the photo?" Bee picked it up and studied it again.

"Why not?" There was always the possibility Piper's attack had nothing to do with Fred's death, though that didn't seem likely, given the fact she was found only yards from where he'd been killed. "Let's say for a minute Levi, who might or might not be spreading rumors of a ghost on the jetty, Amelia, who found out Fred was cheating on her and is seen in that photo looking over her shoulder while one of them passes a package to the other, and Simone, whose husband disappeared under mysterious circumstances and is friends from way back with Amelia, all conspired to get rid of Fred."

Bee squirmed. "When you say it like that, it seems like kind of a far-fetched conspiracy theory."

"But if any of it was true, then what happened to Piper? Why was she so frantic to get Quince out to the lighthouse? And why would someone other than Quince have tried to kill her?"

Bee shrugged. "Maybe she found out something?"

"Could be." But it didn't sit right in Cass's gut. "But what reason would Quince have had to kill Fred?"

"Supposedly, Piper was cheating on him with Fred all last season, and rumor has it Fred was sniffing around Francesca, who Quince really seems to have feelings for, this year. He'd already warned Fred off once. And then there's the treasure. Don't forget the 'ghost' Levi saw out there, and the costume we found would certainly fit Quince." Bee picked up his slice again.

Cass sighed regretfully as she closed the everything box and helped herself to a plain slice. One slice, even loaded, was not going to be enough to help her digest everything that had happened today. Cass sprinkled a packet of grated parmesan over her pitifully bare slice.

After finishing off his slice, Bee said, "So, Levi could have killed Fred, maybe so he'd be free to search for and claim the treasure. Amelia could have killed him because he was cheating on her. I didn't see Simone at the lighthouse, but she was obviously in town at the time, so she could have helped him out the window either out of revenge for Amelia or because he found out she was buying the business, and he was going to try to block the sale . . ."

That was something Cass hadn't considered. And she'd better, since her first phone call of the morning was going to be to Simone to ask her for help controlling the voices.

"And it's also true Quincy could have killed him, because Fred was going after his girlfriend. But has anyone considered Piper could have pushed him?"

"What?" Caught off guard, Cass's first instinct was to defend the young girl, but was it because she didn't think she'd done it or because she'd been hurt? She couldn't be sure.

Bee shrugged. "Not to speak ill, because no one deserves what happened to her, but Piper was mean. And when she confronted Quince in the diner, she obviously had a problem with his relationship with Francesca, so who's to say she didn't find out Fred was interested in her, get jealous, and give him a shove?"

As much as Cass didn't want to believe that, it was more plausible in her mind than Quince having done it. "The biggest problem with some of your theories is that the fall isn't what killed

Fred. It was blunt force trauma to the head. Which means someone hit him over the head with something and then pushed him out the window."

Stephanie started to clear the table. "Maybe the ghost of Samuel Garrison or Thomas the pirate actually did kill him."

Bee harrumphed, then ignored her and turned to Cass. "So, now what?"

"First, I want to try to do Stephanie's reading." Though Cass would have preferred to wait until after she'd spoken to Simone about a shield, it was too late to call tonight, and she wasn't lying awake all night tossing and turning over Stephanie or Tank possibly being in danger. Chief Rawlins's accusations rang loudly in her mind, drowning out everything else. She would not fail anyone else, especially not two of her closest friends. "Then I go to the keeper's house and see if I can get Fred to tell me who killed him."

Chapter Twenty

Cass leaned over Beast, ruffled his mane, and whispered, "You make sure you fetch and return for Bee, okay? No making me look bad."

Bee snickered and grabbed a tennis ball from the drawer. "Of course, he'll return the ball for me. He always does."

Cass just grunted. She couldn't deny Beast listened better to Bee than he did to her. Still, he sometimes got over on him. If not for the fact she'd just had Beast groomed, and didn't feel like having to clean him up again, she'd wish for him to take a nice dip in the bay. Then shake water all over Bee. Or better yet, if Bee had to go wading into the bay after him.

She smiled. "Have fun, you two."

Bee eyed her warily for a second. "Are you up to something?"

"Who? Me?" She fluttered her lashes. "Never."

"Mm-hmm." He headed for the door, having decided to take Beast out and work off some of the three loaded slices he'd eaten before settling down to read. "Come on, boy, let your mama and Stephanie have some privacy."

"Are you ready, Stephanie?"

"As I'll ever be." She settled herself at the table across from where Cass would sit.

Cass considered the basket of paper and pencils. A blank white sheet, ready for her to fill with what might come in Stephanie's future. No. Not right tonight. She needed something straightforward, needed to be able to focus. A life might depend on it. Cass took the crystal ball and set it on the table, then took her seat. "You know I usually try to let my customers know what I'm seeing and how I interpret it as I'm doing the reading, but I really have to work at trying to keep the extra voices out, so could you bear with me if I'm quiet?"

"Of course, Cass." Stephanie straightened in her seat. "I trust you completely. I'll just sit here quietly and let you figure things out, and you can let me know anything I need to know afterward."

Cass nodded. She'd known Stephanie would do whatever she'd asked, and she'd do everything in her power this time to make sure that trust was well deserved.

She tilted her head from side to side, then rolled her shoulders, settling her nerves. Anxiety during a reading was new to Cass, and she didn't want it to interfere. But what had caused the anxiety? The thought of failing Stephanie? Or was it part of a message that Tank or Stephanie were in danger?

Cass rubbed her neck and tried to concentrate on the ball. She looked past the surface, deeper into the distortion that might give her answers, and she opened herself up.

The voices attacked instantly, battering her, begging for her attention. She tried to ignore them, imagined walking into a crowded room with everyone vying to say hello. Projecting an image of Stephanie across the room, Cass focused on her. She walked toward her, couldn't hear anything over the chorus of voices.

An idea struck her. Maybe she didn't have to hear over the voices. Ignoring the chaos, she closed her eyes and shook her head, then opened them again and searched deeper within the ball. She stared straight down, deeper. An image shimmered in the deepest recesses of the crystal. Black? No. Red. Deep red. Blood?

The image swirled and turned, fading in and out. Cass tried to grab hold, tried to steady it.

Dizziness assailed her, followed by a wave of nausea.

She sat back for a moment, opened her eyes to get her bearings and took a sip of her soda to quell the nausea.

Stephanie stared at her and frowned but remained quiet.

Cass massaged her neck for a moment, rubbed her eyes, then tried again. Whatever that image was, Cass had a strong feeling she needed to know. Could it be what would save Stephanie or Tank? Maybe.

It could also be what would hurt them.

Cass blew out a breath and tried to rid herself of enough apprehension to try again.

This time the image came right away. Red. Dark red. Patches of something else. Another color. Not white, too muddied. Gray. Dark red, patches of gray.

Fear tore through her.

"Four. Take him. Four. Help. Four. Needs. fourfourfour. Now."

The image clarified for only a fraction of a second, just barely long enough for her to recognize the shape for what it was. A vehicle of some sort. Red. Patches of gray. Tires.

And it was gone.

Pain throbbed at her temples.

Tears leaked from the corners of her eyes and spilled down her cheeks.

Blood spattered the table from her nose.

Stephanie jumped up and grabbed the roll of paper towels from the counter. She shoved a wad at Cass, placed a hand on her shoulder, and pushed the crystal ball away. "Enough, Cass."

"But I—"

"No." She removed the ball and placed it on the counter out of reach. "That's it."

"But you don't—"

"I said that's enough, Cass. I'm not going to have you hurting yourself to try to do a reading for me." She lifted the hair off Cass's neck and tied it into a knot at the back of her head. "Who knows? Maybe Bee's right and, for whatever reason, things are supposed to play out the way they play out without us knowing what's coming."

It might be time to accept that. But that didn't mean she wouldn't try again after she'd spoken to Simone about helping her create a shield. "I was able to see one thing. I don't know what it means or if it will help, but you need to call Tank and somehow convince him whatever message is trying to reach me has something to do with a red vehicle of some sort with bald tires and patches of gray, maybe primer. And the number four."

"I will, Cass. I promise." She took the bloody paper towels from Cass and handed her a few fresh ones, then grabbed an ice pack from the freezer and put it on the back of Cass's neck. "Here. Keep pinching your nose."

"I'm sorry, Stephanie."

"You have nothing to be sorry for." Stephanie hugged her. "Thank you for trying so hard. And who knows? Maybe that'll be enough to save Tank's life at some point."

Cass nodded.

Bee stormed through the door with Beast on his heels.

A dry Beast. Oh, well. Probably for the best.

He skidded to a stop. "What happened to you?"

"I'm okay, just a bloody nose." Which came out more like *dust a buddy dose* with her nostrils pinched together.

Bee sighed. "What am I going to do with you?"

"I hab no idea."

Stephanie dialed Tank's number and waited, chewing on her bottom lip hard enough to draw a spot of blood. Relief rushed out on a sigh when he answered. "Tank. Do you have a minute?"

He said something too muffled for Cass to hear, and Stephanie walked out the front door.

"Were you able to help her?" Bee asked.

Beast lay his head in her lap, and she absently petted his fur with her free hand.

Cass shrugged and checked if her nose had stopped bleeding. Not completely, but at least it had slowed to a trickle. "I don't know. I hope so."

Stephanie stuck her head back in the door. "Tank's waiting out front to take us to the lighthouse, if you still want to go."

"Yes, just give me a minute to clean up." She stood and tossed the paper towels in the garbage, then tied up the bag and replaced it with a new one.

"Here, I'll get that." Bee took the full bag and started toward the back door. "Wait for me to get back before you leave."

"I thought you were going to stay here with Beast?"

He opened the door and paused. "Do you mind him coming with us?"

"No, not at all. He'll have to sit in the car when we go inside, but I'm sure there's enough police officers up there to make sure he's safe for a few minutes."

"All right." He nodded and started to turn.

"You're coming?"

He held her gaze. "Did you really think I'd let you go out there alone?"

"Bee, seriously, I can't tell you how much I appreciate that, but if you aren't comfortable, it's okay. Tank and probably Luke will be there, plus an assortment of officers and crime scene techs. I'm sure we'll be fine."

"Let me put it this way, while I'm not entirely comfortable going back out to the scene of one murder and one attempted murder, I'm less comfortable letting you go without me. So, it's decided. I'll be right back." He hurried outside to throw the garbage in the Dumpster.

Cass turned to Beast. "Did you have fun with Bee? I bet you were a good boy for him, right? Know how I can tell that? Because he's not soaking wet."

Beast barked.

"Uh-huh. Don't make excuses." While she waited for Bee to return, she put the leftover pizza in the fridge in the back room, then clipped Beast's leash to his collar. "Right after this, we're going to go home and hit the sack. I promise."

Beast yawned and shook out his mane.

Bee rushed back in and locked the back door. "Okay, let's get this show on the road. No sense keeping poor old Fred waiting."

Cass climbed into the backseat with Beast and Stephanie.

Bee jumped into the passenger seat.

She tried to shake off the disappointment that Luke hadn't accompanied Tank. Not like there'd have been enough room in the car for all of them, anyway. Which he'd probably realized.

"Luke is already out there." Tank checked the sideview mirror and pulled out, even though at that time of night the boardwalk was utterly deserted. "He'll meet us at the house."

She tried not to look like it mattered as much as it did. "Have you heard anything about Piper?"

"Still unconscious."

So no answers about who'd tried to kill her.

"What about Quince and Francesca? Did you ever find them?"

"Not yet." Tank came to a full stop at the stop sign, despite the fact there wasn't a car around for miles, red with gray blotches or otherwise, and no one was going to give him a ticket if he didn't. "They both seem to have disappeared."

Cass only hoped they were off somewhere together with Quince desperately trying to make amends. After finding Piper as they had, her concern for Francesca shot through the roof.

Chapter Twenty-one

Cass shifted from one foot to the other as Tank unlocked the front door of the keeper's house.

Luke wrapped an arm around her and pulled her close, the woodsy scent of his aftershave enveloping her in a peaceful haze. "You all right?"

She leaned into him for just a moment, letting go of everything that had been haunting her of late, then she straightened and pulled up her big-girl pants. Though she'd much rather be cuddled together on the couch with him, maybe watching the newest tearjerker that had just released on DVD, she had a responsibility. A responsibility, as Chief Rawlins had so kindly pointed out, that she didn't seem to be taking seriously enough. "Thanks, Luke, I'm fine."

Tank stepped back and gestured for her to enter first.

Luke, Bee, Stephanie, and Tank all followed her in single file.

Chief Rawlins lingered on the porch.

Cass wasn't sure how she felt about that. On the one hand, the chief actually believed in her abilities and had a way of helping her to focus and use them to her full advantage. On the other hand, she didn't want to feel like she had to prove herself to the chief while she was trying to reach out and contact Fred. Either way would leave her feeling self-conscious. Probably best Chief Rawlins just stayed on the porch.

Which she seemed to realize, since she made no attempt to follow them in.

Tank closed the door behind them.

Dim light shone from sconces along the walls in the small foyer. To their right, the door to the museum stood open, the displays also dimly lit. Cass kept the doorway in her mind firmly closed. She didn't know how to separate Fred's from the other voices, so for now, she'd simply block them all and take a look around. See what came to her.

But how to get rid of Luke and Tank so she could have the space she needed to do her thing without worrying about what anyone else thought or expected? A feeling like electricity sizzled across her skin, raising the hairs on her arms and the back of her neck. She looked around the small foyer. Unlike earlier in the day, Cass took the time to notice small details.

Not a large space. Just enough room to have an entryway, with doors leading to a couple of rooms, a hallway that led to the back of the house, and a stairway to the left. A faded, patterned settee, typical for the time period when Kitty Garrison would have lived there, stood sentinel against one wall. An original? Or had someone tried to recreate the feel of the original era.

She sauntered through the doorway to the museum, taking her time, trying to get a feel for the house. Not easy without opening up, but she wasn't ready to deal with anything else just yet.

Shadows crouched in every corner. Yet, each time she tried to focus on one, it skittered away to hide in the deeper pools of darkness.

The display case holding the journal was dark, and Cass moved closer. The dim lighting illuminating all of the other displays was noticeably absent from Kitty's. Maybe because the display was new and the lighting hadn't been installed yet? Or maybe the lighting had been turned off or disabled for whatever reason. Cass moved closer, squinting into the shadows to bring the case into focus.

The overhead lights blazed on, and all of the shadows fled. She glanced over her shoulder to see who'd turned them on.

Tank stood against the wall, hands clasped behind his back. "Oh, uh. Was I not supposed to do that?"

Cass turned away, frustrated, though it wasn't Tank's fault. He didn't know what she needed. Heck, she wasn't even sure what she needed at this point, but she was beginning to think Bee's idea of a little nighttime B and E would have been better than following procedure in this case.

Her second-guessing her choice to do things "the right way" skidded to an abrupt halt when she refocused her attention on the case holding Kitty's display. "It's gone."

"What?" Tank jerked away from the wall.

Luke appeared over her shoulder to stare at the empty case. "What's gone?"

"Kitty's journal. It was in this case when I last came to the museum, but it's gone now."

Tank examined the surrounding area then radioed for a crime scene tech. "What does it have to do with Fred's death?"

"I'm not sure. But something, I think." The image of a red vehicle flashed into her mind, along with a piercing pain in her temple. "Ow."

"You okay?" Tank glanced at Luke then back at her.

She rubbed her temple for a moment, and the pain eased. "I'm okay, thank you. Just tired."

Not a lie.

"Could you do me a favor and hold off on the crime scene techs until I'm done, though?"

"I could do that."

"And something else too." She looked Tank in the eye so she could gage if he was taking her warning seriously. "Did Stephanie talk to you about a red vehicle?"

He frowned, looking more concerned than skeptical.

Good.

"With gray patches. She told me."

Cass laid a hand on his arm. "Please, Tank. I don't know why, but it's important. A matter of life and death. At first, I thought it was Stephanie's, but it may be yours."

A million scenarios flashed through her mind in an instant, someone emerging from the vehicle shooting, the vehicle hitting Tank, an explosion . . . And on and on they went, battering her with the possibilities.

Tank wrapped his arms around her and pulled her close, cradling the back of her head in one hand. He kissed the top of her head. "I'm taking your warning seriously. Stop worrying about me, and see if you can figure out what's going on here. We have a young girl in the hospital who's counting on your help."

She nodded against him, then stepped back, sniffed, and wiped a few tears from her cheeks. "Okay. Thank you, Tank."

He nodded.

Stephanie reached over and squeezed her hand.

"And now, I need to ask all of you a huge favor." And hopefully they'd all understand without being insulted.

Tank, Stephanie, Luke, and Bee all stood staring at her.

Bee might be a problem. But a problem she could live with.

"I need to go upstairs alone." She held up her hands to ward off the automatic protests they all launched.

"Please. I appreciate you all worrying about me, but I really need quiet to be able to do this." *If I can do it at all.*

Bee stepped forward. "You don't really think that's happening, do you?"

"You can all wait right at the bottom of the stairs. No one should be in here this time of night, anyway. It'll be perfectly safe, Bee. And if anything happens, I'll scream, and you can come running."

"Yeah, and if you get another bloody nose like the one I walked in on earlier? Or black out or something?" Bee paced back and forth in the small space, the *clunk, clunk, clunk* of his shoes echoing into the high ceiling.

Cass grinned, trying to make light of it so he'd relax. "If you hear a thud, you have my permission to come running."

Bee snorted.

"Would it interfere with anything if I clear the upstairs first?" Luke asked.

Though she really wanted to walk into everything as it stood, the upstairs rooms had already been thoroughly searched by police and crime scene techs, so it probably wouldn't matter. "Fair enough, just leave everything, lights and all, exactly like they were when you're done."

Tank and Luke jogged up the stairs together, and Cass turned to Bee. "I'll really be okay, Bee."

"I know how you work, Cass, and when you wanted to do Stephanie's reading earlier, I made myself scarce, but this is different. Since we walked in here, even when we found the journal missing, I haven't said a word. I understand you need quiet. I even told Loretta as much when she wanted you to locate Stanley's wallet, which you owe me for, by the way, and I'm calling in the favor right now. And I promise my lips will be sealed, but please let me go up with you."

She started to protest, then thought better of it. She'd already hurt Bee's feelings once by letting Emma spread rumors for her—and look at how that had turned out—and she was going to slip his presence again when she spoke to Simone. She didn't have the heart to blow him off now. As long as he stayed quiet, having Bee there probably wouldn't matter. He was with her so often, his presence would probably not even be noticeable. Besides, he was right; she did owe him for getting Loretta to stop talking, no matter how brief the reprieve.

"Okay, Bee."

"And you know I — wait. What? I can come?"

"Yes, just remember your promise to stay quiet."

He nodded and looked up the stairway just as the upstairs lights flipped off and Tank and Luke started down, then swallowed hard. Bee was not a huge fan of the paranormal, nor of the dark.

Cass bit back the grin tugging at her. She had a sneaking suspicion Bee wouldn't see the humor in the situation just yet.

"All clear." Luke gestured toward the stairway, then leaned on the railing and watched her start to climb.

Tank leaned on the railing opposite him. Apparently, that was all the leeway they were going to give. "Just yell if there's a problem."

Cass ascended the stairs slowly, giving her eyes a chance to adjust to the darkness. Two sconces gave off small pools of light along the narrow upstairs hallway.

The clomping of Bee's thick-soled shoes and his heavy breathing against the back of her neck had her second-guessing her decision to bring him with her.

She stopped for a second to orient herself, took a quick peek into the room that had held the box of lighthouse figures. Still no box. Someone had obviously removed them. Dismissing what she couldn't do anything about, Cass climbed the next flight of stairs and headed in the direction of the room Fred had to have fallen from.

She pushed the door open and paused in the doorway. Moonlight filtered through the sheer curtains adorning the window. Dust motes, probably kicked up from all the recent activity, bounced and swirled in the rays.

Cass lifted the corner of a sheet covering a chair and peeked underneath. Nothing. She walked around the perimeter of the room, altering her course only to walk around the brick fireplace on one wall and the bed on another.

She stopped beside the doorway, took a deep breath, and opened herself up.

Voices pummeled her. Louder than ever. Demanding. Insistent. Unrelenting.

She slapped her hands over her ears. No help, since the voices seemed to be coming from inside her head. If anything, having her ears covered made them louder.

She tried to block them out again.

They forced themselves through whatever shield she might have managed, driving her to her knees.

Bee was at her side in an instant. To his credit, he remained quiet, placing a gentle hand beneath her arm but making no move to help her up until she started to stand.

Once she recovered her equilibrium, he stepped back.

She lowered her face into her hands and took a moment to collect herself. Then she ignored all of the voices and stood in the center of the room. Eventually, they faded to background noise, like a large crowd surrounding her but, thankfully, no longer trying to interact.

She studied the window, approached slowly. She looked out over the lighthouse and the jetty. No ghosts appeared—pirate or otherwise. Had Fred stood in this exact spot in the moments before his death? Had he been looking out over the bay? The lighthouse? Or facing his assailant?

She turned to face the room, ran her gaze over her surroundings, mostly silhouetted in the darkness. One wall was taken up with the fireplace and bookshelves on either side. The wall opposite held a queen-sized canopy bed. A thought occurred. "Did Kitty mention in the journal which room was hers?"

"Um." Bee went to the window and looked out at the lighthouse. "She mentions watching for Thomas to return from her bedroom window, so it would have to have been either this room or the one next to it. At least, they would provide the best view out toward the ocean."

Cass walked into the hallway and entered the room beside it. This room was much smaller, though she couldn't understand why. "Bee, flip the light on, please."

He did as she asked then lingered in the doorway, glancing occasionally over his shoulder and up and down the hallway.

"Something's wrong." The feeling had assailed Cass the instant she'd crossed the threshold.

Bee stiffened. "Do you need Luke and Tank?"

"No. No, it's not like that." At least, she didn't think it was.

She studied the wall where two twin beds stood with a dresser between them. "The other side of this wall is the fireplace in the room Fred fell from."

"So?" Apparently, intrigued by whatever had caught her attention, and happy to be included, Bee entered the room and stood next to her, hands on his hips.

"There's too much space between the rooms." She ran her hand over the wall's smooth flat surface. "Bee, when was drywall invented."

He shrugged. "I don't know. Why?"

"Could you look it up, please?" Cass slid one of the beds farther from the wall, then the other. She ran her hands over the wall behind the beds. Nothing. She reached as far as she could behind the dresser. Still nothing.

"It says here it was invented in nineteen sixteen."

"Come on." Cass returned to the other room and went straight to the fireplace. All brick, blackened in spots. With a wood mantel. It appeared to be original from the time the house was built. The bookshelves, on the other hand, did not. Drywall took up the space between where the fireplace ended and the bookshelves began. Drywall that wouldn't have existed at the time the house was built.

She pushed on the bookshelf closest to the door. It held steady. Then she shoved a shoulder against the one on the other side, only a few feet from where Fred had plunged to his death. Nothing.

Giving up, she studied both sets of shelves.

Bee walked over to the shelves closest to the window and pulled. The entire shelf unit slid easily, and silently, into the room, revealing a gaping black hole. He danced back out of the way, then splayed a hand against the wall beside the window and looked down at the jetty. "Do you think this could have hit Fred and knocked him out the window? Maybe someone was in there and came out without realizing he was standing there?"

From where Bee had ended up when he'd backed out of the way, it was a realistic possibility. But what would anyone have been doing in there? Since everyone else had already left the room, it was possible someone hadn't realized Fred had stayed behind. If Fred had been standing in front of the open window, staring out at the bay or the lighthouse, he could possibly have been hit in the back of the head and knocked out. If not for the lighthouse figure she'd seen. Bee moved closer and examined the wood shelves. He held up a hand in front of his chin, just about the height where Fred would have stood, and studied the shelf at that height. He swiped a finger through a thick coating of dust, then sneezed and brushed off his hand. "If this hit him, someone did an amazing job cleaning it up and then coating it with dust again. There's not even a dark spot on the wood."

Cass shone a light into the darkness. "It's a stairway."

"I'll get Luke and Tank." Bee started for the door.

"Wait." Cass stepped into the opening and bent to shine the light down the stairs. The stairway curved partway down, blocking her view to the bottom. "Not yet. Let me just see."

She turned and studied the bookshelves. "I don't think they open with enough force to have knocked Fred out the window."

Bee bounced back and forth from one foot to the other, vibrating with nervous energy. "So, still a murder. Which means the detectives should be up here investigating, not you."

His eyes went wide and he gasped and started to hyperventilate. "And now my fingerprints are on the possible murder weapon. Oh, my."

"I'm working for the police, remember? And I'll make sure they know I saw you touch the shelf as part of your brilliant investigative technique." She winked and turned back to the stairway. "Any chance you'll stand guard here while I go a few steps down, just to make sure the door doesn't swing shut behind me?"

"Absolutely none." He folded his arms across his massive chest. Bee in full-on protective mode. She wasn't going anywhere alone.

"Fine, then. Come on."

His arms dropped to his sides, and his mouth fell open. "Come on where?"

She started down, her phone's flashlight leading the way. "I just want to see where it leads."

Bee followed, muttering under his breath the whole way.

So much for staying quiet. Oh, well. At least his voice drowned out the others to some extent.

Chapter Twenty-two

Cass descended the stairs slowly, careful to check each step with the flashlight and test it before putting her full weight onto it.

"Hey, Cass. Look." Bee pointed past her shoulder to something on the floor at the bottom. "Is that what I think it is?"

A leather book lay open facedown on the floor, its cover glaring up at them. "Kitty's journal."

She hurried down the last few steps and started to bend to retrieve the book.

"Wait." Bee grabbed her arm. "Put these on."

Cass turned as best she could in the confined space with Bee right on her heels. "What are they?"

"Gloves. Tank handed them to me when we were going up and said to make sure you put them on if you were going to touch anything." He held a pair out to her and struggled to get a pair on his own sweaty hands.

"So why didn't you put them on before touching the bookshelf?"

He shot her a sheepish grin. "He said before you touched anything."

"Uh-huh." With her hands covered, she picked up the journal and leafed through it, then closed it and ran a finger over the cover.

Bee pulled his phone out and used the flashlight to examine the cover. "What do you think it's doing here?"

"No idea." Cass held the book by the spine and shook it out. Nothing dropped out. "It was laying facedown, some of the pages torn."

Bee took the book from her and flipped to the torn pages. "At least no pieces are missing."

"It looks like someone threw it or dropped it there." They'd come to a wall, and other than the small landing where they stood, there was nowhere to go but back up. It seemed where the stairway had turned might have been the second floor, so she judged they were probably back on the first floor. But she'd lost all sense of direction. "Come on, let's go back up and get Luke and Tank."

Bee skimmed the book absently then looked around the small alcove. "Why don't we give the wall a push and see if it opens down here like it did upstairs. Seems foolish to have a stairway that only leads to a dead end. Plus, if the journal is here, someone had to have used these stairs recently."

Bee was right. She should have thought of that, might have if something wasn't pounding through her head trying to get in. She ignored it and pushed against the wall.

It easily gave way, and they found themselves standing in the back corner of the museum, not far from the display where Kitty's book had been. "You think someone just grabbed the book and tossed it into the stairwell? That doesn't make sense."

"It does if that someone wanted to get rid of the journal but maybe not get caught with it in their possession, or didn't have a lot of time to ditch it. I'm sure whoever it was will be coming back for it soon." Bee looked over his shoulder as if worried he'd jinxed himself.

Cass shivered. "Even if that's what happened, it doesn't explain why."

Cass heard voices ahead of them, not of the ghostly variety, but familiar.

The overhead lights flipped on, and Luke and Tank stood in the doorway.

Luke moved toward them. "I thought I heard voices in here. How did you two get down here?"

Cass gestured behind them and explained about the stairway.

Tank peered into the stairway, pulled out his flashlight and disappeared inside. He reappeared a moment later. "I'm going to have to have the techs come in now, Cass."

She nodded absently. It didn't matter; she'd picked up anything she was going to for now. "But I still can't imagine why someone would have tossed the book in there and left it, or why they'd even want to get rid of it."

"Not get rid of it, hide it." Bee held the book up, his finger marking a page. "Seems Amelia or Levi left out a few pages. Or Fred removed them before Amelia gave the transcript to Levi."

"What are you talking about, Bee?" Cass peered at the page he held open, but since she hadn't read the original transcript, she couldn't tell what was wrong.

"I read through all of the pages in Kitty's journal, at least the transcribed copy. Even the pages I didn't read thoroughly, I did skim. Then, if something caught my attention, I read that section in more detail. And this book contains pages that are not included in the transcript, and they most definitely would have caught my attention."

"What do they say?"

"Kitty gives a number of clues as to the treasure's location throughout the missing pages, seems Thomas described where it could be found in great detail when he woke up, but on the last page, she wrote this." He cleared his throat, opened the book, and started to read. "On the last full moon, as spring turns to summer, and the warmth returns to bathe the land, the moon's rays shine directly on the spot the treasure was buried, illuminating the secret entrance."

"Entrance? Like a cave?" Cass couldn't recall seeing anything like an entrance out by the jetty, though the boulder Piper had been found beneath had been loose. She looked back and forth between Luke and Tank. "When we pulled Piper out, I didn't bother looking for anything else beneath the rocks. Did you?"

Luke was already nodding. "We've already pulled that stone out and combed the sand beneath it for evidence, and no one mentioned a cave or an entrance of any sort. Does she give any more details, Bee?"

Bee shrugged. "She doesn't elaborate, and the next page picks up where I've already read. Of course, I have no idea if other pages were taken out, but I could tell you if I skimmed through it all."

"Come on." Tank ushered them outside as officers flooded the foyer and pounded up the stairs. "Sit on the porch and you can read through and see what you can tell us."

When they walked out, Cass inhaled deeply, clearing her lungs of the dampness that had hung over the stairwell from being closed up for so long.

Chief Rawlins sat on the top step petting Beast's head. She stood when she saw them.

Beast moaned and scrambled to his feet.

Tank brought the chief up to speed on what they'd found.

She looked from Cass to Bee. "You think someone found the treasure?"

"When was the last full moon?" Cass asked.

Bee held out his phone, one step ahead of her. "On the night Fred was murdered."

The chief's radio signaled, and she stepped aside to answer.

Cass's gut cramped.

Chief Rawlins returned a moment later. "Luke, Tank, a patrol officer just picked up Quincy Yates, pulled him over for running a red light, driving a red Toyota Camry registered to Francesca Harding."

A red vehicle. Images bombarded Cass.

"We're on our way. Is Francesca Harding with him?" Tank asked.

She shook her head. "I'm sorry to say she's not."

"Yeah, me too," Tank muttered.

Cass figured they were all having the same vision of Piper's battered body, wondering if Francesca had suffered the same fate. Or worse.

He tossed Stephanie his keys. "I'll come by for the car later."

Luke kissed Cass then started away with Tank.

"Tank," Cass called after him. "Be careful. Please."

Chapter Twenty-three

The first thing Cass did when she opened her eyes the next morning was call Stephanie. Still no word from Tank. Cass chose to believe no news was good news.

Second on the agenda was a phone call to Simone.

Simone answered on the first ring with all the warmth of an old friend. "Cass, how are you, dear?"

Cass hopped up and down as she struggled into her leggings with the phone propped between her ear and her shoulder—a task that used to be easier. Could be loaded pizza, among other things, wasn't the best dietary choice, but somehow broccoli and carrots just didn't offer the same sense of comfort. "I'm doing well, thank you. How are you?"

"I am well, thank you."

Now that Simone sat waiting on the other end of the line, it seemed odd that Cass had called her for help when she barely even knew her. Plus, she might even have had something to do with her own husband's disappearance and Fred's death.

"I'm so glad you called." Simone saved her the trouble of having to figure it all out.

Good thing, because her brain clearly hadn't fully woken up yet. She needed coffee. Lots of coffee.

"There's something I've been wanting to talk to you about. A favor I'd like to ask, if you will."

"Oh, uh, of course. What can I do for you?"

"We can discuss that in a bit. First, what can I do for you?"

Simone wanting to ask for her help nudged the door open for Cass to seek guidance from the woman. "I've been having some trouble lately, keeping the voices from harassing me too much to make out any clear messages."

"And you'd like me to help you with a shield."

Cass sank onto the edge of the bed. "I don't have trouble blocking out all of the voices, but I can't let them in selectively like you seem to be able to do."

"Not as much as I'd like, I'm afraid."

It hadn't seemed that way to her. When Simone had been in the shop, only the one voice had been able to reach through to Cass.

"What do you mean?"

"Oh, nothing. Don't worry about it, dear. I'll tell you what. Why don't you meet me at the lighthouse around eight tonight, and maybe we can kill two birds with one stone. I'll try to help you with your shield, and you can try to help me out with what I need."

Kind of cryptic, for sure, and if it wasn't for fear of Tank and Stephanie being in danger, she'd never agree to it. Not to mention the episode Bee was going to have when he found out. And Luke. "Eight? It will already be getting dark by then."

"No worries. There are lights. Besides, I have a feeling what we need to do won't take long."

She had no choice, really. She had to figure out what was going on, and Simone seemed to be the only one with the ability to help her filter out the excess so she could concentrate on what she needed to know. And with Stephanie and Tank somehow needing help, no way could she give up. "I'll see you there at eight then, thank you."

She hung up feeling like she'd just made a deal with a snake oil salesman. "Come on, Beast. Time to eat."

At the mention of food, Beast bounded out of the bedroom, skidded on the hallway's wood floor, and ran toward the kitchen.

Cass trudged more slowly behind him.

By the time they'd returned to Mystical Musings from the lighthouse to pick up her car the night before, it had barely been worth going to sleep. But her eyes had felt like someone was scrubbing sandpaper over them every time she blinked, so she'd fallen into bed for a couple of hours with her mind fully focused on listening to her gut instincts in case Tank needed her.

It hadn't made for a restful night.

Now she knew how Bee felt when she dragged him out of bed before noon.

After feeding Beast and letting him out into the fenced yard to take care of business, Cass made herself a couple of slices of toast with apple butter and a glass of orange juice. She ate standing at the counter, looking out the window into the yard. She'd make coffee as soon as she got to the shop.

Beast dug happily along the fence line, flinging dirt all up over his freshly shampooed fur.

Just what she needed, him escaping the yard when she hadn't

even woken up all the way yet. And needing another bath, to boot. She'd have to go out and fill in the holes later. Again. As for the bath, not happening. She'd have to give him a good brushing when she got to the shop and hope it was enough. She flung the back door open. "Beast, come."

He spread his front legs apart, lowering his body as if bowing, and yipped.

She propped her hands on her hips and twisted her features into her best *I'm not playing around* expression.

Beast jumped back once, then barked, then, apparently realizing it wasn't playtime, sulked as he made his way inside. Triumph warred with pity as he moped through the door. Too much time hanging around Bee, no doubt. "Enough drama, Beast. It's time to go to the shop."

He perked up at that and lunged toward the back door.

Speaking of drama, last she'd seen Bee, he'd decided to stay behind at the lighthouse with Chief Rawlins to read the rest of the journal. She glanced at the clock, barely eight. No way she could call him. She settled for shooting him a text telling him to call her when he got up.

When she pulled into the parking lot at Mystical Musings, someone sat waiting on one of the rocking chairs on the front porch, hidden from Cass's view by the railing.

She clipped Beast's leash to his collar and kissed the side of his face. "Behave, boy, okay?"

Darn, she was supposed to issue commands in a firm voice, not ask questions as if Beast had a choice. Ugh . . . sooner or later she'd get the hang of this. She nuzzled Beast for another moment, then got out of the car with him and headed toward her visitor. Wary of walking up to the stranger unprotected, even with Beast at her side, Cass kept the keys in her hand as she approached.

The woman stood as soon as she saw Cass.

Cass relaxed instantly. "Amelia, how are you doing?"

She sniffed and wiped her eyes, then laughed a little, though it held no humor. "To be honest, Cass, I'm having a rough time. I know you don't open until ten, and I don't mind sitting out here until you're ready, but Simone suggested I come, said you might be able to help me."

Cass hugged her, then stepped back to unlock the door. "Of course, you don't have to wait out here. Come on in."

Amelia petted Beast's head, then followed Cass into the shop with Beast trotting beside her.

"Can I get you something? Coffee, tea, water?" Cass put her bag under the counter, then left the register for later and headed to the back counter to start the coffee and water for tea.

"No, nothing, thank you."

"Please, have a seat wherever you're comfortable." It only took a few minutes to get things started and settle Beast with his basket of toys. She joined Amelia in one of the small private seating arrangements scattered throughout the shop and took a chair to the side of the love seat Amelia had chosen. Close enough to reach out and offer comfort if needed, not too close to make her feel crowded or uncomfortable or pressured. There was no table between them to create any kind of barrier or distance. It was all she could do to make Amelia feel comfortable enough to open up to her.

"I'm sorry, Cass, I'm not even really sure why I came or what I hope to accomplish here." She reached for a tissue from one of the boxes Cass kept on side tables throughout the shop. Contacting deceased loved ones could often be an emotional experience for her clients. "Simone said she left you with a sense of peace she hadn't felt in a long time. And, well, I could really use that right about now."

It seemed to Cass as if Simone's talents surpassed her own, so why not just help Amelia herself? Why send her to Cass? "Would you like a reading?"

"I don't know what I want or need right now." She wrapped her arms around herself and rocked back and forth.

"That's okay, Amelia. We don't have to do an official reading if you're not comfortable with that. We could just sit and chat." She had a feeling Amelia needed a friend more than anything else. "When did you speak to Simone?"

She scoffed. "Last night, multiple times during the night, and again this morning. About three times, so far, this morning."

"And she hasn't been able to help you?" Either spiritually or as a friend?

"Oh, she helps. It's just . . ." She sniffed and wiped her swollen red eyes with the tissue. "It's not the same talking to someone on the phone as it is in person."

"Simone couldn't meet with you?"

"She's not here right now. She had business to attend to on the mainland, and she won't be back until this evening."

Now it made perfect sense that Simone had suggested they meet later on tonight. Nothing sinister. Maybe Bee, Luke, and Tank would forgive her for meeting up with Simone at the lighthouse as night fell, after all. Or at least Luke and Tank might. Bee might take some persuading. Cass relaxed a little. "Why don't you tell me what's been going on and I'll see what I can do to help you?"

Amelia nodded and blew her nose.

Maybe Cass could even help her without having to open herself up to the restless spirits who'd been making her life so difficult of late.

"I'm not really sure what you can do for me, but I'm a wreck." She paused and looked around the empty shop, then frowned. "Is everything we talk about here private, like a doctor's office or something?"

Touchy subject. Cass would never repeat anything she was told by a client in confidence. Unless it pertained to something that could harm someone else. Or if Amelia blurted a confession that she or someone she knew had killed Fred. That would be problematic, because she'd be obligated to pass that information on to the police. "I'm not bound by privacy laws like a doctor is, if that's what you're asking, but I am discreet, I don't take notes, and nothing you say here will be passed on as gossip in any way."

Amelia settled back into the love seat, seemingly satisfied her secrets wouldn't be the next fuel for the rumor mill. "My emotions are everywhere, hurling up and down like I'm on a roller coaster. So much so that I actually feel nauseas at times, like motion sickness or something."

Cass sat back, making herself comfortable, inviting Amelia to take her time, to open up.

"I'm grieving because my husband was killed. And yet, he was on his way to being my ex-husband, and I'm so angry with him for cheating on me that I can't even think straight. So, I can't grieve because I'm angry, but I can't be angry because Fred died, killed by someone he must have trusted to have been alone in a room with him." She sobbed softly. "Or her."

Since one of Fred's injuries had been sustained on the back of his head, Cass had imagined someone sneaking up behind him and hitting him rather than having been face-to-face with him. But Amelia was right. If Fred was in the room with his killer, having some sort of discussion, he'd never have thought twice about turning his back on his companion to look out the window. "Do you think Fred's mistress killed him?"

"You mean one of his mistresses. Apparently there were many." Her cheeks flared red, and her eyes went cold. She sat up straighter and shook her head. "See, that's what I'm talking about. One minute I'm crying hysterically because Fred was killed, and the next I'm taken by such rage that I find it difficult to feel anything for him. Even pity."

There was nothing Cass could say that would ease her pain, especially since some of it stemmed from Amelia's own sense of guilt about how she was feeling.

"And, sometimes . . ." Amelia lowered her voice to a whisper. "I can't help thinking, if one of his mistresses did kill him, he got what he deserved."

She curled into the corner of the couch and sobbed, deep, racking sobs there would be no way to stop before she'd cried herself out. Could be that was just what she needed. Once the emotional dam broke, she might be able to start on the road toward healing.

Cass handed her the box of tissues and moved the wastebasket closer, then sat down beside Amelia and rubbed circles on her back, praying no other customers came in while she was so distraught.

Beast whined and cocked his head, lifting his ears and studying Amelia. After a moment, he lowered his head to his front paws and continued to watch her.

Once Amelia collected herself, and the sobs eased off to soft whimpers, Cass returned to her seat. "Are you feeling better?"

She rested against the seat back. "For now, I guess."

"Unfortunately, we can't choose what we feel. In time, you'll sort the emotions out and come to terms with them. All of them. In the meantime, I can give you a card for a great counselor who's also a friend of mine." Amelia probably needed more than Cass could give her. Even if she could manage to get some sort of connection with Fred, she didn't see what good it would do Amelia.

"Thank you, but I don't need counseling." She blew her nose a few times. "What I really need to know is if you can talk to Fred?"

A sensitive topic Cass didn't have a straightforward answer to. Even if Fred was trying to get through to her, there was no guarantee she could make any sense of what he was trying to say. And she had a feeling, no matter what he might want to say to his wife, it wouldn't do anything to ease her confusion or her pain. "I haven't been able to up until now, and not for lack of trying. I've reached out a few times."

Apparently fully spent, Amelia's tears dried up. "There are rumors you talked to him, that he confided who killed him. Is that true?"

"I'm sorry, but, no. Unfortunately, those are just rumors." Rumors she needed to get stopped before someone got hurt. "And if I had, I'd have passed that information on to the police immediately so they could investigate properly."

Amelia narrowed her eyes and pinned Cass with her gaze. "Would you tell me if you had spoken to him?"

"Of course." While she might not divulge the reason she hadn't been able to reach him, Cass would never have withheld the information from his wife if she had contacted him.

Amelia stood and threw the last of her tissues in the garbage and hooked her bag onto her arm. She brushed her hair away from her face and sucked in a deep, shaky breath. "Thank you, Cass. I appreciate you taking the time to speak with me. How much do I owe you?"

"Oh, nothing, please. I didn't do anything but offer a shoulder to cry on. I'm sorry I couldn't do more."

"Don't be." Amelia ran her fingers through her hair and wiped her cheeks and eyes. "I actually got exactly what I needed."

Chapter Twenty-four

Cass hung her purse over the back of the chair between Luke and Bee as soon as she got to the diner and sat down. "What's up, guys?"

Luke kissed her cheek. "Hey, beautiful."

The intensity in his deep blue eyes set her heart all aflutter.

"Hey, that's my line. Hey, beautiful." Bee kissed her other cheek with a loud smack.

Her heart warmed, a totally different reaction than Luke's greeting brought, but no less tender.

"Hi, Tank, Stephanie." The round table in the back room of the packed diner was large enough for all of them to have plenty of room. Much better than cramming into a booth.

Bee handed her a menu. "I actually just got up a little while ago. I was beat after reading through Kitty's journal again. Stephanie said you were meeting us here for dinner, so I didn't bother calling."

"No problem." She opened her menu, not really hungry, since her stomach was doing the jig at the thought of her meeting with Simone. "Did you find out anything new?"

"Nah, the only pages that were missing from the transcribed pages were the ones regarding where to find the treasure. And we already knew about those." Bee took her menu back and flipped it to the Specials section, then pointed out the hot turkey sandwich. "Chief Rawlins said I could be an official consultant on the case, since I'd already helped with the pirate clothing and again with the journal."

He beamed with pride, and her appreciation for Chief Rawlins bumped up a notch.

"So, the question now is, who had access to the original journal to know what it contained?" Bee opened a small plastic package of breadsticks from a bowl in the center of the table, then waved one around while he spoke. "And who had access to the transcribed pages and would have known to remove those that might point to a location before Levi gave them to me?"

"Levi had access, that's for sure." Stephanie folded her menu and lay it on the table. "As did Fred, who presumably stuck the picture of Levi and Amelia in the folder."

"Amelia had access too." Darn, she should have thought of asking Amelia about the envelope's contents, but the woman had appeared so distraught, Cass hadn't thought of it.

Cass didn't repeat anything of Amelia's visit, since she'd pretty much promised not to. Even though Amelia's parting comment still haunted her. Had she just needed a good cry, as Cass had originally thought? Or had she come in, either on her own or at Simone's urging, to find out if Cass had spoken to Fred? And if he'd named his killer.

Luke cleared his throat.

Tank just looked amused.

"What?" Stephanie frowned.

"Nothing." Luke grinned. "By all means, continue. Who knows? Maybe you'll save us the trouble of actually having to solve this case."

Bee laughed.

It was good to see him let his guard down around the two detectives.

The waitress approached and took their orders.

Cass followed Bee's suggestion and ordered the turkey with mashed potatoes, gravy, coleslaw, and cranberry sauce. It didn't matter to Cass who solved the case, as long as it got solved soon, before she needed to buy a whole new wardrobe one size bigger. Luckily, the leggings she most often wore stretched. But even they could only go so far. "Any word on Piper's condition?"

Tank scrubbed his hands over his face. "No, nothing new. She's still the same."

"Did you get to question Quincy Yates?"

"Huh." Luke lifted a brow. "So, this is what it feels like to be on the opposite end of an interrogation."

Tank laughed.

"You don't know the half of it. Try being on her suspect list." Bee winked at Cass, letting her know her momentary lapse had been forgiven, and bit into one of the breadsticks with a crunch.

"Anyway." She aimed a look at Luke. "Despite you so tactfully trying to avoid the question, did you bring Quince in for questioning?"

"Yeah." Luke swiped a hand over his goatee. "And afterward we had to let him go."

"What?" Bee lowered his breadstick to a napkin. "Why?"

"Because we had no just cause to hold him. He swears Piper was already gone when he reached the parking lot, and numerous other witnesses confirmed his statement."

"Chief Rawlins said he was driving Francesca's car." Her red car. "Did Quince say where she is?"

Cass figured they probably had someone keeping an eye on Quincy, but if he'd already done something to hurt Francesca, he probably wouldn't return to wherever he'd left her. Being that the lighthouse was a hotbed of activity with the police investigation, he'd probably have left her somewhere else.

"No." Luke's jaw clenched. "According to Quincy, they'd driven to the diner in her car. When she stormed out, she didn't bother with the car. Since the keys were in his pocket, he assumed she got a ride with someone, but he didn't want to leave the car in the lot, so he's been driving it. We checked his phone log, and he's made no fewer than a hundred calls to her since."

"What else did he say?"

Luke leaned in and lowered his voice, though being seated in the back room offered more privacy than being in the main section of the diner. "He admits to giving Fred a warning the day before his death, telling him to leave Francesca alone. But he says he left him alive and well. No one has seen or heard from Francesca, so we can't ask her, and until we find her, there's nothing more we can do."

The waitress arrived with their food, and they all sat back to allow her room. She set Cass's plate in front of her.

The aroma of gravy brought back a rush of memories from her childhood, of turkey dinners on lazy Sunday afternoons with homemade cheesecake for dessert. Oh, boy, talk about comfort food.

She thought of bringing up her intention to meet Simone at the lighthouse, but if she did, she'd have an army of bodyguards traipsing all over the place with her, and that's the last thing she needed. Her experience at the keeper's house had taught her that. No, if she was going to be able to work on selectively listening to only the voices she wanted to hear, she would need to focus one hundred percent of her attention on the task. Unfortunately, that meant she had to go alone.

Throughout the remainder of the meal, they ate silently, each of them working through their own thoughts about the murder and who knew what else.

Luke pushed back from the table and stood, then picked up the check. He kissed Cass's head. "Tank and I have to go back to work, and I suggest you guys go home, relax, and watch a movie or something."

Bee stood as well. "Actually, I'm headed to work too. I haven't worked on my designs at all over the past few days, and I'm trying to come up with a new winter line in time for my fashion show."

The three of them left together.

Cass had expected Luke and Tank to have to go back to work, but she hadn't thought it would be that easy to get out from under Bee's surveillance so she could go to the lighthouse alone. Of course, if anyone knew she was headed up there, it would have been a different story.

"What about you, Stephanie? What are you doing?"

She shrugged. "I have some paperwork to catch up on, so I'll probably go home and do that while I worry about Tank being out and around."

A pang of guilt struck Cass, and her resolve to find answers grew stronger. "I'm sorry, Steph, I didn't mean to cause you more stress."

"Don't worry about it." She stood and placed a tip on the table, then slung her bag over her shoulder. "Better he has a heads-up than walk into a bad situation blind."

"If that's even what my vision means. I can't always tell." But once she met with Simone, she hoped to be able to find more answers for her.

"I'll see you later." She squeezed Cass's shoulder and walked out.

And with that, Cass was left alone. She got her stuff together and walked out, then paused in the parking lot and took a deep breath. The scent of a coming storm hung thick in the air.

Thunder rumbled in the distance, followed by a crack of lightning. She'd better hurry. The last place she wanted to be caught in a storm was out at the lighthouse. In the dark.

The thought of stopping to pick Bee up ricocheted through her mind a dozen or more times on the way, but she resisted. By the time she pulled into the gravel lot at the lighthouse, she'd already second-guessed herself about a hundred times. But her every instinct was telling her to trust Simone, so she'd listen to her gut. For now.

She parked as close to the lighthouse as she could get, right beside Simone's Porsche, got out and looked around. With the massive police presence gone, the place seemed way more deserted than she remembered.

Wind tore through the parking lot, whipping Cass's hair around her face. She hurried toward the lighthouse. Whatever vague bit of sunlight might usually be left at that time of night had been swallowed up by the storm clouds.

The bay had turned a dark and choppy black, spraying the cold salt water each time a wave surged against the jetty. She might have made a huge mistake going out there alone. She pulled out her phone, dialed Bee's number, and hit Send.

"Cass." Simone waved from the lighthouse steps.

Too late to change her mind. Besides, Bee was probably already lost in the zone, anyway. Cass disconnected and hurried toward Simone before the storm could unleash a downpour. "Hi, Simone, thank you for meeting me out here. Not the best night for it, though. I'll understand if you'd rather reschedule."

"Actually, Cass, I've waited a long time to find someone who'd be able to help me, and I'm not about to let a little rain interfere with that." She strode down the steps and met Cass on the walkway. "If anything, the storm will be helpful."

"What do you mean?" The memory of what may have happened to Fred when he'd turned his back on someone he might have thought was a friend almost had her turning tail and running.

"Your shield is fine." The wind tangled her long flowing skirt around her legs. "It's a filter that eludes you, one that will allow you to determine which voices to listen to. What you need is help creating a filter. And the growing storm will help with that."

She'd known Simone would understand. "And you know how to create a filter, because you have your own psychic abilities."

"I do, actually." She smoothed her long hair back, but the wind lifted it as soon as she let go. "And I've mastered them quite well. Unfortunately, they don't always work the way I need them to."

Cass could definitely relate to that.

"And in this case, I need to contact someone who was very important to me at one time. There's nothing worse than having abilities that refuse to cooperate when you have a personal stake in the outcome."

That's for sure.

Simone shrugged one slim shoulder. "Anyway, it seems my husband won't speak to me any more after his death than he would during his life."

"Excuse me?" Her radar pinged wildly. How could Simone know her husband was dead? According to Bee's information, which had come from the most accurate source possible, he was simply missing. Cass braced to run.

"I've been trying to reach Andy since he disappeared." She frowned and shook her head, staring into the distance. "Though I can feel in my gut he's gone, I'm not able to reach him. We did not leave things on good terms, and according to his will, his young girlfriend will inherit everything once his fate has been determined. I won't contest it, so I have nothing to gain by investigating his death, and yet, I've searched far and wide for someone who can help me find the closure I need. Despite his philandering, I never did stop loving him."

Cass could understand that. She shook off any misgivings. "So, you'd like me to try to contact him? Out here? Now?"

"Yes." She smiled. "That's exactly what I want."

As long as Simone helped her create the filter, it didn't matter who she tried to reach first. If she was able to contact Simone's husband, great. In the meantime, she'd be learning everything she could, and by the time she was done helping Simone, hopefully she'd understand what she needed to do to find Fred's killer and hear whatever message was trying to reach her about Stephanie and Tank. "Okay. Tell me what to do."

"Walk with me." She started down the walkway toward the jetty. "We won't go far, and we'll head back as soon as the rain starts."

Cass nodded and followed her onto the rocks. She stopped on the same flat rock Bee had insisted Kitty had waited for Thomas on all those years ago.

"Close your eyes." Simone stood just next to her, and still she had to raise her voice. "Have you ever tried meditation?"

"I've tried, but I'm not very good at it." Cass had a hard time unwinding and staying still, making meditation difficult.

"That's okay. Just close your eyes."

With one last look around to be sure they were alone, Cass took a leap of faith and closed her eyes.

"Listen to the wind, let it flow through you." Simone's voice came from right against her ear, as well as from inside her head. "Feel the electricity, the power, sizzling across your skin. Embrace it."

A howl echoed in her head. Goose bumps made a mad dash up her arms.

"Now, open yourself up and use that power, the rush of the wind, to mask some of the voices."

Cass opened her mind.

Like a dam bursting, her shield collapsed and the voices gushed through.

Instead of concentrating on the voices, she listened to the whistle of the wind, the hum of the voices when they merged together as one, crashing like the sea against the shore. She concentrated on the steady hum. Little by little, the wind whipped the voices away, swallowing their sound, masking them with its own. "What's your ex's name?"

"Andrew," Simone answered with no hesitation.

Cass concentrated, opening her mind. Blood trickled from her nose.

"... *lighthouse ... waiting ... pain ...*"

Two distinct voices. Even with Simone helping her shield.

"... *betrayed ... friend ... waiting ...*"

Both male.

"... *now ... betrayed ... why now ...*"

One a familiar cadence, a local. Fred? Not Thomas or Samuel certainly. At least she didn't think so.

"... *push ... not me ... betrayed ...*"

She grasped the other voice, the accent thick, similar to Simone's.

"I think I have him, Simone." How had that happened? Had Simone actually been the one to summon him? Cass had never been that powerful before. "Are you . . . enhancing my abilities?"

"Some."

"Andrew?" Cass asked out loud.

"Betrayed . . ."

She squeezed her eyes closed tighter against the rush of the wind. "Who betrayed you?"

Simone gasped.

"She killed me."

Pain slammed through Cass's head as something struck her from behind. As she started to fall, the world went black.

Chapter Twenty-five

Cass faded in and out of consciousness. Thunder crashed. Lightning sizzled across the sky. Darkness enveloped her.

"*Cass?*" a familiar voice asked.

Black swirled around her. Pain slammed through her head and her stomach lurched. She tried to force her eyes open, but blackness encroached, tunneling her vision until she succumbed.

Motion. The rocking pulled her from unconsciousness, but her head was too heavy. She couldn't lift it from . . . someone's chest? Arms cradled her against a hard . . .

Noooo! Panic clutched her throat, strangling her. Then, merciful blackness.

Cold fingers pressed against her throat.

Don't touch me! she screamed in her mind, but couldn't force the sound from her mouth.

She squeezed her eyes closed tighter, willing the world to stop spinning.

Her cheek scraped across something hard and scratchy. It tore at her face. Cold seeped through her, all the way to her bones. Tears spilled out from beneath her closed lids. She gave up, falling back into the blissful well of oblivion.

Light penetrated the haze of pain.

"*Cass!*" A strong voice, insistent. She tried to ignore it, to crawl back into the cover of the darkness. The voice was unrelenting, growing firmer each time it called to her from within her own mind. "*Cass. Open your eyes.*"

No! She wanted to shake her head but couldn't seem to coordinate the thought with the action.

"*Come on, now.*" The voice changed from demanding to pleading, the accent familiar.

Cass tried harder.

"*Wake up! Now.*"

"Simone?" She forced her eyes open a slit. Pain hammered through her head, but she wouldn't give in. Blurry images shimmered through the tears pooled in her eyes.

She forced her hand into her pocket and fumbled her phone out. Who had she called last? Couldn't remember. Hard to make her fingers work. Why were her hands so cold? She opened the home screen, hit the phone icon, and redialed the last number she'd called.

She struggled to get the phone to her ear. Where had her attacker gone? Simone? Had Simone been the one to hit her?

Thunder crashed and the sky opened up.

Cass welcomed the cool rain. It helped to clear her head.

"Hey, beautiful. Just wrapping things up here —"

Bee? What was he doing here? Hadn't he gone into Dreamweaver Designs to work? Confused, Cass forgot for a moment she'd dialed his number.

"Cass?"

"Bee. Help. Lighthouse."

He'd come. Bee always came when she needed him. He'd call Luke or Tank, but he'd make it to her before they could if he was still at the shop working on his gowns.

Cass got the phone back into her pocket. She didn't want to warn whomever had hit her — Simone? — that she'd called for help if they returned.

The rain continued to pour down on her, clearing her senses. She'd been moved. No longer on the jetty but the beach. She had to get out of there. Had to get up first. She rolled onto her side and struggled to sit. The sand shifted beneath her hand, sending her sprawling.

She could do this. All she had to do was make it to the parking lot. She could lock herself in the car until Bee got there. No way she could drive. Not even just down the road to Mystical Musings.

She finally managed to push herself up to sit, then pulled her knees up and lowered her head to rest on them. Closed her eyes. Just for a moment.

"Cass. What happened?" Bee fell to his knees beside her. "Cass, talk to me. Ah, man, you're bleeding."

"Have to get out of here. Simone." She shouldn't have called him. Shouldn't have put him in danger. Should have tried to scroll through for Luke's number. Or Tank's.

"Is she here?" He stood and looked around, then leaned back over her. "There's no one here, Cass."

"She was right beside me. Except . . ." She'd heard Simone calling to her. Insisting she wake up. But she wasn't here. She was certain the call came from within her head. "I think she might be dead."

Had whoever had hit her killed Simone? Was she lying on the jetty somewhere? Helpless? Stuffed beneath one of the massive boulders as Piper had been?

Her memory of the seconds right before the attack came crashing back, and the air burst from her lungs. "We have to get out of here."

"I don't think we should move you, Cass. I called Luke. Help is on the way."

"No. Have to go. Now." Cass struggled to get to her feet. She had to get Bee out of there. "I was doing a reading of sorts, trying to contact Simone's husband, see if we could locate him."

"You came out here in the dark, in the middle of a storm, to meet up with her? Alone?"

Well, when you put it like that.

"It doesn't matter right now. I think she might have killed him and hit me over the head and left me for dead."

Bee helped her to stand, then let her lean against him. "Are you sensing a pattern here, Cass?"

"What?" She squinted against the headache and tried to clear the fog from her brain.

"Every time you ask someone else for help instead of me, it backfires on you."

"Seriously, Bee?" She was starting to regret having called him.

"Just sayin', honey."

"Bee?" A voice from behind them made Cass's blood run cold.

"Levi?" Bee turned. "Oh, thank goodness you're here. We need help. Cass is hurt."

Levi took off his cap, scratched his head, and put his cap back on. "Sorry, Bee, but I can't do that."

"What?" Bee looked from him to Cass. "Why not?"

By the time his gaze retuned to Levi, the other man held a gun pointed right at Cass, his hand steady, his grip firm and sure. "Start walking, toward the lighthouse. And don't try to run. It makes no difference if I put a bullet in your back, no one's ever going to find the bodies anyway."

"Levi?" Bee braced.

Cass held a gentle hand against his arm to keep him from

charging. "Levi, please. Bee has nothing to do with this. Why don't you just let him go, and I'll do whatever you ask?"

"You're going to do whatever I ask anyway, now start walking." He lifted the gun a bit.

Keeping her hands out to the sides where Levi could easily see them, Cass turned and slowly started toward the lighthouse. "Come on, Bee."

He didn't move, and Cass paused and held her breath, willing him to turn and walk with her. They wouldn't have to stall him for long. Luke should be there any minute.

"What are you doing?" Bee finally turned and started to walk with her, the wind and rain covering the sound of his voice. "I can take him."

She had full confidence Bee could take Levi under normal circumstances, and even in the current situation if Levi wasn't standing too far away for Bee to reach him before he could pull the trigger. But Levi's grasp on the gun didn't waver for an instant, and there was no hesitation in his eyes. She had a strong feeling this wasn't the first time he'd held someone at gunpoint.

She tried to open her mind, search for help. Nothing. The voices that had harassed her so relentlessly seemed to have fled in the face of danger. *Thanks, guys.* But what of the voice that had called to her? Woken her? Certainly saved her life by calling so insistently and giving her the time to call Bee before Levi returned. A female voice, the accent thick. Cass raised her voice to be heard over the storm. "Where's Simone?"

"Don't matter none."

Accomplice or victim?

They'd almost reached the lighthouse. But what to do? Go inside with him, or force him to kill them out there? Once they were inside, Luke would be walking in blind.

Cass staggered and reached out to steady herself against the doorjamb.

"Don't even try it." He stopped before moving into striking distance and redirected the gun to aim it a Bee. "If I didn't need you two for something, you'd already be dead. Open the door. Now."

Not willing to take a chance with Bee's life, Cass did as he said. Rainwater ran in rivulets down her face from her soaking wet hair.

She wiped them away and shoved her hair back as she entered the cool, damp space.

Simone stood at the opposite end of the circular room.

Francesca Harding stood at her back, gun aimed at her.

Bee moved in behind Cass and slid against the wall, halfway between Francesca and Levi.

Cass moved past Bee and stood against the wall beside him but closer to Francesca. If they were going to have any chance at all of fighting their way out of there, Bee's path to Levi needed to be unimpeded. Cass could take care of Francesca. "I don't understand."

"Of course you don't." Francesca sneered and aimed a deadly glare at Bee. "You thought it was so funny when Piper humiliated me in the diner, drew attention to me I didn't need. Well, you're not laughing now, are you?"

Bee kept perfectly still, hands held up in front of him. "Hon, I wasn't laughing at you. And I'm sorry if it seemed that way. Actually, I was cheering you on. It was nice to see someone stand up to that bully for a change."

"Yeah, well, she's not laughing anymore either." Francesca aimed her glare at Levi. "But she's not dead, either, like she was supposed to be."

Bee shifted a fraction of an inch toward Levi.

Francesca frowned.

Cass stood up straighter, putting herself between Francesca and Bee, trying to block her clear view of Bee in case he tried to move again.

"Enough!" Levi leaned over, yanked a large rubber mat off the floor and threw it aside, and pulled open a trap door. "Let's go. One at a time. Bee first."

Bee stood his ground. "What is that?"

"Don't worry. You ain't dying yet." He waved the gun toward the opening.

"No." Bee planted his feet firmly, angling his body in front of Cass. "I'm not going down there, at least not until I know what's down there and what you want from us."

Levi contemplated him for a moment. "Fine. It's a tunnel. It leads to the lighthouse on Gardiners Island."

A chill ripped through Cass. If they went down there and walked beneath the bay to Gardiners Island, which was not that far away, Luke would never find them, even knowing where they were last. Levi was right. They'd never be found. "Why are we going to Gardiners Island?"

"We're not. Yet. First, we're going to see if either of you"—he waved the gun back and forth between Cass and Simone—"can contact good ole cheating Fred and see if he can tell us where the treasure is. And then, Bee here's gonna tell me how to find that treasure. Because I read through those transcribed pages and dug where I thought I'd find it, but it wasn't there."

Bee shifted again and held up a finger. "So, it wasn't you that removed the pages?"

Levi's eyes went wide. "What are you talking about?"

"The pages from the journal."

"*Cass?*"

Her gaze shot to Simone, whose lips never moved, though her voice rang out clear enough in Cass's head.

Simone's brow furrowed in concentration, sweat trickling down the sides of her face. She shook her head once, and Cass turned away.

"... Cass and I found the journal."

She shifted her attention back to Bee.

"You couldn't have. I only had a few seconds before the cops came traipsin' in, and I couldn't get caught with it on me, so I dumped it where no one could find it." Levi mopped the sweat from his brow.

"Yeah, right." Bee mocked. "In the secret stairway that goes from the museum to the room you pushed Fred out of."

"Harrumph. Fred. If he'd have just cooperated instead of being so greedy, none of this would have happened. We were supposed to share the treasure, a fifty-fifty split, until he decided to cut me out." He grinned at Francesca. "Lucky for me he had a penchant for beautiful young women."

"So, Fred wasn't going after Francesca, she was going after him." And had riled Quincy up for nothing.

"Then what were you doing with Quince?" Bee asked Francesca, seeming legitimately interested. Who could blame him? If they ever got out of this, he'd have gossip enough to power the rumor mill for weeks. Maybe even all summer.

"Oh, please," Francesca said. "Quince was a convenient cover. Who'd ever think I was fooling around with that old coot when I had myself the most eligible stud on the island?"

"So you didn't care about him at all?" Bee pressed a hand against his chest and shifted another fraction of an inch closer to Fred. "That's just cold."

She rolled her eyes. "Enough already. Bee, you're here to see if you can find the treasure based on what was written in the journal. Cass and Simone, you two are here to see if you can get Fred, or Kitty, or Thomas, or even good old Samuel—I don't much care who—to reveal the location of the treasure."

Levi once again gestured toward the tunnel. "And then we're all taking a trip over to Gardiners Island to see if we can find the remainder of that treasure. I've heard the stories about treasure being buried there too."

Bee held up a finger. "That would be impossible."

He grinned, pure evil. "Nothing's impossible."

"I beg to differ." Propping his hand on his hip, he took another opportunity to take a step closer to Levi. To the side, though, so as not to make it obvious. "If you know the story of the treasure on Gardiners Island, you also know the Gardiners had to hand it over to the court, except for one diamond Jonathan Gardiner was rumored to have passed on to his daughter, Elizabeth."

"Do you seriously think that's all the treasure buried there?" Levi laughed. "You really are naïve, aren't you?"

Bee sighed.

"Now." Levi waved the gun. "All three of you are going down into that hole."

"Get ready."

Cass shifted her gaze to Levi to avoid her automatic instinct to look at Simone.

"And you say I'm naïve," Bee muttered as he moved past Levi.

"Now." Simone struck Francesca, wrapping her arm around the shorter girl's neck and tightening her grip.

Bee whirled on Levi, almost simultaneously, grabbing his wrist and twisting him against the wall.

Cass lunged at Francesca, frantically grappling to grab hold of the gun.

A loud crack echoed in the chamber.

Francesca froze, giving Cass the instant she needed to grab the gun.

Simone shoved her to the floor and took the gun from Cass, holding it out in front of her, aimed directly at Francesca.

"You broke my arm," Levi screamed.

Bee aimed the gun he'd taken from him at Levi and backed toward Cass. "You're lucky that's all I broke, buddy."

Chapter Twenty-six

Cass dug her feet into the warm sand and leaned back in her beach chair, staring up at the lighthouse. It would be a while before the sight of it didn't bring a chill all the way to her bones.

Bee lifted his sunglasses and looked up the beach toward Mystical Musings. "Seems we have company."

Simone strode toward them, her smile wide. She waved as she approached.

Bee stood and offered his chair, then spread a towel over the sand and sat facing them, his back to the lighthouse. Purposely?

"Thank you, Bee." Simone slipped off her sandals and sat. "The contracts are signed, and I am now the official owner of Bay Island Ghost Tours."

"You changed the name?" Bee squinted against the sun, then slid his sunglasses back into place.

"I thought it best." She crossed one leg over the other, leaned her head back to angle her face toward the sun, and closed her eyes. "It reflects the new direction I'll be taking the tours in and rids the company of Fred's influence."

"Well, congratulations. I couldn't be happier." Cass reached over and gave her a quick hug. "Have you spoken to Amelia?"

She nodded. "I've been staying with her since the incident at the lighthouse."

"How is she?"

"She's holding her own. She's finally coming to realize her relationship with Fred had already ended before he died, when Levi showed her proof Fred had been fooling around with Piper. After that, it was just a matter of filing for divorce. She'll heal. It'll just take time."

"Did she ever?" Bee asked. "File, I mean?"

"No. Amelia and I have been friends for a long time, and when she called me, crying and crushed over Fred's infidelity, I begged her to just file for divorce and be done with him, but she insisted on making his life miserable, payback for duping her into helping him become successful then being unfaithful."

Bee sat up straighter and folded his legs. "So, what did Amelia do to get even with him?"

"She told Levi Fred planned to cheat him out of his portion of the profit and then paid Levi to find the treasure before Fred could."

If Simone had been able to talk her out of her revenge, Fred might still be alive.

"Aha." Bee snapped his fingers. "That's what was in the envelope she was passing to him in the surveillance photo. A payment."

"Apparently, Fred wasn't a very trusting man," Simone said.

Bee snorted. "Untrustworthy people usually aren't."

"Very true, dear. In the end, Levi betrayed her and tried to find the treasure for himself."

"Is that how you ended up buying the company?"

"Yes. The tour company had always been in Amelia's name, since she'd applied for the original loan to start the business, and when she found out he was cheating on her, she offered it to me first. First, because she knows I'm an avid history buff." A slow lazy smile spread across her face. "And even more so because she knew the addition of the paranormal aspect would entice me."

"So Amelia knew you were psychic?" Cass asked.

"You can't be such close friends with someone without picking up on what they can do." She shifted her gaze and her smile to Bee.

Cass frowned. She'd asked Bee numerous times how he'd known Simone was going to attack Francesca, and each time he'd insisted he hadn't. Now that she had them both together, it was a good time to find out the truth. "Bee swears he didn't hear you tell him to attack, yet he went after Levi an instant after you attacked Francesca. It happened almost simultaneously. So fast I'd have sworn it was a coordinated attack."

"And it was." Simone shrugged. "In a sense. Bee might not have been able to read me, but I could read him."

Bee lurched forward. "You were in my head?"

"You could say that."

"Great." He slapped his hands over his ears as if afraid his thoughts might leak out. "I'm going to need to make a tinfoil helmet."

Simone's smooth, easy laughter seemed to mollify Bee, and he leaned back on his hands, still sulking but not as aggressively.

"Don't worry, Bee. It's not like that. A good number of things led me to anticipate what you were going to do, not the least of which was your feelings for Cass. There was no way you were allowing her down into that hole if you could stop it."

"No, there wasn't." Bee's cheeks flared red, and he changed the subject. "So, Simone, what made you become such an avid history buff?"

She tilted her head, narrowed her eyes, and studied him. "I love gossip and, after all, what is history but gossip from the past?"

"You're doing it again, aren't you?" Bee slapped his hands against his temples, fingers spread wide to cover as much of his head as possible. "Stay out of my head. It's creepy."

"No, Bee. I promise I'm not in your head. Even though I managed to call out to Cass in the instant before we attacked, because she is psychic as well, mostly my talents run the same as hers. I can read people very well, my instincts are strong and I trust them, and I can hear the dead speak."

Bee choked.

Simone just laughed, the two of them seeming to understand each other. Despite Bee's reluctance, Cass could tell he'd become quite fond of her.

"Will you be moving to Bay Island to oversee the tours?" Cass warmed to the idea of Simone hanging around. It had been nice having someone around to talk to who understood the issues she was having.

"No, actually, I've hired Quincy Yates to run the company, so he'll be staying year-round, and I'll be popping in and out." She sat up and turned to face Cass. "Right now, I need to head back to the city and speak to the detectives in charge of my husband's case."

Cass recalled the last words she'd heard before being knocked out. "He's dead. I'm sorry."

"It's okay, I really knew it already, though he was too stubborn, even in death, to reach out to me and let me help. I saw and heard the same thing you did, though. And a couple of the detectives on the case know me and trust my abilities. Now that we know his mistress was the one to kill him, we have a direction to head in." She stood. "Thank you for helping me with that, Cass. I can't tell you how much I appreciate it."

Cass and Bee stood as well, and Cass hugged Simone. "No problem. That's what friends are for."

And Simone had become a friend, from the first moment she'd felt that instant bond with her to the moment she'd fought by her side.

"And thank you, as well, Bee. If not for you, Cass and I both would have died in that tunnel." She wrapped her arms around his neck and hugged him fiercely.

Bee blushed all the way to his hairline. "Yeah, well, like Cass said, that's what friends do."

She kissed his cheek. "Well, I am very proud to call you my friend then, and if there's ever anything you need, you just call. In the meantime, I hope you'll both keep in touch."

After promising they would, they watched Simone walk back across the beach.

Bee watched her go, then picked up his towel and shook it out. "You know, I was prepared not to like her."

"And how did that work out for you?"

He laughed.

A loud rumbling from the direction of the lighthouse caught their attention, and they turned to watch the heavy equipment they'd brought in to move some of the boulders and dig up the treasure Bee had been able to pinpoint from the journal's description. "I can't wait to see what they come up with."

"Me neither, I—"

"Cass!" Luke ran toward them from the direction of Mystical Musings. "Bee!"

Cass stiffened as the image of a red vehicle drove through her head.

Bee grabbed her arm. "What's wrong?"

"Hurry." Luke ran faster. "You have to come."

"Where?" Bee wrapped an arm around Cass and held her against him.

"The hospital. Tank's already there, and an officer that was closer to the house already picked Stephanie up."

Chapter Twenty-seven

Cass closed her eyes, letting the hum of the tires against the smooth pavement lull her.

Luke had refused to tell her what was going on, though he did say Tank was all right. The image she'd seen as he ran toward her down the beach haunted her, flashing over and over in her mind. Bee sat beside her in the backseat, holding her hand. Whatever had happened, they'd get through it together.

Luke pulled to the curb in front of the emergency room and jumped out of the car.

Bee and Cass followed suit.

With Luke and Bee on either side of her, Cass braced herself for the worst and strode through the ER doors.

The barrage of voices assailed her. Not from within her own mind but from the crowded waiting room filled with hushed voices, pain-filled cries, and soft sobs. She blocked it all and followed the hallway Luke led her down.

Tank emerged from a curtained area at the end of the corridor, his eyes red and swollen. He held his arms wide. "Cass."

"Are you all right?" She rushed into his embrace. "What happened?"

He held her close for another moment, then gestured toward a small waiting room.

Cass went in but didn't sit.

Bee stood at her side, her rock, as always.

Tank faced her, his eyes bloodshot, his expression grim. "Cass, I just want you to know none of this would have happened if not for you."

Her heart stopped for an instant, then thundered heavily against her ribs.

"They found the lighthouse figure used to kill Fred in the tunnel beneath the lighthouse, and I was heading back out there, when I noticed a car next to me. A beat-up red Nissan with patches of gray primer and a partially blocked license plate whose last three numbers were four, four, four."

Butterflies fluttered in her chest along with the mamba her heart was doing. She covered her mouth to hold back a sob.

"I never would have given it a second glance if not for your warning. But, because of you, I did. And there was a child in the backseat. A little boy. Tears ran down his cheeks and he glanced at the driver and back at me, and I just knew something was wrong. Since he wasn't in a car seat, I had just cause to pull the car over." Tank's voice hitched.

Bee sniffled.

Cass squeezed her eyes closed, dreading whatever would come next, willing him not to tell her.

"Stephanie's with him now."

Her eyes shot open.

"He's been abused, Cass, and he's being removed from his father's custody. His mother apparently died a few years ago, and we can't find any relatives as of yet. Stephanie and I have applied for emergency custody."

Tears prickled the backs of her lids, and she had no hope of holding them back.

Bee grabbed her hand and strode out of the room to the curtained-off area Tank had come from. He yanked back the curtain and slapped a hand over his mouth.

Cass slid her arm through his elbow and sobbed softly.

Stephanie put a finger to her lips and pulled the sleeping child closer.

"She's the only one he'll let touch him. He's four years old, and his name is Aiden. His father says he's on the autistic spectrum."

"Oh, dear." Bee cried softly.

"It'll take some time, but the father's not objecting, and there's no way the courts will return custody to him, so we're working on arranging a private adoption. And it's all thanks to you. You saved him, Cass. You saved our son."

About the Author

Lena Gregory is the author of the Bay Island Psychic Mystery series, which takes place on a small island between the north and south forks of Long Island, New York, and the All-Day Breakfast Café Mystery series, which is set on the outskirts of Florida's Ocala National Forest.

Lena grew up in a small town on the south shore of eastern Long Island. She recently relocated to Clermont, Florida, with her husband, three kids, son-in-law, and four dogs. Her hobbies include spending time with family, reading, jigsaw puzzles, and walking. Her love for writing developed when her youngest son was born and didn't sleep through the night. She works full-time as a writer and a freelance editor and is a member of Sisters in Crime.

To learn more about Lena and her latest writing endeavors, visit her website at www.lenagregory.com/, and be sure to sign up for her newsletter at lenagregory.us12.list-manage.com/subscribe?u=9765d0711ed4fab4fa31b16ac&id=49d42335d1.

Made in the USA
Monee, IL
19 July 2020